The RIVER of FIRE

Also by Patrick Easter

The Watermen

The RIVER of FIRE

PATRICK EASTER

Quercus

First published in Great Britain in 2012 by

Quercus
55 Baker Street
7th Floor, South Block
London W1U 8EW

A CIP catalogue record for this book is available
from the British Library

ISBN 978 0 85738 057 9 (HB)
ISBN 978 0 85738 058 6 (TPB)

10 9 8 7 6 5 4 3 2 1

Typeset by Ellipsis Digital Limited, Glasgow

Printed and bound in Great Britain by Clays Ltd, St Ives plc

Map drawn by Jamie Whyte

For Julia and Emma

The RIVER of FIRE

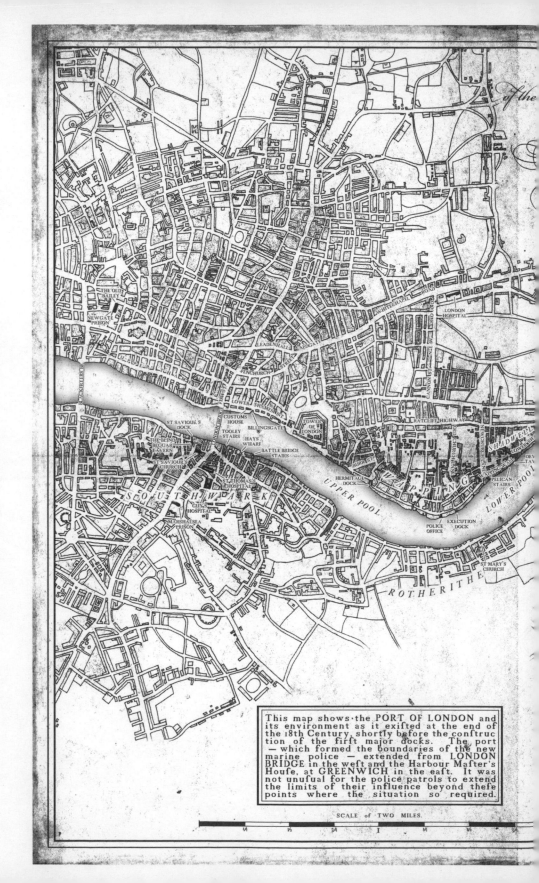

This map shows the PORT OF LONDON and its environment as it exifted at the end of the 18th Century, shortly before the conftruction of the firft major docks. The port — which formed the boundaries of the new marine police — extended from LONDON BRIDGE in the weft and the Harbour Mafter's Houfe, at GREENWICH in the eaft. It was not unufual for the police patrols to extend the limits of their influence beyond thefe points where the situation so required.

SCALE of TWO MILES.

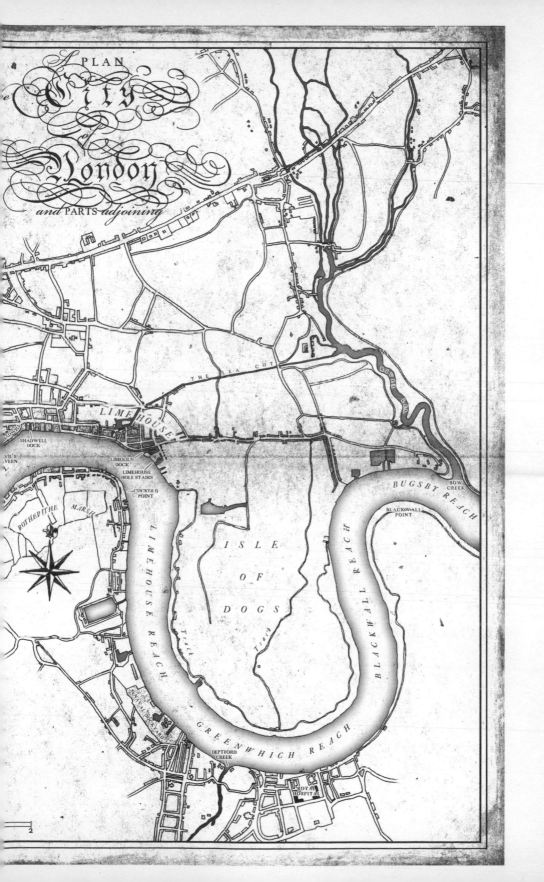

There is a glossary of historical and
nautical terms on page 371.

CHAPTER 1

March 1799

The Port of London

Moses Solomon woke with a start and stared out over the Thames. The inky blackness of the night was pierced by the shimmering light of several dozen lanterns on the ships lying at anchor in the Lower Pool.

His heart was racing. Something had woken him.

He struggled onto one elbow, the joints of his thin frame stiff from the damp air. He glanced up and down the narrow passageway that led off Wapping Wall, in a desperate need for reassurance in the loneliness of the night. He could hear nothing except the gentle gurgle of the tideway oozing its way to the distant sea and the low moan of the wind. He looked towards the river where a lantern hung from a wrought-iron arch over Pelican Stairs, spilling its dull, yellow glow onto the steps.

Solomon shivered and drew his threadbare coat about him, turning up the collar and holding it to his throat. Perhaps he'd imagined whatever it was that had woken him. He struggled to stay awake, his eyes drooping.

Then he heard a splash. His looked towards the river. This time there was no mistaking the sound or where it had come from. He shaded his eyes from the faint glare of the lantern and stared into the night. A heavy length of timber bumped against a mooring pole at the foot of the stairs, making him jump.

It spun out of sight and the silence returned.

He remained still, peering at the shifting shadows that were like so many demons in his mind, listening to the sounds of the moving river. Then he stood and crept to the head of the stairs, his heart hammering against the wall of his chest.

A movement cut across the extremity of his vision, a flash of white in the water. He swivelled his head. A man's face appeared, fleeting and indistinct, seeming to struggle with the fast-flowing tide. Solomon ducked out of sight and pressed his body against the passage wall. He struggled to breathe, felt tightness across his chest. He wanted to run, but couldn't. Thirty seconds passed; then forty, and still he didn't move, his eyes riveted to the place where he'd seen the face.

A heavy *clump*. Close by. Then the sound of laboured breathing and of someone climbing the river stairs below him. Solomon scrambled away, gulping for air, his mouth dry. He reached the top of the passage and turned right, ducking into the porch of the Devil's Tavern.

Behind him, the footsteps had stopped.

Solomon stood as still as he was able, his body trembling, his ears straining to catch the least sound. From the river end of the passage, a loose stone rolled over a wooden step and thumped onto the tread below, the sound magnified by the still of the night. Solomon eased himself away from the tavern door and crept to the corner of the building from where he could see down the passage. A young man was standing less than thirty feet away. He was bent over, one arm outstretched, braced against the wall of the tavern, his chest rising and falling as though exhausted and out of breath. Suddenly he straightened and looked out over the river. He seemed to have been startled by something.

Then he turned.

The lantern over the arch shone on a face stiff with pain, the young man's wide-spaced eyes wet with tears, his teeth clamped over his bottom lip, his shoulder-length hair hanging limp about his face. He appeared to gather himself then started up the alley, his progress slow and irregular, his left leg dragging behind him in the dirt. Solomon backed into the doorway of the tavern. The young man drew level. His clothes smelt of fish and sea water. He stopped and glanced nervously over his shoulder, along the way he had come.

Solomon waited, barely breathing, certain he'd be discovered. He felt the sweat forming in the filth-stained creases of his brow and begin to roll down over his eyes to the folds of his thin neck. He knew what to expect if he were seen. The beating would follow as surely as the coming dawn. It had happened before. On countless occasions. He was a hatseller and ragman accustomed to walking the streets, used to the insults and worse of those that passed by.

He tensed. The stranger had turned west, towards the City, was limping away from him, the scraping noise of his boot fading into the night – the stamp and drag of a man in pain.

He expelled a lungful of air and waited for his pulse to slow. He leaned forwards, out of the doorway, searching the street. There was little to see beyond the reach of his arm. He crept to the corner of the tavern and stared down the length of the alley, the splash of yellow light from the lantern on the arch his only point of reference.

He found himself wondering what had happened to the young man, why he'd been limping. He remembered the look of fear on the lad's face as he'd turned away from the river and the light had caught the look in his eye. He thought again of the noise that had woken him. An explosion; a sudden burst of noise, like the discharge of a gun. Gunfire would explain the boy's injury. A knot of fear formed in his stomach. He realised there wasn't another landing place within a quarter of a mile of where he stood.

If the young man was being pursued, his pursuers would have to come this way.

He had to leave.

Then Solomon caught the sound of a voice, low and indistinct. He listened, his head on one side. It had come from the river, of that he was sure. But where, exactly? Perhaps from a watchman on one of the ships. He dismissed the idea. The voice had been too close for that.

He cupped his hands behind his ears and waited to hear it again. He wanted to be sure. There was a soft splash, an oar entering the water followed by the familiar thud and creak of the leather sleeve striking the thole pins.

It was enough. He pushed himself away from the tavern, slipping on wet cobblestones as he did so. He reached out a hand to save himself, the sudden movement dislodging the pile of hats he was wearing. They tumbled to the ground.

He searched for them, keeping one eye on the passageway, his thin pulse racing. He found three. One was still missing. He couldn't spare the time to find it. He heard the voice again. Much closer. He caught sight of the missing hat, picked it up and hurried away. It was then he realised he was no longer wearing his *kippah*, his skullcap. His stomach tightened. He thought of going back. He'd no time; would return to look for it in the morning, when it was safe. He scuttled along Wapping Wall, his long black coat flying behind him.

*

Out on the Lower Pool of the River Thames, a skiff slid through the water, its bow wave barely causing a ripple on the smooth surface. In the stern, a tall figure sat hunched over the tiller, his eyes scanning the Shadwell foreshore, his narrow face set in a frown of concentration. He reached up to anchor his battered tricorn more firmly on his head.

Pierre Moreau was not normally troubled by the ups and downs that were, regrettably, a feature of his professional life. Quite the reverse. As a *commissaire de police* in Paris, responsible for investigating the activities of the enemies of the French Republic, he prided himself on his composure, his ability to get things done with the minimum of fuss. But on this occasion matters had gone seriously wrong. It should never have happened.

He wiped away a trickle of perspiration from his forehead and glanced at the short, thickset frame of his companion who was, at that moment, leaning back on the oars. André Dubois – soldier, thief, assassin – had failed him; the young Englishman had escaped.

Perhaps the fault was his. He had, after all, agreed to Dubois being brought back from the Italian campaign to assist in this operation. No one had compelled him to do so. And he could hardly claim not to have known what he was like: the fellow had been one of his informants.

Moreau shook his head at the memory. He had not long arrived in Marseille when the two of them had met – he a comparatively inexperienced police officer, still in his middle twenties, Dubois several years his junior, a hot-headed street fighter with a volcanic temper, whose weapons of choice were the knife and the garrotte.

It had not taken him long to appreciate the value of someone like the young Dubois in terms of the information that he might provide. And he had accordingly made it his business to cultivate the relationship to what he saw as their mutual benefit. The courtship had, however, seldom gone the way Moreau would have wished, his new protégé making frequent and extravagant demands for protection from the consequences of his freewheeling criminal activity.

And if the policeman in him had hoped that his assistance on these occasions would buy him the information he craved, he was often disappointed. Yet, despite these drawbacks, the morsels of intelligence he was able to extract from his volatile informant were sufficient to make the association worthwhile, at least for the time being.

But with the passage of time, Dubois's reputation for violence spread and it became increasingly difficult for Moreau not to appear complicit in his activities. In the spring of 1794 the bodies of two men were found by police close to the Marseille waterfront. They had been garrotted and suspicion inevitably fell on Dubois, more especially since he was known to have fought with both men in the days preceding the murders.

The *commissaire* had not seen his informant after that. Within months he had been promoted and moved to Paris, all thought of the erstwhile Dubois rapidly fading from his mind.

Moreau turned to look at the faint glow of a lantern on the north bank of the river, examining it carefully. It seemed to be in the right position. He steered the boat towards it, his mind still on the subject of his informant. For reasons he'd never been able to discover, his colleagues in Marseille had been unable to find sufficient evidence to charge Dubois with the double killing, despite the very public nature of the offence. No one, it appeared, had seen anything, and there the matter rested.

Now, nearly five years after Pierre Moreau had last seen him, he and Dubois were again working together on a mission that was as dangerous as it was important to the outcome of the war against England. The instructions received from Monsieur Jean-Pierre Duval, the *ministre de la police* in Paris, had left little to the imagination.

'Information has been received from a reliable source that requires our immediate action if advantage is to be taken of the opportunity it presents,' Duval had said. 'I want you to undertake the operation. It is, I regret, dangerous. If it were not, I should have sent someone less able. Your assistant on this occasion is André Dubois, a person with whom you have, I believe, worked in the past.'

Moreau glanced again at the shoreline. The light was closer now, the buildings on either side looming out of the darkness, the black roofs stark against the deep purple of a pre-dawn sky.

If he had expected the military to have knocked a bit of sense into Dubois, he was disappointed. While active service in Italy had curbed the more obvious excesses of Dubois's violent nature, it had not eradicated them. A report from his *chef de brigade* spoke of a determined if insubordinate and quick-tempered soldier whose willingness to engage the enemy was matched only by his ability to take offence, leading to numerous scraps with his own comrades.

The report reminded him of something else Monsieur Duval had told him about his new assistant.

'Shortly after you left Marseille,' said the *ministre de la police*, 'Dubois's father died. I cannot recall the reason – the pox, I believe, but it matters not. He was a highly successful captain of a corsair operating under a *lettre de cours*. Before the war, he would often take his son with him. In the course of his business, they visited Gibraltar where the boy learned to speak English. You may feel this qualification to be of some benefit to the present assignment.

'After his father's death, the vessel, still operating under a *lettre de cours*, passed to his son. As you can imagine, the young Dubois was immediately filled with dreams of riches. Unfortunately, the dreams were not matched by his skill as a commander. Almost immediately he fell victim to a British man-of-war which seized the vessel. The lad spent the following six months as a prisoner in England. To my certain knowledge, Dubois has never forgotten that incident and bears a deep and lasting hatred for the British. From your point of view, then, your assistant has both strengths and weaknesses. He is a useful man to have with you in a fight and his excellent English is an advantage. On the other hand, you will know better than I that he is extremely volatile, a confirmed criminal and, I suspect, may take any opportunity to kill while in England. You will have to watch him carefully.'

Moreau knew he couldn't have it both ways. Dubois might be the scum of the earth but he would have been worthless as an informant – and as his assistant on this operation – had he not been. He had always known, even before his conversation with the *ministre de la police*, that with the advantages would come the liabilities. He just hadn't expected things to start going wrong quite so soon.

He pushed the skiff's tiller hard over and swung the small craft up into the ebb tide, the swirling water pushing the vessel's bow towards the base of Pelican Stairs. Another few seconds and the hull was scraping silently against one of the mooring poles at the foot of the oaken steps.

'Wait here a moment.' Moreau waved his assistant back onto his seat. 'If the boy is still in the area I don't want to lose him for want of a little care.'

Climbing out of the skiff he crept up the stairs and looked over the lip of the river wall. It was, as he had suspected, deserted. A knot formed in the pit of his stomach. The young man's escape was not going to help matters.

He glanced up into the night sky. The first trace of grey had appeared, low down on the eastern horizon. He shivered in the cold damp air. Time was running out. He beckoned his companion and the two men moved cautiously along the narrow passage towards Wapping Wall.

'*Citoyen* Moreau.'

Moreau stopped and looked round.

'What is it?'

'It's still warm.' Dubois held out a small black skullcap. 'The owner was here in the last two or three minutes. He may have seen us. Or the boy.'

What Moses Solomon wanted, more than anything else, was somewhere to lay down his head and sleep; somewhere he'd be safe, somewhere he'd not be disturbed. Beyond that, he was too tired to think. He shuffled along a still deserted Wapping Wall, stopping frequently to look over his shoulder, glances that served no purpose but to fuel his anxiety.

And Solomon knew what it was to be anxious, to be followed, tripped, kicked and beaten for the sport of others. The treatment had left its legacy. He walked with a permanent limp where a hurled stone had once smashed his right knee. He'd learned, over the years, to be circumspect about where he went and what he said, yet it wasn't always possible to avoid trouble.

It was the lot of a Jew, especially one as advanced in years as he was; a Jew who followed the old ways and dressed accordingly. He was often called upon to pay the price for the sin of being different. There had been a time in his youth when he had thought the cost too high, had wanted to abandon the certainties of his forefathers and meld into the fabric of the host community. But he had not done so. He didn't know why. Judaism had made demands on every aspect of his life, demands that he had often struggled to make sense of and which the world beyond seemed unable to comprehend. It was only with the onset of old age that he had come to value the traditions by which he lived, and learned to accept the disdain of those outside the narrow confines of his faith.

Solomon noted the streaks of grey in the sky behind him. Soon the streets would be full of men making their way to work – the lumpers, coopers, rope-makers, coal-heavers and the rest. He both looked forward to and dreaded the dawn with its inherent perils and opportunities. But for the moment all was quiet, the street deserted. He still had time to sleep, if only for an hour or so.

He had almost reached the junction with New Gravel Lane when he heard the sound of rapid footsteps approaching from behind. He slipped into a doorway and listened. The footsteps were getting closer. They belonged to more than one person. He stared into the gloom. It was too early for anyone to be going to work.

The seconds passed. Then the dim outlines of two men appeared. The shapes became clearer. They were looking for someone, their heads turning this way and that as they drew closer. He was reminded of the injured boy he'd seen by the river stairs, the hunted expression in his eyes as he'd turned away from the Thames. He'd been frightened of something. A shiver of apprehension ran down Solomon's spine. He closed his eyes. The footsteps stopped close to where he stood. He shrank back into the doorway. Beads of cold sweat ran down the side of his face. He fought down the urge to reach up and wipe them away.

A voice spoke, low and guttural, in a language he didn't know. He peeped through half-closed eyes, his knees threatening to give way from under him. He could see two men. One taller than the other. They were standing with their backs to him, conversing. No, not conversing – arguing. He could hear his own breathing, loud and rasping.

The men stopped talking. They had turned and were looking at him. The taller of the two came towards him. He was holding something in his hand. It was a *kippah*. His *kippah*. Solomon stared at it in shocked silence. The man spoke.

'Is this yours, old man?'

Solomon nodded.

'What were you doing by the stairs?'

Solomon didn't answer, too afraid to speak.

'I asked you a question, old man. What were you doing by the stairs?'

'It's on account of where I sleep.' Solomon's eyes remained fixed on the roadway. He'd learned not to meet the gaze of others, to challenge their authority.

'Why did you leave?'

'I heard someone coming and I were afraid.' Solomon swallowed, his throat dry.

'We're looking for a young friend. Did you see him?'

'No, your honour, I regret I did not.' Solomon ducked as he saw the shorter of the men take a step towards him, a knife in his hand. The man stopped, prevented from coming any closer by his companion's arm across his chest. Solomon closed his eyes again. If he was to die he wished they would get it over with. He could hear them talking to one another. Then the sound of retreating footsteps. He opened his eyes. The men were leaving. His *kippah* was on the ground at his feet. He stooped and picked it up, his pulse still racing.

CHAPTER 2

'Mr Pascoe, sir?' Tom Pascoe was dimly aware of a man's voice outside the door, calling his name. He pulled the blanket over his head, turned over and settled back to sleep. With any luck whoever it was would go away and stop bothering him.

'Mr Pascoe, sir?' The same voice. It had an insistent quality.

Tom opened first one eye, then the other and stared at the door of his room, a deep scowl of hatred on his face. The bastard just wasn't going to give up.

'Can you hear me, sir? It's me, sir. Kemp.'

'Hear you?' grumbled Tom, pulling the blanket free of his face and swinging his tall, athletic frame out of the bed. 'I'll warrant the whole of fucking Wapping can hear you.'

He pulled on a pair of breeches, still damp from the previous night's patrol, and drew out a watch from one of the pockets. A little before eight in the morning. He'd been asleep less than an hour. Still scowling, he crossed the room and opened the door.

'I regret this intrusion, sir.' Waterman Constable John Kemp raised a hand in salute, his bear-like frame filling the doorway. 'His honour Mr Harriot sends his compliments and says if you is at leisure he would be pleased to see you, sir. Hart and Ruxey are already on their way.'

'If I'm at leisure?' said Tom, raising a sarcastic eyebrow and running his fingers through a tousled mane of yellow hair. 'Don't Mr Harriot know we've been up all night?'

'Aye, sir, he knows right enough. Says the matter won't wait, sir. Seems a lugger's been sent to the bottom. She's in the Lower Pool, sir. Could be the crew's still on board.'

'A lugger?' Tom was suddenly awake. 'Did Mr Harriot say any more about it?'

'I regret it extremely, sir, but that were all he said.'

'Very well,' said Tom, stifling a yawn. 'Present my compliments to the magistrate and tell him I'll be there directly.'

He nodded as Kemp knuckled his forehead and turned to go. Closing the door he wandered over to the window. The early morning sunlight was streaming through a thin layer of ice covering the panes, the fractured shards of brilliant white, spilling onto the bare boards of his room. He scratched away a patch of the ice with a thumbnail and peered out over the rooftops of St Catherine's. Columns of grey-black smoke curled into the sky from a thousand chimneys. Beyond them, the silver thread of the Thames wound its way down past Wapping to Limehouse where it swept south, past the King's fleet at Deptford and on to the distant sea. Even from this distance he could hear the dull roar of the port and see the ant-like comings and goings of wherries, lighters and bumboats weaving in and out of the ships in the Lower Pool. He turned away, remembering what Kemp had said about a sunken lugger.

'It could be the same one,' he murmured. He wasn't one to jump to conclusions. But the coincidence was too great to be dismissed. He wouldn't normally have been surprised by the failure of a particular vessel to materialise, particularly when the information had come from an informant. He'd learned, since becoming a river surveyor with the marine police, not to place too much store by what those irredeemable villains told him. They were only ever as good as the source from which they got their information – the garbled stories exchanged in smoke-filled rooms, the muttered snippets of private conversations never intended for the ears of others, the second rumours that were the currency of idle chatter.

He knew only too well that few snouts ever checked the accuracy of what they'd been told, even if they had a mind to. The risk of asking questions far outweighed the benefits, at least so far as the informant was concerned.

But on this occasion the snout had been one of his more

reliable sources, the details quite specific. The lugger was to arrive shortly before midnight at a wharf on the Southwark shore, not far from London Bridge. Even the absence of the name of the wharf or any information about what was being carried had not caused Tom to doubt the veracity of the claim. It was enough that the man had assured him the cargo was valuable.

And unlawful.

Tom walked over to the basin in the corner of his room and poured in some cold water from a pitcher. He splashed some onto his face and then towelled himself dry. Shaving would have to wait for another time. He searched for his shoes and the white silk blouse he'd been wearing last night, eventually finding both behind the door where he'd tossed them an hour before. Finally, slipping on a battered and faintly grubby blue uniform coat with white facings, he headed out.

Twenty minutes later he was knocking on the door of the resident magistrate's room at the police office at 259, Wapping New Stairs.

'Come in.' John Harriot sat frowning at the pile of papers on his desk. Tom smiled in spite of his tiredness. He knew that, at fifty-five years of age, Harriot still preferred patrolling the river to wading through the never-ending stream of demands emanating from the Secretary of State for the Home Department. The magistrate's grim-faced expression softened as Tom's head appeared round the door.

'Ah, Mr Pascoe. The very man. Thank you for coming in. I've got something I need you to deal with as a matter of urgency. Do help yourself to coffee.'

'Thank you, sir.' Tom walked over to the polished mahogany sideboard opposite the fireplace, picked up the silver coffee pot and poured himself a cup. Spooning in a generous quantity of sugar, he turned to face the magistrate. 'How can I help?'

Harriot did not answer immediately. He reached for his pipe and lit it, the deep lines of his forehead cast in shadow by the flickering flame, his broad face drawn in concentration.

'Early this morning,' he said, 'a fishing lugger was discovered on the bed of the river, a little upstream from Shadwell Dock. The sinking appears to have been deliberate.'

'Do we know anything about the vessel?' said Tom. 'Where she comes from? Who owns her? That sort of thing.'

'No, nothing at all. Why d'you ask?'

'It may be nothing,' said Tom, sipping his coffee. 'But I spent most of last night keeping watch on the south bank, close to the Bridge. I'd been told to expect a fishing lugger at around high water. The information suggested she'd be carrying something of particular interest to us.'

'And she didn't show up?'

'No, she didn't.' Tom leaned forward and put his coffee on the floor beside his chair. 'Do we know what happened to the crew of your lugger?'

'That's the point, sir,' said Harriot, sucking his pipe. 'There's every reason to think they may still be on board.'

André Dubois stood at a second-floor window of one of the numerous warehouses lining the south side of the Thames below London Bridge, the property of a merchant sympathetic to the Revolution. Dubois knew nothing about him. If the fellow had a name, he was not privy to it. He gave a dismissive shrug and let his eye follow the forest of masts down through the Pool of London towards the Isle of Dogs.

He couldn't see where the lugger had gone down; didn't need to. It was enough that he knew she was at the bottom of the river with the bodies of her two crew. He had no regrets about what he'd done. Once the argument had begun, it would not have been safe to let them go. He stole a glance at Moreau. The latter was sitting at a small, square table, his head in his hands. The *commissaire* did not look happy.

Dubois returned to his thoughts. The incident with the boy was an altogether different matter. Once the decision had been made to kill the other two, it naturally followed that the boy would also have to go. And Dubois would have succeeded if only he'd been given sufficient time to take aim. As it was, he'd merely inflicted a wound.

The potential consequences were serious. The lad knew where they had come from and had seen what had happened to his two friends. It didn't require much imagination to guess what he would do with the information. And once the authorities knew of their presence in London, the whole operation would be at risk – not to mention their own lives. He blamed Moreau. The *commissaire* had effectively prevented him from killing both the boy and, later, the old Jew.

He'd never been able to understand Pierre Moreau's reluctance to take a life. He didn't dislike his colleague. He had a grudging respect for the man who'd often protected him from the consequences of his behaviour. And he'd needed that protection in an existence that, despite the occasional periods of high exhilaration, had been filled with more than his share of darkness. Indeed his life, both in Marseille and at sea, had seemed to comprise a constant, churning fear that led to repeated and violent confrontations with those who crossed his path. No, he didn't dislike him. He just wished the fellow would recognise that it was sometimes necessary to take a life.

He remembered the day he and Moreau had met, when the latter had caught him crawling out of someone else's home with a handful of silk handkerchiefs and a pocket full of francs. Dubois smiled sardonically. He'd made the mistake of assuming his greater bulk and physical strength would quickly overcome the tall, slightly stooped figure of authority standing between him and freedom.

It hadn't taken long for him to be disabused of the idea. Almost before he knew it, he was lying face down in the dirt of the Marseille waterfront, a calm voice prevailing on him to stop struggling.

He'd not enjoyed the experience but had been relieved to be spared the customary beating meted out to recalcitrant felons judged unable to see the error of their ways. Moreau had, in that regard, been different from the norm, and had instead sought a mutually beneficial bargain with his new prisoner.

Yet despite the difference in approach, Dubois had found it hard, if not impossible, to trust the policeman, more particularly when the terms of the bargain had included becoming an informer. He'd bridled at the notion of providing information almost as much as the implied expectation that he would, somehow, mend his violent ways.

He shook his head. He'd not been ready – still was not ready – to give up the life he had been used to. Violence and all that it entailed was so much a part of him that he could not begin to contemplate the possibility of forsaking it. Apart from any other consideration there was the attitude of those with whom he consorted to be reckoned with. Giving up violence as a means to an end would certainly have been regarded by them as a sign of weakness and an opportunity to settle old scores.

The result had been a difficult relationship between the two of them that had often teetered on the point of collapse, only to be rescued with the occasional pieces of information that Dubois had felt able to provide to his police handler.

Perhaps predictably, he had only begun to appreciate Moreau's influence on his life when the latter had been transferred to Paris in 1794, three years before he himself was drafted into the army.

Those three years had been amongst the roughest of his young life. The almost simultaneous death of his father and the departure of Moreau for Paris had exposed him to the pent-up anger of those amongst whom he plied his trade. In consequence he had felt obliged to hone his skills with the knife and the garrotte as never before. His only escape had been aboard the corsair he had inherited from his father, an escape that was soon to be snatched from him.

To this extent his relationship with Moreau had changed nothing except the ability to evade the consequences of some of the less serious of his escapades – that and the rather more dubious reputation amongst his fellow travellers, of enjoying police protection.

From that perspective, the army, when it finally arrived in his life, appeared to offer some respite from the fear and drudgery of his existence. Even the imminent prospect of battle in the mountains of northern Italy had seemed preferable to the state of constant anger and regret that were so often a feature of his life in Marseille.

But discipline, and the respect for rank that was its bedfellow, did not sit easily on Dubois's shoulders. In the early months of his army service he came close to forfeiting his life in front of a firing squad as one incident of insubordination followed another. Yet out of the chaos of his existence, the army began to recognise and harness those peculiar skills that the new recruit had cultivated on the putrid streets of his youth. To his undoubted abilities with the knife and the garrotte was added training, by the army, in the dark art of silent murder. And with this talent he was sent behind enemy lines to wreak such mischief as his fertile mind could devise.

The order to report to the office of the *ministre de la police* in Paris, a year or so after his arrival in Italy, was as unwelcome as it could be. But then any missive containing the word *police* was likely to cause serious concern in his mind, particularly where the reason for the order was not explicit. His sense of relief at being told he was to work to Pierre Moreau could then have been more the product of a temporary absolution for his tortured mind, than any real happiness at the prospect of rejoining his former handler.

'Just for a change, you'll do what you're told, Dubois,' hissed Moreau. 'Killing the old man would have achieved nothing. He knows nothing and even if he did, it is extremely unlikely he would go to the authorities. What could he say? That two men stopped to talk to him in the middle of the night? Killing him would only draw attention to ourselves at a time when we need to concentrate on our operation.'

Anger welled up in Dubois's throat and his fingers gripped the length of twine he always carried. He did not like being told what he could and could not do.

A bitter north wind swept through the Lower Pool carrying with it a light drizzle of freezing rain. Tom wiped the damp from his eyes and looked over to the Shadwell bank. A clutch of watermen and their skiffs was gathered around a large, tub-shaped lugger of about sixty feet in length, lying on the hard, directly off the Devil's Tavern on Wapping Wall.

'In the King's name, lay away there,' cried Tom, his hands cupped round his mouth. Heads turned and the skiffs fell back, leaving a channel through which the police galley made its way. A minute later it was alongside the stricken vessel.

'Your honour?'

Tom looked at the slight figure of Joe Ruxey seated at the bow thwart of the police galley. The lad could be no more than about twenty – perhaps a year or two less. He'd joined the marine police fewer than three weeks previously from the East India Company where he'd spent the last eighteen months on the China station. Tom realised that was all he knew about him.

'Aye, Ruxey, what is it?'

The boy jutted a pale, pointed chin to where a hole had been punched through the lugger's strakes, just below the waterline. Tom nodded.

'Anyone know anything about this?' he said, looking round at the watermen and gesturing to the damaged hull.

For a moment, no one said anything.

'Saw her anchored in the channel last night.' The voice caught Tom unawares. He turned to see a man of about sixty, lounging in the stern sheets of his boat, his lined, weather-beaten face staring out from behind a white nicotine-stained beard, an old nor'wester jammed down round his ears. 'A little after sunset, it were. She were all right then.'

'See anything of her crew?' said Tom.

'Can't say as I have.' The man paused and looked around at the men in the other boats. In a younger man his hesitation might have seemed the result of uncertainty. Tom waited for him to continue.

'Some say they's still aboard but there ain't no one as wants to look. I were out again afore dawn this morning.' The man spat out a plug of tobacco, watched it hit the water and then turned back to Tom. 'Saw the tips of them masts – just the trucks, see – above the water. It were a mercy she weren't rammed by nobody.'

Tom glanced at the still ebbing tide. Soon it would turn. He reckoned on less than three hours to do what needed to be done before the lugger was again submerged. He ran a practised eye over its bluff bow, the bulge in her hull amidships and the overhanging square transom. There were no markings aside from her name – *Mary-Anne* – painted in large white letters on her stern. Nothing to indicate her home port.

'Where's she from?' said Tom.

'Don't rightly know,' said the man, stroking the underside of his beard. 'But if I had to guess . . .' He pointed at the hull. 'I only ever seen luggers built that way on the south coast. Somewhere around Hastings would be my guess. I reckon if you was to look, you'd see she's got a triple keel an' all.'

'What d'you know about the damage to her hull?'

The man's eyes narrowed. 'Naught, your honour, and that's the truth.'

Tom stood up and leaned his hands against the lugger's damp strakes, his head peering over the rail at the thin layer of slime coating the deck and what was left of her sails. The deck itself was on a single level, sloping up towards the bows but levelling out midships and continuing aft on an even plane. Between the two masts were the hatches – one large, one much smaller – each raised a few inches clear of the deck. His eye fell on the forward, smaller hatch, its cover held in place by a series of timber wedges.

'Poor bastards.' Tom hauled himself over the rail and looked back into the police galley. 'Lay along there, Ruxey. I want the forward hatch cover off just as soon as you like.'

The boy didn't move, his eyes turned towards the shattered strakes, his face paler than usual.

'Bear along there, lad.' Tom's voice was sharper.

Slowly, the boy slid off his seat and clambered unsteadily up onto the lugger's deck, his eyes avoiding the forward hatch, his head bowed.

'You all right lad?'

Ruxey nodded mutely.

'Best you get back down,' said Tom, jerking his thumb at the police galley. 'Send Hart up in your place and tell him to bring a lantern.'

The boy turned away, his head still bowed. He looked close to tears. Tom raised an eyebrow. It was scarcely credible that the boy had not dealt with death before; not after eighteen months at sea. There had to be some other reason for his reluctance. A clattering of boots told him Sam Hart was on his way.

He and Sam had worked alongside one another since the earliest days of the new police. The friendship had grown despite the cultural and religious differences that separated them – Tom an Englishman with the King's commission as an officer in the Navy, Sam a Jew and an immigrant, forced to adapt to a way of life that was at once alien and threatening to his survival.

Tom didn't wait for his friend's arrival. Knocking away the wedges, he lifted the hatch cover and dropped it onto the deck. The strong smell of fish and damp clothing rose through the opening. He waited a moment for the air to clear, grateful it was not a deal worse, before dropping to one knee and peering into the black void of the crew's cabin. Behind him, he heard Sam approaching.

'I'm going down, Sam,' he said, without looking up. 'There'll not be room for both of us. I'll let you know what I find. Did you bring a lantern?'

Taking the light, he swung his legs over the cross-coaming and descended the ladder. Nearing the bottom, he looked around the cramped, low-beamed space measuring no more than seven feet in length and about six feet at its broadest point, narrowing to about a foot at the bows. On either side of the companion ladder, fixed to the hull and running parallel to it, were two narrow bunks separated from one another at the bow by a crude table. Above this hung a storm lantern.

Tom stepped off the bottom rung of the ladder and into about a foot of water, his foot brushing against something soft. He bent down and held the lantern close to the surface of the water, the light reflecting back into the cabin. He stretched out his free hand, his fingers coming into contact with material of some kind. He caught hold of it and drew it towards him. It was heavy and difficult to move. He let go and moved his hand further along. Suddenly, he stopped, his fingers grasping strands of human hair.

Again he shone the lantern. This time the light fell on the body of a man. It was lying face down, its arms outstretched above the head as if, in life, the man had been reaching for something, his fingers curled inwards.

He turned the body over, letting the light spill onto a grey face, the skin wrinkled like that of an old man, the mouth open, the pale lips drawn back over the black stumps of what remained of his teeth. He swung the lantern along the length of each arm, then the torso and finally the legs. There was no sign of any injury.

He was about to turn away when he again noticed the claw-like shape of the man's hands. He lifted one of the arms and examined the hand, noting the roughness of the skin, the ingrained filth and the broken fingernails he'd seen so often before amongst his former shipmates. But there was something else. He picked up the lantern and shone it onto the tips of the fingers. All five digits showed signs of recent damage to the skin. For a moment he continued to look at them. There was no obvious reason for the injuries. Turning the hand over, he looked at the nails. Nothing. Then he noticed a sliver of wood lodged under one. He took a knife from his belt and eased it free.

He stood up and looked round the rest of the tiny cabin. A second body lay on the larboard bunk, curled up, foetus-like, its head pressed hard against the after bulkhead. Like its companion, the body was of a young man of around twenty, dressed in the red and white striped, three-quarter length trousers and canvas jerkin of a fisherman. Tom bent over him for a closer look. Here, too, the only signs of injury were to the fingertips, slivers of wood below several of the fingernails.

Tom turned away and climbed up the companion ladder into the daylight, gratefully filling his lungs with the cold air of a late winter's morning.

'Two of them,' he said, in answer to Sam's questioning look. 'Pass me the hatch cover, will you?' He examined the underside. 'Thought so,' he muttered. 'They were still alive when the lugger was sunk. They tried to get out. You can see scratch marks, where they tried to escape.'

Tom glanced over the side to where bits of driftwood were floating slowly upstream. 'Tide's on its way in. We ain't got time to wait for the next low tide to have a proper look round. We'll have to float her in towards the bank.'

'How are we going to do that, sir?' said Sam. 'There's a bleedin' great hole in her side.'

'I'd not forgotten,' said Tom. 'We'll put a barge either side of her, pass three or four lines under her keel and wait for the tide to lift her. Soon as that's done we'll take her to shallower water.'

It took a further four hours before the tide had risen sufficiently to manoeuvre the *Mary-Anne* into position a little way downstream of Pelican Stairs and for Tom and his crew to complete an ultimately fruitless search of the lugger.

'Kemp,' said Tom, his stockings, breeches and coat now an almost uniform mud-brown. 'You and Hart bring the bodies up. Lash them one each side of the galley. They'll need to go to Wapping for the post-mortem.'

CHAPTER 3

'You're telling me there's no obvious reason why the vessel was sunk and the crew murdered?' John Harriot eyed his dishevelled surveyor with a faintly disapproving gaze.

'That's about the size of it, sir.' Tom stood close to the fireplace, the palms of his hands held towards the flames, a cloud of steam rising from his damp clothing. 'There's some suggestion that the vessel involved comes from Hastings or thereabouts. In the absence of any other infor-mation, I propose going there. See what I can dig up. We'll not get far until we know the identity of the victims and the reason for their journey to London.'

'I agree, Mr Pascoe. Will you go alone?'

'Aye. I did consider taking Hart but there's other work needs doing while I'm away. There's a coach leaves at first light tomorrow.'

'Let it be so,' said Harriot. 'By the by, where have you put the bodies?'

'Usual place. In the basement.'

'Very well. Let the coroner know before you leave.' Harriot picked up a sheaf of papers. The interview was over. Tom didn't move. 'Is there something else, Mr Pascoe?'

'As a matter of fact, there is, sir,' said Tom, choosing his words with care. 'What can you tell me about Ruxey?'

'Not a great deal.' Harriot leaned forward in his chair, his elbows resting on his desk, his hands cupped round the bowl of his pipe. 'As you already know, he came to us from the East India Company where he spent most of the last eighteen months or so in and around Canton and Shanghai. The various reports I've seen suggest he was honest, sober and industrious in the execution of his duties. Is there a problem?'

'Anything else?'

'Only the odd detail or two, not all of it flattering. He was apparently disliked by his shipmates, was considered surly and uncommunicative with a tendency to outbursts of bad temper. Aside from that, as I've already said, he was well thought of by the officers.'

'Did he ever see any action?'

'Yes, several times, in fact,' said Harriot. 'The most recent was in the Straits of Malacca when his convoy was caught by a French squadron. It was, apparently, a lively action. Several dead, I believe.'

'Very odd,' said Tom.

'What is?'

'When we went aboard the *Mary-Anne* this morning he behaved as if he'd never seen a dead body before. I was hoping, sir, you might tell me something that would help explain his reaction.'

'I regret I can't help you there, Mr Pascoe, but I dare say he'll get over it in time.'

'I certainly hope so,' said Tom. 'I'll let you know how he gets on.'

A fine curtain of rain was falling as Tom left Harriot's office and walked up Old Gravel Lane towards the London Hospital. He wanted to see Peggy in spite of her likely rejection of his overtures of friendship. She'd never got over the attack and had made it only too apparent that she no longer wished their friendship to continue. He slowed his pace, a sudden tightness in his throat. The man responsible for that attack was dead, yet it had made no difference to her attitude towards him.

She'd not told him what had happened. He'd only learned of it through Harriot. The man concerned had been arrested and indicted to stand trial at the Old Bailey; would have done so but for the decision of the Grand Jury not to proceed.

Whether it was the initial incident or the subsequent refusal of the jury to support her, the result had been the same. Peggy had withdrawn into herself and, it had seemed to Tom, held him at least partly to blame for what had happened. Nothing he had been able to say or do since that day had made any difference. She no longer wished to see him as once she had.

He thought back to the early days of his friendship with her, of how their initial shyness in each other's company had given way to a flowering of affection and trust. He remembered their growing sense of ease in each other's company, when they had been able to confide their innermost thoughts, safe in the knowledge they'd not be betrayed.

Yet the journey – at least in the early days, had not been an easy one. He'd found it hard to convey to her the sense of his own inadequacy at the loss of his sea-going command in the spring of last year. His occupation had always defined who he was as a person and contributed to his sense of self-worth. It had been some time before he had been able to adjust to the change in his circumstances and accept the new reality that was now his life.

Nor, for much the same reason, had he welcomed the opportunity of the post of river surveyor with the new marine police. Quite apart from any other consideration, he had doubted the ability of a force of sixty or so men to overcome the entrenched criminality of the fifteen thousand souls who laboured under conditions so appalling as to render their behaviour at least understandable, if not acceptable.

Despite these reservations, his friendship with Peggy had grown, the two of them often walking together in the garden quadrangle of the London Hospital in Whitechapel or taking a boat on the Thames as far as the gardens at Vauxhall, the hours slipping by in a state suffused with happiness. As spring had passed into summer, Tom had become aware of the depth of his feelings for her. With the arrival of the cool winds of autumn, he had come to believe that his future lay with her, a future which now seemed doomed.

At the top of Old Gravel Lane, he paused before turning into the wide, crowded thoroughfare that was the Ratcliff Highway, the air heavy with the smells of rotting food, dung and unwashed bodies. For a brief moment he stood and watched the multitude shuffling about its uncertain business. At a nearby fruit stall a group of barefooted children were helping themselves to whatever their nimble fingers could reach. A few yards behind, half a dozen straggle-haired girls – they could not have been older than ten or twelve – were busy pawing at the pockets of some sailors brought to anchor.

He moved on, threading his way across the highway before turning up Cannon Street, towards the Whitechapel road and the London Hospital, his thoughts returning to Peggy.

The entrance hall of the hospital was a large, bright, rectangular area with a stone-flagged floor and a high ceiling. Into the right-hand wall had been set two hatches at which a queue of people presently stood patiently waiting for their medicines to be dispensed. At the far end, opposite the main door, two marble pillars marked the entrance to a corridor that extended along the entire length of the building.

Tom crossed to the corridor and turned right, passing as he did so a series of doors, each one labelled with the name of its intended occupant or purpose: 'Apothecary', 'Physicians' Room', 'Bleeding Room', 'Privys', and so on. From somewhere came the sounds of clattering plates and the raised voices of what he imagined to be the scullery maids.

Arriving at the western end of the building, Tom turned into a lobby and descended some steps at the bottom of which was a door with a small glass panel set at about eye level. He stopped and looked through. The Receiving Room was full. He couldn't see Peggy. He opened the door and entered, his eyes sweeping over the two or three-score people that were present. Then he saw her. She was standing close to one of the examination rooms, tending to a heavily built man of about forty, his left arm missing, the sleeve of his coat pinned across his chest. She was thinner and paler than when he'd last seen her. He walked over.

'Why, Tom, it's you. Pray, what, sir, brings you here?' The tone was neutral.

'Joy, Peggy.' Tom hid his disappointment. He thought he'd grown used to the coolness of his reception. He glanced awkwardly at her patient. 'If you is at leisure, I should like to speak to you privately.'

'I . . .' Peggy smiled, a tight, nervous smile that played about her lips. She looked away. When she looked back at him, the anxiety seemed to have gone from her eyes. 'I am, as you see, otherwise engaged but, if you will but wait, I shall be at leisure. I will ask Miss Squibb to accompany us.'

It had stopped raining and a fresh smell of damp earth rose from between the dead stalks of the flowers when, a few minutes later, the three of them reached the quadrangle at the rear of the hospital and began to walk along the moss-covered flagstones. After a moment or two, Tom slowed, leaving Charity Squibb to walk on ahead. Soon, she was out of earshot.

'Peggy, I wanted to see and speak to you on—'

'Forgive me, Tom, but I think I know what it is you want to say,' said Peggy, holding up her hand. 'But you, of all people, should understand how my life has been lived since . . . since . . . well, since that day. I know it has been hard for you, as it has been for me, and I am grateful for your most particular friendship and understanding.'

There was a curious edge to her voice, welcoming yet distant, as though speaking to a stranger. The barrier he had hoped removed was still there. He said nothing, his eyes fixed on hers, waiting for her to continue.

'I regret it extremely but I can do nothing to alter the state of my mind, at least for the present,' she said. 'The image of that villain Boylin is always before me and even though he no longer lives, I fear his coming. You may think it madness but . . .'

'Dearest Peggy.' Tom stretched out a hand towards her. She shrank away, her eyes widening in fright.

'Peggy, forgive me.' Tom let his arm fall to his side. 'I had not meant to alarm you.'

But it was too late. Peggy turned and ran quickly towards the garden steps, followed by the faithful Miss Squibb.

CHAPTER 4

The coach from London clattered to a halt in the narrow confines of Market Street, Hastings at shortly before eight the following evening. Tom stretched his limbs and peered out of the window. A faded image of a swan painted on a wooden board creaked to and fro above a set of double doors. A man stood in the entrance, his face red and beaming, his large, saucer-like ears protruding from the sides of his head like those of a bat.

Tom got down from the coach and massaged the small of his back, grateful that the long and uncomfortable journey was finally at an end. If they'd hit one pothole since they'd left London, they must have hit a thousand, each one a bone-jarring, coach-swallowing, wheel-breaking specimen.

'Welcome, sir, to the Swan,' said the beaming man. 'A hearty meal and as much as you care to drink awaits you. Come in, come in.'

The town seemed deserted when, an hour or so later, Tom left the Swan and walked down the sloping street towards the distant sounds of the sea. Emerging onto a shingle beach, he looked down onto the moonlit water, the foaming white crests of the waves roaring up the beach before sliding back down again, the wind tearing at the hem of his greatcoat.

He scrambled down the steep slope of the beach, past a series of tall wooden structures, to where he could see a dozen or so fishing luggers drawn up on the foreshore. From somewhere close by, a seagull climbed noisily into the night, wheeled and disappeared.

Tom walked over to the nearest fishing boat, his eye taking in the same rough, clinker-built strakes and the triple keel boards he'd first seen on the *Mary-Anne*. She had the same bulge in her hull, the same overhanging stern below a square transom and the same bluff bow. He checked another boat and then a third. All were built the same way.

He thought of the wreck lying in the Lower Pool of the Port of London and of the men who'd died in her. There seemed little doubt they'd come from this town. Behind him, a bell tolled the hour. He turned and looked back at the town, lost in the deep shadow of the Bourne Valley, the twin harbour lights the only visible sign of life. Tomorrow he'd see the local magistrate and anyone else who might help him identify the bodies he'd seen in the

Mary-Anne. With luck he'd also discover the reason for the journey that had taken them to their deaths.

Richard Ball, jurat of the town of Hastings, stood in the low-beamed living room of his home on Fisher Street, his back to the fire, eyeing Tom with a look of mild curiosity. He did not, it seemed, often receive strangers in his home, especially those from London.

'Let me understand the purpose of your visit to Hastings,' said the jurat, scanning a letter of introduction Tom had given him. 'It is to conduct an investigation into the deaths of two men whom you suspect came from this town?'

'That's correct,' said Tom.

'May I ask what makes you think the men came from here?'

'I don't know for certain that they do. What *is* apparent is that the vessel in which the bodies were found was built here. The design is identical to the luggers I've seen on the beach.'

'What, pray, was the name of this vessel?'

'The *Mary-Anne*. Does the name, sir, mean anything to you?'

'Indeed it does,' said Ball, adjusting a pair of steel-framed spectacles on the bridge of his nose. 'The *Mary-Anne* is owned by a man named Will Sutton, or, as he's known in these parts, Surly Will.'

'You know him?'

Ball didn't answer immediately. He picked up a brass scuttle from the hearth and threw some coals onto the fire. When he looked back, there was a thoughtful expression in his eyes.

'Aye, I know him right enough.' Ball rested his arm on the mantelpiece. 'You think he is one of the men that died?'

'It's possible. I need more information before I can be sure. What do you know about him?'

'Doesn't have many friends,' said Ball. 'Lived with his father on Fisher Street, no more than a hundred yards from here. They were both fishermen, chopbacks we call them, like most of the men here. I often used to see father and son coming and going from the place they called home – in reality an old boat, sawn in half and upended in what used to be someone's garden.'

'A boat?'

'It's not unusual. Many of the families on this side of the Bourne stream live in abject squalor. There's not a square inch of land behind most of the houses in these parts that hasn't had some kind of structure put on it to act as someone's home.'

'And chopbacks,' said Tom. 'Where did they get that name from?'

'Oh, it's an old story. About thirty years ago some fishermen out of Hastings boarded a Dutchman with the intention of stealing her catch. They were beaten off, leaving one of their number behind. The Dutch skipper decided on a summary execution of the unfortunate man and hanged him from the fore-yardarm. The Hastings men, by this time reinforced, again attacked and sliced the skipper's back with an axe. Hence chopbacks.'

Tom nodded, couldn't help wondering if the fishermen of Hastings still had the same capacity for violence.

'You said you used to see Surly Will with his father. Is that no longer the case?'

'The father died about eighteen months ago. He was a widower. Had been for many years. After that, I saw less of the son,' said Ball, his face lit by the flickering flames of the fire. 'About a year ago, the lad decided there was more money to be had fighting the French than fishing. Fortunately for him, their Lordships of the Admiralty disagreed and refused his request for Letters of Marque.'

'I own their Lordships did him a favour,' said Tom. 'From what I saw of the *Mary-Anne*, his first encounter with a Frenchman would have been his last. But I interrupt you, sir.'

'For a while I heard nothing more of the fellow. I imagined he'd gone back to the fishing trade. But I was wrong. The next thing I heard was that he and a man named George Dighton – better known round here as Bulverhythe George, were running tea, silk and everything in between from across the Channel.'

'Bulverhythe George?'

'Aye. The lad comes from Bulverhythe, a small village a

mile or so down the coast. The name just stuck with him.'

'I'm sorry. You were telling me about Surly Will,' said Tom.

'Yes. He was seldom far from trouble,' said Ball. 'Was apt to be a little too quick-tempered and would often get himself into scrapes. They were harmless enough in themselves and to begin with none of us was particularly concerned. But that all changed when his father died and Surly was left to his own devices. With no one to control him, his fits of violence became more frequent and more serious. With the exception of Bulverhythe George, the few friends he had dropped away and, for a while, he was left isolated within the community. All we knew was that he continued to go out on the *Mary-Anne*, supposedly to fish. The problem was that there were seldom any fish on board when he returned, usually four or five days later. If he was asked, he'd either ignore you or tell you to mind your own business.'

Ball moved away from the fireplace and settled himself into a chair opposite his visitor. For a second or two he stared at the glowing embers in the grate, his hands joined together as if in prayer. Without looking up, he said, 'Not long after he had been refused his Letters of Marque, Surly began seeing much more of his friend Bulverhythe, and the two of them would often be seen putting to sea on the *Mary-Anne*.'

'Had they known each other long?'

'From boyhood. I used to think they got on well but about two or three months ago they had a falling out over

45

something. I think they got over it but for a while things were a little strained between them.'

'And you've no idea what it was about?'

'No, not really,' said Ball. 'It would be too easy to explain it in terms of their characters. Bulverhythe is very much the quieter of the two and didn't hold with violence. It may be that he didn't like something that Surly had done.'

'But something drew them back together again?'

'Yes. As fishermen they were not a success but they always seemed to have enough money to live on. It became increasingly obvious that they were engaged in smuggling.'

'Were they never caught?'

'Oh indeed, sir,' said Ball. 'They were brought before me and my fellow jurats on several occasions. At their most recent appearance, we committed them to the town jail, but it made no difference. Not even the confiscation of the goods they were running seemed to work. It got to the point where we were considering taking Surly's boat from him but that would have consigned both of them, as well as Bulverhythe's mother and father, to the workhouse, so we chose the lesser of two evils and let him keep the boat.

'Then, last summer, they began to disappear for weeks on end. There are those who say they were running goods direct to London, yet no one was ever quite sure.'

'London?' said Tom. 'Why would they sail there? Wouldn't it have been quicker and more profitable for them to bring goods ashore here and travel overland?'

'It does seem strange, doesn't it?' said Ball.

'Unless,' said Tom, after a short pause, 'the two of them had found a more profitable cargo than tea, coffee or silk.'

'Like what, sir?' said Ball, looking quizzically at his visitor.

'I've no idea, sir,' said Tom. 'I was merely considering the possibility. There's no chance that someone other than Surly Will and Bulverhythe George could have taken the *Mary-Anne* to London?'

'I'd be surprised,' said the jurat. 'Fishermen must go out if they are to survive. A journey to London would mean the loss of the boat for several weeks, not just a day or so.'

Tom glanced towards the window as a group of men trudged past. When he looked back, he said, 'You've mentioned Bulverhythe George. Is there anything further you can add about him?'

Ball gave an apologetic shrug. 'As I told you, I saw him often enough, but seldom spoke to him. The rector knew him better and would, I'm sure, be happy to help you.'

He stopped and looked at his visitor. 'You mention Surly and Bulverhythe but not the third man. You do know there were three men on that lugger when she left Hastings?'

'What?' said Tom. 'No, I didn't know.'

'Yes, I was on the beach – we call it the Stade round here – about three weeks ago when I saw the *Mary-Anne* putting to sea. She was some distance from the shore but I could plainly see three men aboard.'

'Any idea who the third man was?'

'No, I'm sorry, I can't help you there. The fellow had his back to me, but I'm certain the other two were Surly and Bulverhythe.'

'And no one has been reported to you as missing?'

'Not yet,' said Ball.

'Is there anyone I could ask?'

'You could try talking to one or two of the fishermen, although I doubt you'll get anywhere. They're a contrary lot and that's a fact. You'll find them drinking in the Cutter at this hour of the day.'

'Anyone in particular?'

Ball thought for a moment.

'You might try Stevy but I suspect you'll get less out of him than anyone else. Keeps himself to himself. Lives alone in a hovel up beyond the Slough. Nobody knows his surname. He rarely talks to anyone except Surly and Bulverhythe, although God knows what he has in common with those two.'

'Local lad, is he?'

'No,' said Ball. 'He's not. Arrived in the town about six years ago. Local gossip has it that his mother was from the other side of the Irish Sea; died some years ago. Nobody seems to know anything about the father.'

'Is it possible he was the third man on the *Mary-Anne*?'

'No. I've seen him about the town in the last day or so.'

CHAPTER 5

It was early afternoon, the winter light already beginning to fade when Tom left the magistrate's house and walked down Fisher Street, towards the beach. His conversation with Ball had gone some way to filling in the many gaps in his knowledge. He now knew the name of the owner of the *Mary-Anne* and the person with whom he habitually sailed. For a while, he'd been tolerably confident that they were the men who had died. But the news that a third man may have accompanied them to London now served to confuse matters.

He stopped at the bottom of Fisher Street and gazed out over the beach with its scattering of boats drawn up on the pebbles. The wind of the previous night had gone, the sea now a placid calm of grey stretching to the horizon. Close by, a group of fishermen had bent their backs to the hull of a lugger. One of them barked an order.

'Hunch up!'

'Oooh!' The fishermen straightened, their backs still pressed to the lugger's hull. The vessel slid a foot or two down the slope to the sea, the keel riding on a succession of greased boards.

'Hunch up!'

'Oooh!'

'Hunch up!'

Tom looked back at the town, crouching in the bowl-like embrace of the valley. Over to his right was the building he was looking for.

The Cutter tavern was a four-storey structure facing the sea, its scruffy, shiplap cladding worn to a silver-grey, its bleached signboard swinging in the cold winter breeze. Alongside was the lower harbour light, perched on top of a high lattice tower.

Tom crossed to the tavern door.

The room he entered was about forty feet square, its walls and ceiling covered in a yellowish film of tobacco stain, the air thick with the smell of stale beer and fish and smoke. Down the centre were some tables and benches on which sat perhaps twenty or thirty men. Against the left-hand wall a wood fire burnt in the grate, tended by a ruddy, round-faced man of about fifty, his large, vein-streaked nose suggestive of a lifetime of drinking. Tom assumed he was the landlord. He let the door slam shut behind him and made his way over to the fireplace as the room fell silent.

'Don't often get strangers in 'ere.' The landlord's breath smelt of beer. 'You visiting?'

'In a manner of speaking, Master Landlord,' said Tom. Behind him he could hear the low rumble of conversation stirring back into life. 'Down from London for a few days on business.'

'Oh, aye? What kind of business would that be?' The voice was suddenly wary.

'It's of no importance,' said Tom, aware of the change of mood. He wondered if news of the deaths had already reached the town. 'Know Surly Will, do you?'

'As it happens. What you want him for?'

'Nothing important. What about Stevy?'

'He ain't here.' The landlord's eyes swept the room. 'Might be in later.' He turned back to the fire. It was clear the conversation was over.

Tom looked round the room, silent once more, the men's unsmiling faces turned towards him. He had the feeling the publican had more to tell him. The fellow had looked apprehensive, his eyes darting between the fireplace and the men in the room.

'Well, thankee, Master Landlord. I'll not take any more of your time.' Tom turned away and walked to the door, the room still silent, the men watching his progress.

Stepping outside, he crossed the small square to a nearby building and melted into its shadow to wait. Five minutes later, the door of the tavern opened and a figure emerged into the moonlight. The man stopped and looked around as though searching for someone.

'Your honour?' The voice was low and hoarse. Then, more urgently, 'Your honour?'

'You looking for me?' Tom stepped out from the shadows and into the moonlight.

The man spun round and stared in Tom's direction before walking uncertainly towards him.

'I must speak with you, your honour,' he said, a hand outstretched, his voice hesitant. Tom recognised the landlord. 'You was asking after Surly Will.'

'Aye, so I was. What of it?'

'My name is Harry Fearne. My boy Toiler were with Surly, three, maybe four weeks ago. We ain't seen him nor Surly since. I'm afeared for my boy. I couldn't say nothing when you was speaking to me on account of everyone were listening. I must know, sir. D'you have some news of my boy?'

'My business is with Surly Will,' said Tom. 'Of your boy, I know nothing. But what makes you think he's with Surly?'

'He left these shores in Surly's boat and he ain't come back. Toiler don't usually have nothing to do with him nor his mate Bulverhythe George, neither.'

'Tell me about them,' said Tom.

'Aye, but not here,' said Fearne, glancing nervously at the door of the tavern. 'The lads what drink in my establishment wouldn't care for it if they saw me speaking with you, like.'

'Where, then?'

'By the White Rock.' Fearne pointed a finger along the coast to where a promontory jutted out into the sea about half a mile away. 'I'll meet you there at first light tomorrow.'

Close to the tavern wall, a faint rustle of leaves disturbed the stillness of the night as Stevy watched Tom and the landlord go their separate ways.

The police galley rocked alongside the narrow pontoon at the bottom of Wapping police stairs, a bitter north wind whipping the surface of the Thames into angry flecks of spume. To the east, over the Isle of Dogs, a weak sun struggled into an unwelcoming sky, its pale disc dimly seen through banks of cloud on the horizon.

Sam Hart stepped into the galley shivering despite the heavy canvas jacket he was wearing. Like the rest of the crew, he was carrying a short length of carved timber and a straw-lined sack. The former, which he now put down on the arms' chest, would serve to provide him with a dry seat while the latter would keep out the worst of the wind. He stepped into the sack, secured it with a length of twine around his chest and sat down.

'Where we heading for?' John Kemp slid an oar between the thole pins and glanced at Sam.

'Pelican Stairs. Some cully were seen coming ashore on the night them poor sods on the fishing lugger were turned off. We've to find him. There's folk round there what I know. They might be able to help. Now, if you's ready, stand by to cast off.'

The strong ebb tide caught the galley's bows, carrying them round in an arc to face downstream, the oars of the police crew driving her through the water down past the endless tangle of ships, each surrounded by its own fussing flotilla of lighters, skiffs and wherries.

'Master Hart?'

'Aye, Ruxey, what is it?' Sam looked at the newest member of the crew.

'I were wondering about those men you was talking on just now. The ones that died. D'you know who they were? Their names, like?'

'Nay, lad. It's too early for that. Don't expect to hear nothing until Mr Pascoe gets back. Why d'you ask?'

'No reason.' Joe Ruxey hesitated, turning away as if anxious to avoid further questioning, the hint of a blush in his cheeks. 'I were just interested.'

Sam let it go. He had other things on his mind. The instructions from Tom Pascoe had been quite clear. He was to make enquiries of his network of informants and discover the identity of the man who'd been seen coming ashore at Pelican Stairs on the night of the murders.

Sam mentally ran through a list of half a dozen people he knew in the area who might be able to help. He sighed. It would be difficult persuading any of them to talk. It wasn't that they would not want to help him under any circumstances. Far from it. The majority had known him since he was a child; belonged to the same close-knit community of Ashkenazi Jews as his father. But the relationship was at once an advantage and a drawback.

On the one hand he was able to call on information that no gentile could obtain. But on the other, there were rules that had to be followed if he were not to breach that code of conduct to which all Jews subscribed. Informing was frowned upon. Informing on another Jew more so. The Jews had a word for it – *moser*.

He sucked a lungful of air through clenched teeth as he thought through his options. He had, over the years, drifted away from his faith and the community of which he had been a part. He had found it difficult to reconcile the rabbinic traditions and the way of life they imposed with that of a nominally Christian population and its distractions. It wasn't something he was proud of. Later, when he might have been expected to think more deeply about what Judaism had to offer, it was too late. He'd grown out of the habit of worship and lost the ability to pray.

Nor had that been the only reason behind his decision to leave. He had seen for himself the physical and mental abuse to which the faithful were routinely subjected by a population seemingly inured to the sufferings of their fellow human beings. But if he was honest, he had to admit that those who endured the most did so as a consequence of the choices they had made. The way they dressed and the way they spoke, together with a widespread reputation for criminality, made them a target.

Sam glanced over his shoulder. A line of brigs, barquentines and a snow were clubbing down on the tide, their kedge anchors dragging the bottom of the river, their foremast t'gallants billowing in the stiff breeze. Soon they would begin their turn into Limehouse Reach, the first of many changes in course, on their long journey to the open sea.

'Ain't this where you wanted to go?' Kemp's voice broke in on his thoughts.

'Thankee, Kemp,' said Sam, recognising the black and white timber frame of the Devil's Tavern, a flight of wooden steps to its left. He put the tiller hard over and watched the galley swing up into the tide, her bows at an angle to the rushing water, edging her towards the steps.

'Ship starboard oars ... easy now,' said Sam, watching the rubbish-strewn Thames slapping and gurgling its way past the mooring poles. 'Hitch on and make fast.'

The galley slid smoothly to a halt alongside the bottom step.

'You come with me, Ruxey,' said Sam, climbing ashore. 'Stay with the boat, Kemp. I don't want no thieving bastard having it away as soon as our backs is turned.'

Sam ran up the steps and into the passageway, the walls

on either side liberally covered with torn and fading sheets of paper. He didn't look at them. He already knew what they were. All the river stairs had their fair share of posters carrying descriptions of the bodies found drowned in the tideway.

'There's a cully I knows,' said Sam as he and Ruxey turned into Wapping Wall and headed east. 'Ain't much happens in these parts without him getting to hear on it.'

Fifteen minutes later they turned off the main thoroughfare into Labour in Vain Street, a dank, narrow, rubbish-strewn alley, hardly wider than the mouth of a cesspit, most of its grime-covered buildings teetering on the point of collapse, their roofs sagging, their doors and windows more often than not missing. Sullen-looking women stood in the empty doorways, barefooted children clutching their mothers' long skirts as they watched the two constables walk past.

Arriving at the end of the lane, the two men stood in front of a sad-looking three-storey building, all of whose windows and doors had been removed. Sam studied it for a few moments. Then, waving at Ruxey to follow him, he stepped over the threshold and walked down a narrow hallway, past a ruined staircase to a room at the back. Here, as at the front of the house, the windows had been removed as had many of the floorboards. Sam stopped in the doorway and looked round. The room appeared empty but for a pile of rags in one corner. He walked over and prodded them with the toe of his boot.

'As Abraham is our father in faith,' mumbled a voice, 'leave me to sleep.'

'Joshua?' said Sam, bending down. 'Joshua, it's me, Samuel. Show a leg. I want a word with you.'

The bundle stirred and a gaunt face appeared. 'Samuel?'

'Aye, it's me,' said Sam, smiling. 'D'you not remember me?'

The gaunt face came fully into view and a pair of coal-black eyes gazed at Sam.

'Aye, aye, I remember you well enough. You and your father also. He of blessed memory.' The old man paused, his tired, bloodshot eyes swivelling from Sam to Ruxey and back again. A thought seemed to come to him and he began to shake. 'What is it you want of me?'

'It's nothing,' said Sam, stretching out a hand and placing it on the old man's shoulder. 'A friend needs my help but I cannot find him. I was told you might have seen him. He came ashore at Pelican Stairs a few nights since. Some say he were hurt. Now he's disappeared.'

'I ain't seen naught of your friend,' said Joshua, staring at Sam, an anxious look in his dark eyes. 'But I heard folk speak of him at the synagogue.'

'What folk would that be?' coaxed Sam.

The old man remained silent, his jaw moving up and down, his eyes fixed on the floor in front of him. Sam was beginning to think he'd not heard the question when the man spoke.

'As I recall, it were Moses Solomon. I'll not be sure, mind, but I think it were him.'

'And you say he was in the synagogue. Which one was that? Gun Yard? Cutler Street? Where?'

'I don't rightly recall.' Joshua rubbed his forehead with a gnarled finger, his eyes drifting away to fix themselves on the remnants of the far wall. 'It might have been Rosemary Lane.'

Sam sat back on his haunches and ballooned his cheeks.

'Thankee, Joshua,' he said, getting to his feet. Then he reached into his pocket, drew out a coin and pressed it into a dirt-encrusted hand. 'Keep well.'

CHAPTER 6

It had snowed in the night. Tom pulled his old navy great-coat about him and headed out of Hastings along the lane that would take him to Priory Water and the hills beyond. A fresh flurry of snowflakes tumbled out of a slate-grey sky. Around him men and boys were trudging in the same direction, trousers tucked into thigh-length sea-boots, thick wool jackets worn open to the weather, bright spotted handkerchiefs tied around their necks. Above them, the ruined battlements of a Norman castle seemed to look down at them from the craggy summit of the West Hill.

He branched right and began climbing, gently at first and then more steeply. He was alone now; the fishermen turning off towards their boats on the Stade. He could have remained with them a little longer and taken the coastal path, past the Gunner's House, to the White Rock. But he wanted to be on his own. Away from the prying eyes that would otherwise have followed his every move.

A chill breeze gusted along the coastline ruffling the soft snow that had gathered in the nooks and crevices of the cliff face. A dozen or so seagulls swooped with effortless grace over the grey surface of the sea, their mournful shrieks like the call of the damned.

He paused and looked back through the pre-dawn gloom to the tall, black-painted net shops and the score of capstans used to haul the big luggers over the stone beach. The men were mere specks now, moving between the boats, making ready to put to sea. The sights, the sounds, the smells brought back memories of long ago when, in his father's boat, Tom had chased the herring off the Northumberland coast as far south as Yarmouth. He remembered the harshness and hunger of those days and nights spent at sea, when a man's ability to feed his family depended on the vagaries of the wind and the moon. He remembered the seasons of plenty and those when the fish didn't come, the boredom and, aye, the sudden onset of danger when the weather would change in the blink of an eye and send the little boats scuttling before the storm, chased by the white-tipped breakers that threatened to overwhelm them.

A sudden movement caught his eye, down amongst the jumble of warehouses, smithies, carpenters' shops, wood stores and tanneries that stood at the edge of the town. The area was dark and deserted at this early hour. For a while longer he remained still. Then he shook his head and resumed his climb.

The track curved away from the sea, upwards towards a solitary corn mill at the summit, its rust-coloured sails turning slowly in the wind. Passing it, he dropped down the other side towards the craggy shape of the White Rock.

'I was afeared you'd not come, your honour,' said a cold-looking Harry Fearne, landlord of the Cutter, as he emerged from behind a large boulder. He beckoned Tom to follow him and led the way along a narrow path hewn into the face of the rock until they reached a stone platform over-looking the English Channel.

'These are Spanish, are they not?' said Tom, nodding at a number of cannons mounted on the ledge, all of them pointing out over the sea.

'Aye. They was taken off a man-of-war. If Bony ever comes this way, we might even get to use them.'

'If Bony gets to within range of these, we'll all be in trouble,' said Tom. 'But, pray, tell me about your boy.'

'Toiler?' Harry Fearne looked out across the white-crested expanse of sea, a pensive look on his face. 'It's a long story. Robert Thwaites is how he were christened. I told you he were my boy and, in a manner of speaking, he is. His real father is dead. Lost overboard in a proper sou'westerly blow about ten year ago. Toiler and his kid sister, Josephine, took it hard and for a long time we didn't see neither of 'em down on the Stade. But I made it my business to look after the boy and Josephine too. Came to regard 'em as me own, like. Then, bit by bit, they started coming down to the Stade again. Sometimes it were just Toiler and sometimes both of 'em. Toiler were the quiet one of the two and he'd just do his work and go home again. But his little sister were into everything and would talk to all the lads free and easy. I didn't give it no thought then, but after she disappeared, I wished I had.'

'Toiler's sister disappeared?' said Tom. 'When did that happen?'

'About five year ago. One day she were here and the next she'd gone. It nearly drove their mother mad with grief. And young Toiler weren't much better. For months we all searched for her, hoping she were alive, that maybe she'd gone to Rye or Pevensey or some such. But she never come back and we had to accept she'd gone for good, maybe swept away in a storm, same as her father.'

'You said you didn't give it any thought, then,' said Tom. 'What did you mean?'

'Surly Will,' said Fearne with a knowing downward jerk of his head. 'He and Toiler were about the same age while Josephine were about two years younger. Them three and another lad what we call Bulverhythe George used to play together when they was nippers.'

Fearne walked to the edge of the cliff and looked back at Tom. 'About two or three months before she disappeared, I see her and Surly alone. I didn't know what it was but they seemed different, like they was sweet on each other.

Then, all of a sudden, it were finished. As I said, I didn't give it no thought at the time But now ...'

'Did she ever see the other boy, Bulverhythe, on his own?'

'No, but that don't mean he weren't sweet on her, too,' said Fearne.

'How old was she when she disappeared?' said Tom.

Fearne puffed his cheeks and considered for a moment. 'About fifteen, I reckon. No more.'

'What happened after that?'

'Her brother – Toiler, like – took over his father's boat and went back to fishing but his heart weren't in it no more. He seemed to get over it but every now and then I'd see him staring out to sea and I knew he were thinking of his sister. Then, about four months since, I sees him talking to Surly and Bulverhythe George. It were strange. Toiler's got nothing in common with those two villains. They stopped being friends when they was nippers. Went their own ways, like.'

'Was that the only time you saw them together?'

'Aye, though I did hear from some of the other lads that Toiler were seeing quite a bit of Surly.'

'So he often went out in the boat with them?'

'No, that's the strange thing. I only ever saw him go out in the boat that once.'

'I've heard it said Surly and Bulverhythe sailed to London several times. Had you heard that?' said Tom, changing the subject.

'Aye,' said Fearne.

'What were they doing there?'

'Don't rightly know. The old Reverend Coppard could likely tell you more. There ain't much he don't know about in this 'ere town.'

Tom walked up West Hill from his meeting with Harry Fearne, his hoary breath rising into the cold March air. He stopped and looked up at the great sweeps of the corn mill he had passed earlier, seeming to wave to its neighbours at Ore and Fairlight and Baldslow.

He thought of Toiler, wondering what the lad had been doing on the *Mary-Anne* with Surly, a man whose company he'd not shared since boyhood. They had nothing in common and yet had chosen to sail with one another. Was it possible there'd been an argument between them which had led to murder? Or had the crew of the *Mary-Anne* simply fallen victim to a robbery that had gone wrong?

Ahead of him the long grass quivered in the snow. Tom saw the sudden movement and halted, his senses alert. Nothing stirred. He waited for a moment, then walked on, irritated by his reaction. It had probably been a rabbit or some other small creature. His mind returned to his interview with the landlord of the Cutter.

There was no warning.

A blinding flash and the roar of exploding gunpowder rent the air ten, perhaps twelve paces in front of him. Tom felt the tremor of something passing close to his left ear. He dropped to the ground, his eyes searching the slope above him. A man leapt to his feet and was running towards him, a knife in his hand.

Tom rolled onto his back and yanked at the sea-service pistol wedged in his coat pocket. He could hear the man's footsteps, the swishing sound of his boots through the snow-covered grass.

He waited, knew he'd only get one chance. He judged the moment, rolled onto his stomach, palmed the cock of his gun with his left hand while his finger tightened round the trigger. He aimed and pulled hard. He felt the savage kick-back of the weapon, saw a tongue of flame spit from the muzzle and a plume of smoke belch into the morning air, obscuring his view.

He jumped to his feet, tossed the gun aside and drew his cutlass, staring through the drifting smoke. Slowly it cleared. A body lay in the snow, the eyes open, a small, neat hole in the centre of his forehead.

CHAPTER 7

Wapping Street was busy by the time Sam Hart left the police office and turned left. His search for Moses Solomon had got him nowhere. The hat-seller had not been seen in any of the synagogues in Rosemary Lane nor those in Houndsditch. He crossed the bridge at Hermitage Dock before turning right towards Smithfield and Butcher Row. There was still the synagogue at Duke's Place, a little to the north of Aldgate, that he hadn't tried and it was to there that he was now headed.

The synagogue was an ornate, three-storey building wedged into a corner between two rows of terraced houses in Duke's Place. Sam crossed the square and mounted the steps in front of the building.

'*Shalom aleichem.*' He was greeted at the door and handed a black skullcap and a white, tasselled prayer shawl.

'*Aleichem shalom,*' said Sam, draping the garment over his shoulders and putting on the cap before going inside.

He sat down at one of the benches near the door. The interior was, he guessed, about a hundred and twenty feet long and roughly seventy wide. To the left a triple row of arched windows extended the length of the building and reached almost from floor to ceiling, the whole bisected by an upper terrace in which sat a number of women. Down the centre of the synagogue, and suspended from the high, vaulted ceiling, were a number of chandeliers, each one containing upwards of sixty lighted candles.

At the far end, past a raised dais with its brass handrail, and hidden behind a scarlet curtain hanging between two marble pillars, was the resting place of the Ark. He looked round. The benches were filling, the worshippers all draped as he was in their white *tallit* and wearing a *kippah*. Many were sitting, others stood, bent forward, rocking to and fro, their hands held up in front of them, palms facing backwards.

From somewhere near the front, the rich, full voice of the cantor rose into the air, joined now and again by the rest of the congregation, the sound swelling through the high-arched interior, rising and falling in a melodic chant.

Behind Sam, the door of the synagogue squeaked open, daylight flooding in. Sam turned. The stooped figure of an old man shuffled in, his gait familiar.

The cantor was still singing. The congregation rose to its feet, obscuring his view of the newcomer. Sam turned to face the front. The scroll containing the Torah was being carried in procession up the central aisle, the worshippers moving towards it, touching it as it passed. He risked another glance over his shoulder, could see the old man clearly now. It was Moses Solomon. He breathed a sigh of relief.

He'd not seen the fellow for weeks; had not needed to. They were not friends in the ordinary sense of the word. The old man was a ragman and hat-seller, a sometime petty thief, a source of information, to be made use of as and when required.

He shook his head, uncomfortable with the direction his thoughts were taking him. Solomon did not choose to speak to him; did not give information without cost to the code by which he lived.

Sam pushed aside his concerns. He would try and obtain the information he wanted without recourse to the blackmail that he had in mind. Yet he wondered if he was not about to ask too much of the old pedlar. Quite apart from the Semitic principles involved, the life of an informant was a dangerous one, more so for an elderly man, physically unable to protect himself.

Sam was suddenly aware of the sound of shuffling feet. Around him, men were leaving. The service was over. He got up, removed his shawl and the skullcap and followed them. He could see Solomon's bent figure making its way in the same direction. He caught up with him as he emerged into the square.

'Moses.' Sam lifted the collar of his coat against a cold, driving rain. 'A moment of your time.'

The old man ducked at the sound of his name, a momentary look of fear in his clouded eyes as he turned to face Sam. As recognition dawned, he raised a trembling hand in salute, his fingers bent, as though grasping for some unseen object.

'Forgive me, master.' Solomon's eyes rested for a moment on Sam's face before looking quickly round Duke's Place, now almost deserted. 'I regret I did not recognise you.'

'It's nothing.' Sam glanced back at the synagogue as the last of the worshippers emerged and hurried on their way. 'I came here in the hope of seeing you.'

'You are not here for *Pesah*?' An anxious look.

'No, I regret not.' Sam looked down at his hands, embarrassed by the admission. He might no longer practise his faith but there were times when he did not like to be reminded of the fact.

'Was there some little service you required of me?' The coal-black eyes fixed themselves on Sam.

'Shall we talk inside?' A gesture at the entrance through which they had just come. 'Out of this wind?'

They made their way back across the square, the tins tied round the old man's waist jangling noisily as he climbed the stone steps. Inside, the grey winter light struggled through the rows of arched windows. An acolyte had lowered the candelabra and was putting out the last of the candles. Sam led the way to one of the side benches and waited for Solomon to catch up.

'There is something, you might be able to do for me,' said Sam, searching the old man's careworn features. 'You sometimes sleep, do you not, by the river, alongside the Devil's Tavern?'

Solomon stared at the stone floor. Somewhere, a door slammed shut. The acolyte had finished his duties and was gone. They were alone.

'How is it you know where I sleep, your honour?'

'You know how it is. People talk,' said Sam. 'That's where you sleep, is it not?'

'Aye, when there's not a warmer bed to be found,' said Solomon, his hands shoved between his knees, his head bent forward.

'Did you see anything unusual while you were there? Anything you want to tell me about?'

'No, Master Hart. I see nothing.'

'Someone swimming in the Thames and coming ashore at the stairs?'

'No, sir. Nothing, I swear.'

Sam gazed steadily at the old man. He had hoped it wouldn't be necessary to take the path he'd now set himself.

'The thing is, Moses,' he said, 'I want to help you but you're making things very difficult for me. I've heard you've been up to your old tricks again.'

'Not me, your honour,' said Solomon, shaking his head, a tremble in the voice.

'The Bow Street lads are looking for someone of your description,' said Sam. 'Seems there's a witness. And the witness has said that a cully who looks like you bought some stuff what was stolen from a house. The Runners have asked for our help.'

Solomon's face paled.

'D'you understand what I'm saying, Moses? What I want you to do is think carefully and tell me if you saw anything down by the stairs a few nights since, and I might forget to say anything to them boys from Bow Street.'

'It is forbidden to speak, your honour.' Moses turned his pleading eyes on Sam.

'I understand what you're saying, Moses, but this is important. Two men have died and we need to find out who did it. I need your help. I've heard you saw a cully come ashore that night. I want you to tell me about him.'

The ragman turned his head away, his lower jaw moving rapidly from side to side, his bloodshot eyes fixed on the scarlet curtain at the front of the synagogue.

'I were asleep, close to the stairs – the one's you's been talking of.' The voice was barely audible. 'I were woke by something. It could've been a gun. I don't know. Anygate, I listened for a while but hears no more and I thought I must've been dreaming. It were then when I sees this cully swimming in the river. I hid and saw him come up them stairs.'

'Did he see you?' said Sam, getting up and walking to an adjacent bench.

'No, he never saw me.'

'What did he look like? Young? Old? Fat? Thin?'

'He were no more than a boy,' said Solomon. 'Dark hair what was curly. And broad in the face.'

'What happened then?'

'Naught. He went up the alley and that were the last I saw on him.'

'You said you thought you heard a gun. Had someone been shot?'

'Only the lad,' said Solomon. 'Leastways I think he might have been. On account of he was limping and looked like he were in pain.'

Sam nodded slowly, watching the motes of dust dancing in the pale sunlight that was slanting in through the tall windows. He'd found the man he'd set out to find but the real prize still eluded him. The description of the man seen swimming ashore had been barely adequate and without something better the chances of finding him were slim in the extreme. Sam leaned forward, his elbows on the bench in front, his chin resting in the cups of his hands.

'There's always the hospitals,' he murmured.

'What's that, your honour?' Solomon threw him a startled glance.

'Nothing,' said Sam. 'What did you do after the boy disappeared? Did you go back to sleep?'

'No . . .' Solomon's eyes swivelled from side to side, searching the empty hall. 'I went away. I were afeared the lad would come back and find me.'

Sam paused. Something was missing. The old man had removed the pile of hats he routinely wore and placed them on the bench beside him. He glanced at the bare head and noted the absence of the skullcap. 'You're not wearing your *kippah*. Have you lost it?'

Solomon's hand flew to the top of his head.

'I have it in my pocket. I forgot to put it on.'

Sam watched the old man draw the cap from his pocket and place it on his head. He could see traces of dried mud on it. He didn't believe the explanation. Wearing the *kippah* was, for a practising Jew, as natural as eating and sleeping.

'You didn't just forget, did you, Moses?' said Sam. 'Something happened down by them stairs which you haven't told me about.'

'I thought I were a dead man,' said Solomon, glancing up and down the synagogue as though to satisfy himself he'd not been overheard. 'They had my *kippah*. They knew I had been in the passage by the tavern.'

Sam continued to press the old man for answers he would have preferred not to give. He couldn't claim to enjoy the process. He perfectly understood the mental struggle through which Solomon was going. But he had to know the truth.

Half an hour later he left the old hat-seller sitting on

the bench and went outside into the pale light of the morning. It was quiet now but for the patter of the rain. He thought of the old man he'd left behind in the synagogue. He remembered the expression on his face, the hesitant voice and the way he had refused to meet Sam's gaze when answering questions. He sympathised, could understand why Solomon should not wish to involve himself in a matter that was of no concern to him. Except that now, he suspected, it probably did concern him. Sam shook his head and hoped he was wrong

Somehow he didn't think he was.

CHAPTER 8

Peggy knelt on the floor of the receiving room of the London Hospital. The thigh wound was a mess, fragments of bloody cloth protruding from the pulped and swollen flesh. She glanced at the patient's white face, beads of perspiration standing out along the hairline. He looked to be in his early twenties, his long, tangled hair reaching down to his shoulders, a pair of thick eyebrows meeting over the bridge of a beak-like nose. She cradled his head as it thrashed to and fro with the onset of a fever. She looked round the room for anyone who might have brought him to the hospital. There was no one.

She got to her feet and hurried over to the duty surgeon's examination room, knocked and went in. Three men, identically dressed in black, were bent over the figure of a patient lying prostrate on a long wooden table in the centre of the room.

'Yes, what is it?' Mr William Blizard, Principal Surgeon

at the London Hospital, did not look up.

'If you please, sir, there is an object which I believe you might wish to examine as a matter of urgency,' said Peggy, addressing the surgeon's broad back.

Blizard stopped and looked at her from beneath his left elbow, an eyebrow raised in surprise.

'And what, pray, makes you think that, nurse?'

'The object, a young man, has been shot, sir.' Peggy let her eyes drop under the surgeon's relentless gaze. 'In the leg, sir. He is presently without his senses and showing signs of the fever.'

'If you will pardon me, Dr Headington.' Blizard nodded to his companion, and reached over for his coat. 'I won't be long.'

He followed Peggy out of the room and dropping to one knee beside the injured boy, examined the wound. After a moment or two, he said, 'This is not recent. Do we know how he came by his hurt or where he's been these two or three days since?'

He didn't wait for an answer. Turning back to the injured boy, he prodded the area around the wound with the tips of his fingers, with only the occasional grunt to mark the progress of his investigation. At last, he clambered to his feet and wiped his hands on his handkerchief.

'He's certainly been shot,' he murmured, gazing at the wound from under a pair of bushy eyebrows. 'The question is, do I leave the ball where it is or try and remove it?'

Peggy remained silent.

'Be so good,' he said, 'as to inform Dr Headington that I should be glad to see him as a matter of urgency in the cutting room. I propose to remove what I suspect to be a lead ball from this object. I want you there as well, Miss Tompkins.'

Peggy nodded, beckoned the porters and watched as they carried the new patient out of the receiving room. She felt her pulse quicken at the prospect of what was to come. She'd been to the cutting room many times, witnessed many an operation. The experience never got any easier.

She sighed and looked round for Dr Headington.

The Reverend William Coppard, Rector of the Parishes of St Clements and All Saints, Hastings in the county of Sussex, nodded gravely as he listened to the story. Nothing much surprised him any more and while he was sympathetic to the loss of life, he couldn't pretend he was affected by it in any real sense of the word. Death was, after all, an inevitable consequence of life and everyone had to meet it at some point or another. It was, for him, a routine everyday occurrence that called for the observance of certain formalities, but no more. He had, long ago, learned to divorce himself from any emotional involvement in the grieving process.

'Yes, yes, Mr Pascoe,' said the reverend, as he and Tom walked along the seafront below the cliffs of the West Hill,

'I certainly knew Stevy. He was not what I would have called a hothead.'

'Any reason why he would want to kill me?' said Tom.

'I'm tempted to say his motive had something to do with your visit to the Cutter last night. Many of the men are involved in smuggling and would not take too kindly to any questions that might unearth their activities.' The reverend laced his fingers across an ample stomach before going on. 'I say I'm tempted but I don't really believe it. There has to be some other, more compelling, reason for Stevy to have acted as he did.'

'Like what, sir?'

'All I can say for certain is that Surly Will and his friend Bulverhythe George have been up to something that they and, presumably, Stevy, are anxious to keep quiet. Stevy's attempt on your life may have been connected with that.'

'I see,' said Tom, gazing out over a grey sea, streaked with white, the waves marching, rank on rank, towards the beach like some invading army. 'Was he close to the two men?'

'I wouldn't say close, Mr Pascoe, but he was certainly in their company more often than anyone else, more especially these few last months. I got the impression that whatever the other two were up to, Stevy was in it too.'

'What about his background?' asked Tom. 'What sort of man was he?'

'Now there's a question,' said the rector, puckering his

lips. 'He was a very clever young fellow. He had obviously received something of an education at some point in his life because he could read and write. He came to Hastings shortly after the outbreak of war in '93 but never became part of the community. The only people he was ever known to have contact with – and then only infrequently – were the two men I've already mentioned.'

'And what about Toiler?'

'Toiler, sir?' said the reverend, his bushy eyebrows shooting skywards. 'What has he to do with all this?'

'He was with Surly and Bulverhythe on board the *Mary-Anne* when she sailed from this town three weeks ago,' said Tom.

'You do surprise me,' said the rector, sucking in his cheeks. 'He's the last person I would have expected to have anything to do with those men.'

'Yet, sir, something persuaded him to join them,' said Tom.

'D'you see that light?' Coppard pointed to a spot, part way up the little bowl-shaped valley in which the town nestled. 'The large lantern on top of a wooden tower? No, no, a little to the left of St Clement's. Yes, that one!'

Tom nodded.

'That light,' continued the rector, 'and another one close to the Cutter, is often all that stands between a safe landing and death for the fishermen of this town. They rely utterly on those lights, especially when the south-westerlies are blowing and the sea is doing its best to drown everyone. The men must line up the two lights or risk disaster. And for what, sir? For what?'

Tom opened his mouth, decided he hadn't the first idea what he was expected to say and closed it again, wondering what all this had to do with Toiler.

'Well, sir, I shall tell you for what.' The reverend wagged a fat finger in the air and breathed in deeply. 'For nothing, sir. The fish they catch seldom brings in sufficient for the men's daily needs, certainly not enough to justify the risks they take. It would be surprising, sir, were they not to seek other ways of making a living.'

'Like smuggling?' said Tom.

'Aye, sir, like smuggling,' said the rector. 'I do not condone it but it is a fact. They will carry anything across the Channel that brings them a profit.'

'Are you suggesting that hunger may have driven young Toiler to throw in his lot with the other two, and engage in this trade?' said Tom. 'And if so, why did Stevy not also go?'

'That I can't say,' said the rector, cocking an eyebrow.

Tom reached into his coat pocket and taking out a plug of tobacco, bit off a chunk. 'Then what of the disappearance of Toiler's sister? What effect did that have on him?'

'So you know about that, sir.' Coppard rubbed his chin with the palm of his hand and glanced at Tom with small, bead-like eyes. 'I don't know that I'm qualified to say anything on the subject.'

'Pray, what d'you mean, sir?'

'This is all very difficult, Mr Pascoe. I am a minister of the church and, as such, have certain responsibilities, not the least of which is the pastoral care of my flock. They must have confidence in my ability to respect their privacy.'

'I understand your difficulty, sir, but I am in the process of investigating the deaths of two of your parishioners. If the disappearance of this young woman can be linked to the deaths, then I beg you to tell me what you know.'

For a moment or two the rector said nothing, his eyes scanning the horizon. When he spoke, it was more to himself than to Tom.

'Am I released from my vow of secrecy?' he mused. 'After all, he's probably dead now.'

'I don't follow . . .' began Tom.

'In matters of this kind,' said the rector, 'a priest is bound by rules of secrecy. He may not, sir, divulge anything said to him in confession. I was merely reminding myself of that rule. But in this case, I conclude that the death of the person concerned releases me from my obligations.'

'I'm exceedingly glad to hear it,' said Tom.

'About two months ago,' said the rector, 'Surly Will came to see me and said he had something to tell me.'

Tom inclined his head in what he hoped was an encouraging sort of way, and waited for the rector to continue.

'He told me that about a week before Toiler's sister disappeared, he'd found her walking alone close to the cliffs of the East Hill. They had, until a short time before, been seeing quite a lot of each other but that had now ceased. He tried to speak to her but she refused his advances. He lost his temper and raped her.'

'Let me, sir, get this straight in my mind,' said Tom. 'Surly comes to you two months ago and tells you about an incident that took place – what – five years ago? Is that right?'

'Yes. I suppose it must have been preying on his mind.'

'And as a result of that incident she left the town?'

'It certainly appeared to be part of the reason,' said the reverend. 'But from what I understand it was not the first time Surly had used violence towards her. In fact it seems to have been a regular occurrence. I suspect the girl simply decided that she could take no more.'

'What did Toiler have to say about it?'

'He didn't find out. At least, not then.'

'But later?'

'It's quite possible Surly confided in a friend at the same time he spoke to me. If he did . . .' Coppard shrugged. 'Word soon gets around a small community like this.'

CHAPTER 9

The cutting room at the London Hospital was situated in the eaves, its high, sloping ceiling given over entirely to a skylight window through which a weak sunlight presently streamed. Along the length of the wall below the window was a series of stepped terraces, each level protected from the one above by a brass handrail at about chest height. A coal-fired stove occupied one corner while, in the centre of the room stood a narrow wooden table about seven feet long and about waist height, above which hung a lighted oil lantern. Below the table were a number of tin pails, placed there for the reception of discarded limbs and other detritus. Next to the table was another, smaller one on which had been laid out a bow saw, two bistouries, a catlin, a set of trephines and various other items of the surgeon's trade.

Peggy followed the porters into the room and watched them lift the barely conscious young man on to the larger of the two tables. She wished Tom were with her to calm the anxiety she felt. It was odd she should think of him now, when she had least expected to. She had considered him out of her life, a part of her existence that had faded into obscurity. And yet ... She closed her eyes, acutely aware of how she had behaved towards him over the past months, of her dismissal of his offer of friendship, of her failure to recognise her true feeling towards him. But how could it have been otherwise? Boylin's attack had destroyed the innate trust with which she had hitherto viewed the human race and awakened in her a cynicism she'd not known she possessed. The effect had been to push the only person she had ever loved to the outer reaches of her life.

An image stole into her mind of a tall, broad-shouldered man with long hair, the colour of straw, tied at the nape, his face furrowed with deep lines about his eyes, a vertical scar, faint now with the passage of time, running down the right side from his eye to his chin. He was wearing a blue coat with white lapels that had seen better days, the colour faded through long exposure to the elements. On the left shoulder was a bright flash of blue where once had resided the single epaulette of his Master and Commander rank in the King's Navy. He was smiling at her. She could have sworn she felt the rough skin of his hand brushing against her arm.

The image faded, replaced by that of her nemesis, the man responsible for the unhappiness of the past few months. She frowned. The mental torment of what had occurred that afternoon was still with her. Less often, perhaps, than in the past but still there. The nightmares had ceased. So, thankfully, had the fear of going alone beyond the gates of the hospital and the cold sweat with which she used to greet each new day. Yet the residue of self-loathing and the mistrust of men still lingered.

The door to the cutting room opened and two men came in. The first, the younger of the pair, was carrying a large glass container filled with what appeared to be malt whisky. Behind him, Peggy recognised the stooped figure of the apothecary in his customary black coat and breeches. The two men walked to the table in the centre of the room where the younger man decanted a measure of the amber-coloured liquid into a glass tumbler and handed it to his companion.

'Here lad, drink this,' said the apothecary, holding the tumbler to the patient's lips. 'It'll help.'

Ten, twenty, thirty minutes dragged by. From time to time, more spirits were offered and accepted. No one spoke. At last, the apothecary approached the table, examined the patient, and nodded to one of the porters. The man left the room and a moment or two later there came the clanging sound of the bell mounted outside the theatre door.

Almost at once, Peggy heard the sound of running feet. The door burst open and a noisy, jostling group of about a dozen young men rushed in and made their way to the terraces. Behind them came several porters who walked to the table in the centre of the room and joined those already there. No one appeared to take any notice of the now inebriated patient, seeming to prefer to continue such conversations as the bell might have interrupted.

A short time later the theatre door again opened and into the room walked the sombre figure of Mr William Blizard accompanied by Dr Richard Headington, the duty physician, followed by the surgeon's dressers and his two assistant surgeons. At once the general hum of conversation died away.

'Gentlemen,' said Mr Blizard, removing his coat and looking up at the students lining the terraces, 'this is a case of a gunshot wound where the ball has entered the object's right thigh and is embedded deep within the soft tissue. The hurt is some days old and there is evidence that an attempt has already been made to extract the ball. I suspect my task has, in consequence, been rendered more difficult. It is, gentlemen, a procedure I would not have undertaken but for the presence of other foreign matter within the wound. Those of you who have spent time at your studies will recall my considered view that injuries of this type are best left alone to heal of their own accord, unless there are pressing reasons for intervening. I do not, I think, need to add that Dr Headington, here, is in full accord with my proposals.'

Blizard rested the tips of his fingers on the operating table, his forehead creased in concern, his eyes on the boy in front of him. Peggy guessed what he was thinking. She'd seen that look of fearful anticipation before; a horror of the pain he was about to inflict, the prospect of ending the patient's life. She saw Blizard's hands tremble slightly as he mopped his brow with a handkerchief and looked up to face his students again.

'You will note, gentlemen,' said the surgeon, clearing his throat, 'that my first task is the removal of debris from the wound. After that I shall attempt to extract the ball itself.'

Blizard peered at the group of porters surrounding him.

'Take a strong grip on the object, but tenderly if you please. Mr White, be so good as to place the pail just here, on the floor. Mr Harvey, I will thank you for my instruments.'

Peggy stepped further back into the corner of the theatre, her thoughts returning to Tom. She tried to push them to one side but it was no use. The harder she tried, the greater the clarity of Tom's image in her mind's eye. Could she blame him for what had happened with that unpardonable wretch, Boylin? Tom could not have known what was about to happen.

A sudden scream pierced through her consciousness. She looked up to where the porters were struggling to hold the patient still, the young man's back arching upwards, his outstretched fists clenched into a tight ball. Then he fainted, his body limp, his head lolling to one side. On the terraces, a student raised a hand to his mouth, his face suddenly grey. A colleague slipped a supporting hand under his elbow, steadying him.

Blizard resumed his work, inserting pincers into the wound. Beads of perspiration stood out on his face. He raised one shoulder as though for extra force on his implement, pressing downwards, his teeth bared. Then it was over.

'There you have it, gentlemen.' Blizard waved the pincers in the air, a small lead ball clamped in the cup-like jaws. He paused and turned to one of his dressers. 'Thank you, Mr White. You may swab the wound and dress it. Then we must leave the patient in the capable hands of Nurse Tompkins here, and trust that the fever does not carry him off.'

Peggy looked across at the unconscious figure on the table. She didn't know anything about him – not even his name. She wondered how he had come to be shot. In so far as she had thought about it at all, she had assumed the injury to be accidental. But what if it were not? Might someone be looking for him?

Well before dawn, while the town of Hastings still slept, Harry Fearne left his room at the Cutter and walked up Market Street in the direction of the parish church of All

Saints. A cold north wind was blowing down the valley, carrying with it fresh flurries of snow.

Following his meeting with Tom Pascoe at the White Rock, he was no nearer to discovering what might have happened to Toiler or why he should have chosen to join men he shared nothing in common with. He had endlessly turned the matter over in his mind in an effort to answer the questions and still got nowhere.

He would not have given Stevy a moment's thought, but for the shooting incident. Like Toiler, Stevy was not someone he would have expected to form a relationship, however loose, with Surly and Bulverhythe. And yet now that he came to think about it he had, on occasion, seen the three of them down on the Stade talking together.

The publican continued his climb up the side of the valley, stopping from time to time to catch his breath. Soon he was crossing the upper pastures of the West Hill. He had no clear idea of what he wanted to achieve, only a sense that a visit to the hovel that Stevy had called home might produce some clue as to why he had attacked Tom Pascoe and, by inference, what Toiler had been doing in the company of Surly and Bulverhythe.

Close to the summit, he saw a large oak standing alone amidst a thicket of brambles at the side of the footpath. He noticed a gap in the undergrowth leading towards the base of the tree where, he already knew, Stevy had built his home. He stepped through and came to a clearing in the midst of which was what appeared to be a collection of sticks about six feet high with an entrance at one end. He paused. It didn't seem right entering the home of a man so recently dead. He steeled himself, took out a candle from his coat pocket, lit it and went in.

The interior was bare but for a strip of sailcloth along one side that appeared to have acted as a bed. On it were some scraps of old carpet and a threadbare blanket. Next to this was an iron cooking pot, a battered pewter plate and a tin drinking mug. Fearne crouched and let his eyes take in the scene. There was nothing of interest to him. Nothing that might help him to understand what had happened to Toiler and the others. Disappointed, he began to turn away when he caught sight of a charred scrap of paper, half-hidden beneath the sailcloth. He leaned over and picked it up.

It was blank on one side. On the other there appeared two wavy parallel lines that ended where the paper had been burned. A cross was drawn immediately to one side of the lines and close to the charred edge. Throwing the scrap to one side, he lifted a corner of the blanket and peered underneath. An area of the earth appeared to have been recently disturbed. He bent down and scratched at the surface. It was still loose. He scooped out some of the earth, his fingers rubbing against something solid. He dug some more. A cloth bag, tied at the neck, came into view. Catching hold of it, he pulled it out. It was heavy and it jangled with a metallic sound. Below it was another bag. Then two more. He loosened the string at the neck of the first one and tipped its contents onto the bedding. A large number of gold coins fell out. He moved the candle closer and counted them. There were two hundred and fifty. He opened the other three. All of them contained gold coins, perhaps a thousand in all. He couldn't be sure but they looked to be French.

He suddenly felt afraid and, scrambling to the hovel's entrance, he peered out. There was no one around. He went back inside trying to imagine how Stevy might have come by such a fortune. Had he stolen them? If so, then from whom? What was clear was that he couldn't leave them here. But if he took them, what then? How would he explain his search of a dead man's home? On an impulse, he replaced the coins, picked up the heavy bags and slipped them into his coat pocket. He'd think about what to do, later.

He remembered the charred piece of paper and wondered if that had anything to do with the money. Stooping, he picked it up and stuffing it into his coat pocket, walked out into the clearing.

The hammering on the front door of the Cutter, an hour and a half later, surprised the landlord. It was still early and he was tired after his climb up the slopes of the West Hill. He looked at the door and then at the plate of meat pie and gravy that was his breakfast. Whoever it was could wait. He reached over and cut himself a thick slice of bread. The hammering began afresh. Fearne frowned, wiped his mouth with the sleeve of his shirt, and got up to open the door.

'You the landlord?' The man standing outside the door was probably in his mid-forties, tall and strongly built, his face weathered, his prominent nose broken. Fearne noticed that the left sleeve of his threadbare coat was empty and pinned across his chest.

'If it's a drink you want, we're not open,' said Fearne, raising his voice against the roar of the surf.

'It's you I want, mister.' The stranger pushed past Fearne and seated himself on one of the benches. He pointed to the seat opposite. 'Sit. I ain't got all day.'

Fearne tried to place the stranger's accent. It wasn't local. More like London.

'Know Surly Will, do you?' A quick, upward jerk of the chin.

Fearne hesitated. There was no reason why he shouldn't answer the question. But something warned him to be careful. He thought of the money he'd brought down from Stevy's place. Luckily it was hidden. It was the first thing he'd done when he'd got back to the Cutter.

'Aye,' he said. 'I see him from time to time.'

'Where is he?'

Fearne had the uncomfortable feeling that whatever he

93

said was going to end badly. Whatever the reason for the stranger's interest in Surly Will, he was unlikely to want to hear that he was dead.

'I ain't seen him close on three weeks,' he muttered.

'What of the cully they call Bulverhythe George? Know him, do you?' The stranger leaned his forearm on the table.

'Bulverhythe?' Fearne looked up. 'I ain't seen him, neither.'

'That's too bad,' said the stranger, an impatient edge to his voice. 'Where've they gone?'

'I . . .' Fearne studied the back of his own hands, noticed the onset of liver spots on the wrinkled skin, vaguely surprised by the discovery. He'd be no match for this scrub, if it came to it. Even with only one arm, the stranger would take him. 'I hears they went to London. Both of them. They ain't come back.'

'Was there someone else with them?' The eyes had narrowed, the forehead creased. 'A lad named of Stevy?'

There was an odd cadence in the man's voice. Fearne had the feeling the man was somehow afraid of the question and the answer it might bring.

'Aye, there was a third lad,' stuttered the publican. 'But it weren't Stevy.'

For a moment he found himself wondering, why him? Why had the stranger chosen to approach him for answers to his questions? But he knew the answer. It was his own fault. He'd bumped into one of his regulars on the way

94

down and made the mistake of telling him that he'd been up to the hovel. The story had doubtless gone round the town in no time and it was only natural the folk in the town would refer all enquiries to him, especially those concerned with Stevy. Fortunately, he'd managed to keep quiet about the coins.

A look, halfway between fear and relief seemed to inhabit the stranger's face. He got up from his bench and walked to the tavern door. Opening it, he stood in silence looking across the small square towards the turbulent sea. He turned and faced the publican.

'If Stevy's not with them, where's he gone?'

Fearne's pulse surged. He hesitated.

'Well?'

'Likely he's up the West Hill, where he lives,' said Fearne, avoiding the man's stare.

'Been there, 'ave you?' The man brought his face close to Fearne's. 'How d'you know where he lives? You been snooping?'

'No!' Fearne looked round the empty room. There was no escaping the man's questions. 'Everybody knows where he lives.'

He didn't see the man's hand reach towards him. It wasn't until the fingers closed round his throat that Fearne was aware of anything at all. He clutched at the iron fist, tried to wriggle free, could hear the gurgling noise from within his own throat.

'You's lying to me, cock.' The voice was rasping now, the breath stale. The man released his grip. 'No one lies to Jim Clarke. You understand, mister?'

'He's dead,' said Fearne, feeling his throat with the tips of his fingers. 'Stevy's dead.'

'What's that?' The man staggered, the colour draining from his face. 'Dead?'

Fearne watched him. A moment of silence passed.

'How? Tell me, damn your eyes, afore I throttle you.'

'He were shot.' Fearne edged along the wall, his eyes bulging with fear. 'Don't know no more than that.'

'Who did it?'

'Don't know.' Fearne didn't look up.

'You're lying to me, you pox-ridden death's head on a mopstick. Tell me who did it.'

'The constable what came down from London.'

'A constable? What's his name? Where's he now?'

'Don't know where he is,' said Fearne. 'He never told me no name, neither.'

Again the man lunged at him, throwing him to the floor. Fearne curled himself into a ball, his hands over his head.

'I'll not be asking you no more.' The stranger leaned over the still figure of the publican, his finger wagging.

'It were Pascoe. That were his name. I remember now.' Fearne closed his eyes, waiting for the blows he was sure would fall. He dared not move, dared not do anything which might provoke a further beating. When nothing happened, he half-opened his eyes. The man was still staring at him.

'Pascoe, you say? Where will I find the scrub? What's he look like?'

'As God is my saviour, I don't know. How would I? He were down from London and now he's gone. As to what he looks like . . .'

The stranger listened to the description. He straightened and paced up and down the taproom, stopping occasionally to look back at Fearne.

'Did this Pascoe go searching Stevy's place?'

'He might 'ave done.' Fearne covered his face as the man came towards him. 'He never said nothing to me.'

There was silence. Fearne felt the sweat of his fear trickle down his neck. The door of the tavern slammed shut.

The man had gone.

CHAPTER 10

Tom Pascoe approached the Swan on Market Street, satisfied he had, for the time being, extracted all he could from his visit to Hastings. Outside the hotel, the coach for Tunbridge Wells was being made ready, the ostler backing the last of the horses between the shafts. Tom glanced at his pocket watch. There was still a few minutes before it departed.

He turned in through the front door and peered into the waiting room. It was occupied. A man was sitting hunched over the fire, his coat drawn closely about him, his hat pulled down over his forehead. He looked up as Tom came in through the door, his eyes widening for a fraction of a second as though he knew him. Then he turned away.

The surveyor walked to the far end of the room and sat down, an involuntary smile of pleasure crossing his lips as his thoughts turned to Peggy. He imagined her going about her work – her small, swift steps, the sway of her hips, her smile, how she would brush away an errant strand of hair. He imagined she would be helping her patients with their breakfast about now. After that would come the preparations for the daily ritual of prayers and Bible reading followed by the surgeon's and the physician's rounds. Then ... He chuckled to himself. She was seldom far from his thoughts.

'If you please, gentlemen, the coach for Tunbridge Wells departs in two minutes.' The coach-driver's voice was muffled, his head swathed in a scarf, the high collar of his coat seeming to dwarf him.

Tom stepped through the front door across the pavement and up into the waiting coach. He looked round for the man who'd been in the waiting room. There was no sign of him. Nor had the fellow appeared when, a minute later, a blast of the coach horn warned of their imminent departure. Tom shrugged. Perhaps he'd been mistaken. Perhaps the man had not intended to travel at all. There was a sharp crack of a whip and the squeal of iron-shod wheels on the cobbled surface, and the coach jerked forward to begin its journey.

Soon they were clear of the tollgate on the London Road and were climbing the steep incline that would take them to the village of Ore where the turnpike turned left on its way to Battle. Tom looked back the way they'd come. Below him lay the parish church of All Saints, its square tower rising above the serried rooftops of the town, dark against the brilliant blue of the sea.

He shifted his gaze. Further to the right, far beyond the limits of the town, a thin column of smoke rose from the lime kilns on the Priory. The other side of the smoke, hidden by the lip of the West Hill, was the White Rock where he had spoken to Harry Fearne about Toiler. Tom took a small chunk of tobacco from his pocket and bit off a piece, his thoughts going over what he'd been told about the boy and the friendship that had existed between his sister and Surly Will.

It wasn't until after his visit to the Reverend Coppard that things had begun to fall into place. If Toiler had only recently discovered that his sister had been raped, and by whom, it would explain his sudden desire to join the crew of the *Mary-Anne*.

He turned from the window and rested his head against the back of his seat. The descriptions of the two bodies matched those of Surly and Bulverhythe. And there didn't seem to be much doubt that the third, surviving, member of the crew was Toiler. If the rape of his sister had provided Toiler with a motive for killing Surly, his presence on board the *Mary-Anne* also provided him with the opportunity.

Tom felt uneasy. Why would Toiler wait for the *Mary-Anne* to arrive within the Port of London before committing murder? And why would he then sink the boat? It made no sense. If he was responsible for the deaths, he had also effectively marooned himself many, many miles from home. And what was the *Mary-Anne* doing in the Port of London in the first place? The most simple explanation, that she had been engaged in smuggling, seemed far from the mark. And even if she were found to have been carrying smuggled goods, that in itself did not explain why Toiler should have chosen to commit murder so far from home.

Nor did the explanation of smuggling explain Stevy's involvement. All that was known about him was that he had spent time with Surly and Bulverhythe. Yet he'd attempted to kill Tom. It didn't seem credible that he would do so to prevent the detection of a smuggling operation. There had to be more to it than that.

Tom's eyelids grew heavy as the coach rocked and jolted its way through the countryside. Battle, Sedlescombe, Hurst Green, Robertsbridge – the towns and villages came and went in a blur of soporific stupor, interrupted only by a change of coach at Tunbridge Wells, for the journey to London.

Richard Ball was a busy man. His duties as a Hastings magistrate made sure of that. He picked up another letter from the pile lying on his desk and held it up against the light. The complaints hardly varied from one day to the next – animals fouling the Bourne stream, neighbours failing to maintain the paving outside their homes, noise from the Cutter or the Bell. He sighed and rubbed the tiredness from his eyes.

There was a knock at the front door. He glanced at the carriage clock on the mantelpiece. Just after seven in the morning. He was not expecting anyone.

'Yes, Mary, who is it?' said Ball as the maid appeared beside his desk.

'If you please, sir, it's Harry Fearne, the landlord of the Cutter. Says, if you is at leisure, he would like a word. Says it's about young Stevy.'

Ball clucked his tongue in irritation.

'Tell him I'm extremely busy. And if he's got anything to say about Stevy he should save it for the inquest.'

He watched the maid leave the room, heard the murmur of voices and the click of the front door closing. For a moment he found himself wondering what old Harry Fearne could possibly have wanted at this hour of the morning. He half thought of calling him back. The fellow was not the sort of person to call round if he didn't think it important.

His eye caught sight of the pile of letters on the desk. He really could not spare the time to see him for the moment. He'd drop round to the Cutter as soon as he had time. Maybe tomorrow or the day after. It couldn't be that pressing.

Standing in the shelter of the old Norman castle, later that morning, Richard Ball hunched his shoulders against the

March wind and gazed fondly at his friend, the Reverend William Coppard. The latter was lying on his stomach, perilously close to the edge of the cliff, straining for a better view of a waxen chatterer he thought he'd seen a moment or two before.

'Dash it, I can't seem to find the fellow,' said Coppard, climbing to his feet and wiping the snow from his coat. 'Did you see him, dear boy? Reddish-brown. Black throat. Crest on his head. No? What a pity. Now, what was it you was saying to me?'

'We were, as I recall, talking about that fellow Pascoe and his enquiries. What did you make of it all?'

'Strange business,' said Coppard, still peering over the cliff. 'Mind you, I'm not at all surprised about Surly and young Bulverhythe. They were always going to catch it sooner or later. But Toiler? He's a different kettle of fish. I simply can't see him getting involved with those three.'

'Three?' said Ball, glancing at the reverend. 'Who's the third?'

'I suppose I was talking about Stevy.'

'Ah, I'd forgotten about him,' said Ball. 'By the by, I had old Harry Fearne knocking on my door earlier this morning. Told my housekeeper he had something to tell me about Stevy.'

'Did you speak to him?'

'I'm afraid I sent him away. Told him to keep whatever he had to say for the Inquest.'

'So you haven't heard, sir,' said the rector, looking up sharply.

'Heard what, my dear fellow?'

'It might be an idea to have a chat with him. It seems he was paid a visit by some cove he'd never met before. He thinks the fellow might have come from London. Anygate, the man apparently wanted to know where he could find young Stevy. When Harry told him the lad was dead, things got a bit nasty.'

'I'm sorry to hear that. Is he all right?'

'Nothing he won't get over,' said the rector. 'But that's not what I'm talking about. As soon as this fellow discovered Stevy had been shot, he demanded to know the name of the man responsible. Harry, it seems, was sufficiently frightened to tell him that it was our friend Pascoe.'

'What of it?' said Ball. 'If this man knew the boy, it's only natural he should ask the question.'

'Normally, I would, sir, agree with you,' said the rector. 'But in this case Harry believes the fellow means to kill Pascoe.'

Harry Fearne stood at the door of the Cutter watching a fishing boat navigate its way through the heavy swell towards the beach. His throat was still sore although the redness had begun to fade. He only wished he could say the same for the state of nervous anxiety the stranger's visit had left him with.

'Good afternoon, Harry.' Fearne turned to see Richard Ball walking towards him along the coastal path. Next to him was the rotund frame of the Reverend Coppard, his black cassock covered in grass stains.

'Why, mornin', gentlemen,' said Fearne, wondering what the two of them should want him for.

'Can you spare us a moment?' It was Ball again. 'In private.'

'Certainly, gentlemen.' Fearne felt his heart miss a beat. He was regretting picking up the bags of gold coins from Stevy's place. He should have insisted on seeing the jurat this morning and giving them to him. He led the way into the taproom and through the door to his private parlour at the back of the house.

'I believe you had an unwelcome visitor this morning,' said Ball as soon as the three of them had sat down. 'And from what I've heard the fellow is looking for Mr Pascoe. Is that right?'

'Aye, sir, it is,' said Fearne. 'He didn't say so but I believe he wants to turn off the constable.'

'Did he say why he wanted to kill him?' said Ball.

'It were on account of he shot Stevy.'

'Do you know where the man is now?'

'I heard he were taking the coach for London,' said Fearne.

'We've heard he didn't get on it,' said the rector. 'Any idea why he might have changed his mind?'

'No.' Fearne's head jerked up. 'Except I hears Master Pascoe were travelling on that there coach.'

'We must get word to Pascoe,' said Ball. 'I'll go to London myself; at first light tomorrow.'

'Tomorrow might be too late, your honour,' said Fearne. 'If that scrub what attacked me wants to get to London afore Master Pascoe, then all he's got to do is hire a horse from the Swan. He could be in London afore Mr Pascoe and be waiting for him.'

'Then I shall ride on the instant,' said Ball. He paused for a moment, looking at Fearne. 'Why d'you suppose this fellow came to see you if he was after Stevy?'

Fearne hesitated, his face reddening. 'He must've heard I went to the place where Stevy used to live. I'd hoped to find something what might help me find Toiler.'

'And did you?' asked Ball.

'No, but . . .' Fearne stopped and looked pleadingly at the Reverend Coppard.

'What have you to tell us, Harry?' asked Coppard, gently.

'I found some coins.'

'D'you have them with you?'

'Aye.'

'Best you show them to us, then.'

Fearne put down the bags on the table in front of him, opened one and tipped out its contents. For a long moment there was a stunned silence as the three of them stared at the hoard.

'You found these at Stevy's place?' said Ball.

'Aye, they were buried under the place where he used to sleep.'

'They're French, of course,' said Ball, examining one of the coins. 'Where do you suppose Stevy got hold of them? D'you know?'

Fearne shook his head.

'Did you find anything else?' asked the Reverend Coppard.

'Only this.' Fearne extracted the charred piece of paper from his pocket and handed it to Ball.

'Can't make head nor tail of it,' said Ball, holding it up to the light. 'Could be connected with the money, I suppose. If it is, it's too serious for us to deal with. You don't get this amount of money for a little bit of smuggling. And since Mr Pascoe has an interest in the case, I intend to hand the coins and the paper over to him to deal with. Doubtless he will know what to do. I shall warn him about the threat to his life, at the same time.'

CHAPTER 11

André Dubois smiled when he heard Toiler had been traced – a dry, cynical smile. The lad knew too much to be left alive. He'd brought them across the Channel. Knew their names. Could not be trusted to keep silent about their presence in London. Several times he, Dubois, had been on the point of going out and looking for the lad himself; would have done so but for Moreau's insistence that he stay put.

'You're a fool, Dubois,' his colleague had told him more than once. 'You know nothing of this town. How long d'you think it would be before you were discovered? Leave the boy to our Irish friends. They will tell us as soon as they find him.'

And so they had – apparently. He'd been seen going into the house of an apothecary in Pillory Lane, not far from the Tower.

'Doubtless for treatment to his hurt,' Moreau had said.

Dubois glanced at his colleague. He didn't look at all

well. His face was pale and glistening with sweat. During the night he had cried out several times, as if delirious.

'If he's still there,' said Moreau, gulping for air, 'he is not to be harmed.'

Dubois turned away, irritated by the implied criticism. Two years of military discipline had done little to curb his natural peevishness. If anything, his experience had given free rein to his irascibility, cloaking it with the fraudulent respectability of war. For two years he'd been encouraged – ordered – to kill in the name of France. Now all that had changed and he was expected to play by a different set of rules – rules he neither understood nor had any intention of obeying.

'Naturally, the same applies to the apothecary.' Moreau was still talking. 'You have caused us quite enough difficulty already.'

The winter sun had long since set behind London Bridge and the Thames was in darkness but for the blaze of the ship-borne lanterns whose reflections danced across the water in sparkling beams of light. Dubois leaned against the wooden sash of the window and looked down the length of the Pool towards the Tower, the latter's grim battlements squat against the blue-black sky. Somewhere out there was the boy they had allowed to escape.

'Come, it's time we were going.' Moreau's voice cut across his thoughts.

Crossing the river, they passed under the arch of St Magnus

the Martyr and turned right down Lower Thames Street, still busy with the hurry of traders coming and going from the legal quays. Ten minutes later, they had edged their way past the Custom House and the nearby fish market at Billingsgate and were climbing Tower Hill towards the dark grey walls of the Norman castle. Once there, they would turn down towards the river and Pillory Lane.

Dubois quickened his pace. It had, for him, been a tedious few days cooped up in the warehouse with little or nothing to occupy his time. Toiler's escape and the resulting fear of detection by the English had forced on him a period of inactivity that he'd found difficult to bear. His patience was running dangerously thin.

Moreau had told him little about what they were expected to be doing beyond the fact that it was important for the success of the war. He was being treated as a child, not to be trusted with the detail of the operation; as though his sole purpose was to make sure no harm came to Moreau.

They walked down Pillory Lane on the eastern extremity of the City of London. He felt inside his coat pocket for the coil of thin twine he always carried.

'That's the house,' said Moreau, nodding in the direction of a large, stone-built house on the opposite side of a deserted street.

Dubois looked around. They were standing in the shadows of some warehouses. A little further on was the

Thames, quiet and invisible at this hour, the air tainted with the smell of a tannery. He looked back at the house Moreau had indicated. A light shone in one of the ground-floor rooms. He checked the other houses. They were in darkness. They'd not be disturbed.

He followed Moreau across the lane and waited while he knocked on the door. Moments later it swung open.

'May I help you?' A grey-haired man stood in the opening.

'Forgive me, sir,' said Moreau, bowing, 'but I was looking for the apothecary.'

'I, sir, am the apothecary. Have you need of my services?'

'I seek news of my friend who was sent to you with a hurt to his leg. Is he well? His name is Toiler.'

'I regret I cannot discuss my patients or their ailments with anyone other than themselves.' The apothecary shook his head.

Dubois felt a surge of irritation. His hand slid to his coat pocket, his fingers encircling the loop of twine.

'I understand perfectly,' said Moreau with a small wave of the hand. 'But he is with you?'

'I'm sorry . . .'

The apothecary got no further. Dubois lifted him clear of the floor and pinned him against the wall of the entrance hall.

'Put him down, *Citoyen* Dubois,' snapped Moreau.

Dubois released his grip and watched the shaking apothecary with an amused expression on his face.

'I apologise for my friend,' said Moreau. 'The fact of the matter is that we need to find your patient without delay. It would be in your interests were you to cooperate with us. Otherwise ...'

Moreau's voice trailed off.

'He ... he came to me but is no longer here,' said the apothecary, still shaking.

'When did he leave?'

'I cannot now recall.'

'You do not, sir, appear to understand the position in which you find yourself,' said Moreau. 'My friend here is difficult to control and were he to consider you unhelpful, I could not answer for what he might do.'

The apothecary's eyes darted between the two Frenchmen, his hands clutching at his chest.

'There was little I could do for him,' he said, his voice barely audible. 'He stayed with me one night. I suggested to him that he should go to the London Hospital in the Whitechapel road. He may be there.'

'Thank you, *monsieur*,' said Moreau, turning to leave the house.

Dubois followed him to the door and stopped.

'I've dropped something. I'll catch up with you.' He waited until his superior had crossed the street before turning a pair of cold, expressionless eyes towards the trembling man behind him. His hand dropped to his coat pocket.

Minutes later he joined Moreau on the corner of Pillory Lane, his breathing a trifle quicker than usual, but otherwise unchanged. He did not speak. He did not consider it necessary to do so. *Citoyen* Moreau was unwell, and was, in his opinion, no longer fit to make the decisions that were needed. The old Moreau would never have left him on his own in the house; would have known what he intended to do. It was better this way.

They walked on.

Shortly after eight o'clock that evening Tom finally arrived at the Bolt-in-Tun Inn and climbed down from the coach into the busy surroundings of Fleet Street.

'Give you joy of your safe return, sir,' said a familiar voice at his elbow. Tom looked round and smiled, his weariness quite forgotten.

'Why, Sam, was you waiting for me? Never mind, never mind. I'm famished. Will you not join me in something to eat? We can talk there and—' Tom stopped and stared across the street.

'What is you looking at, your honour?' said Sam, following the direction of his gaze.

''Tis naught,' said Tom, after a brief pause. 'I thought I saw someone I knew. I warrant I was mistaken.'

On the other side of Fleet Street, Jim Clarke scratched at the stump of his left arm and shrank back into the evening crowd, his teeth clenched. He moved a pace or two to his left, to get a better view of the man who'd just arrived on the Tunbridge Wells coach. It was, he was quite sure, the same cully he'd seen at the Swan in Hastings, earlier in the day. The description the publican had given him of Tom Pascoe had not been perfect, but it had been enough.

A tremor ran through his body. Grief and anger welled up inside him in equal measure. Stevy was gone. Nothing would bring him back. A desire to even the score with the man responsible overwhelmed him.

And then there was the money. There was no doubt that it had gone. He'd been up to Stevy's place on the West Hill and searched for it; had seen the disturbed earth, the hole in the ground below Stevy's bed. Someone had got there before him. He looked across the street at Pascoe. He had to get it back – and quickly. There was more involved than his pride or even his sense of grief. The money wasn't his and he knew what to expect if he couldn't account for it.

He watched Pascoe, and a second man who'd met him off the coach, cross the courtyard and enter the inn. He settled down to wait. He doubted either of them would be going anywhere for an hour or two.

The stump of his arm started to itch again, reminding him, as if that were necessary, of the moment of its loss. The memory raced through his brain as it had done a thousand times before, each vivid second indelibly etched in his mind, terrifying in its clarity.

They had been riding east all day, he and his comrades of the 22nd Light Dragoons; the vanguard of a relief column bound for Antrim, on the shores of Lough Neagh. Not that he knew that at the time. Nobody had thought to tell him – or anyone else in the one hundred and fifty strong column. But he'd guessed they were heading for trouble; the same trouble they'd faced yesterday and the day before and the day before that ever since the uprising had begun. He'd often wondered if there was a single Irishman in the whole country who'd not tried to kill him at one point or another.

They reached the town in early afternoon; dusty, tired and thirsty from the long march. In the distance he'd been able to see columns of black smoke curling up into the deep blue of a cloudless sky, a sure sign of the trouble that lay in store.

The column didn't stop. There was no time for that. Just kept moving forward, the jingle of harnesses, the clop of their horses' hooves. They were on the outskirts of the town now, green bunting hanging from deserted windows as if a talisman against the coming of Death. He remembered those strips of green mocking his presence in their midst, those flags that grinned and spat in his face – the green of the rebels of Ireland. If anything had spurred him on, it was those flags.

He can see the rebels now – a thickly pressed horde, ragged clothes hanging limp about their shoulders, a sea of staves and pikes and flags over their heads, the din of their voices an unearthly howl heard through the swirling smoke of the fires. He closes his eyes, feels the heat of the summer sun on his back, the sweat on his grime-ridden face. His gut is churning, his throat is dry. He looks up. The mob is still there. Hundreds of them. Perhaps a thousand. Maybe more.

A bugle sounds. The pulsating, nerve-jangling notes of the Charge. His horse's ears prick up and point forward, her nostrils flaring in excitement. He pats her flank, urging her onward. His own fear matches hers.

They are flying now, she and he and the rest of the column, the dragoons' lances levelled, the thunder of hooves loud in his ears. There is a blinding flash and the roar of a cannon. He can't see where it's pointed. Too late now to do anything anyway. He fixes his eye on one man and the scrap of green bunting tied to his pike. God, it's hot. Not a cloud in the sky. Another flash from the mouth of the cannon, the ear-splitting roar seems very near. Around him, his mates are falling. He can hear their screams and see their horses stumbling, pitching onto their necks. There's a sudden rush of wind close to his chest. A cannon ball. What fucking idiot gave the order to charge? Too late now.

His horse is galloping. She's not responding to the pull of her reins. He yanks back. Still nothing. He looks down. The reins lie on the horse's neck. He's puzzled. Looks again. He must have dropped them. The bugle is sounding once more. The retreat. He can't stop her. His left arm is gone.

Don't be stupid. You're looking in the wrong place. But it *has* gone; torn from below his shoulder. His tunic awash with blood, the sleeve dangling uselessly by a thread or two. At his shoulder is a stump of bleeding flesh and bone.

He's amongst them now, his lance embedded deep in the chest of the man with the green flag on his pike. The mob is scattering before the flaying hooves of his mare. It won't last. It can't. Some shit will get him soon. He's holding the reins in his right hand now. A pike is jabbing at him. He ducks. It misses him. His horse is running free, back to what's left of the 22nd. The bodies of his mates lie, unmoving, in the dirt. Christ! What a mess. There must be twenty or thirty of them – poor sods.

He looks over his shoulder. The mob is running away. The bugle again. Another charge. He's grinning. Our turn. No quarter. Hack the bastards down. There's blood everywhere. The mare tramples on the fallen—

Clarke's eyes snapped open. He stared about him; remembered where he was. He grimaced, looked across at the Bolt-in-Tun, his heart beating faster than it should. It was always the same when his thoughts turned to the events in Antrim. The door of the tavern was opening, two men coming out.

He ducked back into the shadows. It was Pascoe, accompanied by the same cully who'd met him off the coach. The two men crossed the courtyard and turned left down Fleet Street towards Ludgate Hill. He dropped in behind them, his hand feeling for the butt of his pistol.

CHAPTER 12

Peggy walked the length of Harrison Ward, checking each of her patients in turn. It was nearly midnight. She shivered. She did not enjoy the night shifts. They always seemed to go on and on with not much to occupy the hours, particularly in winter. Not that she and her room-mate, Charity Squibb, had to do it very often. The nights were normally covered by the watchers but a bout of sickness had reduced their availability.

She opened the door of the stove and shovelled in some more coal. Her patients were mostly quiet although a few tossed about, mumbling in their sleep. From time to time she'd hear one of them cry out.

She replaced the coal shovel and looked up. The ward was in darkness except for a candle burning in its sconce at the nurses' table and another carried by Charity Squibb. Her colleague was at the far end of the room accompanied by two porters. Huge shadows danced above their heads, thrown by the candle's guttering flame as they gathered round one of the beds. One of the patients had died and Charity had offered to be the one to accompany the cadaver to the dead house. She'd known of Peggy's reluctance to perform the duty ever since her unfortunate meeting with Boylin on just such a trip.

Peggy watched their departure before resuming her measured stride along the ward. From outside the windows came the low moan of the wind and the occasional patter of raindrops on the glass.

She stopped when she reached the boy's bed. He appeared to be sleeping. She bent over him and felt his brow with the back of her hand. He seemed over the worst of the fever but was still far from well. She straightened his blanket and was about to turn away when he opened his eyes.

'How are you feeling?' Peggy smiled down at him.

The young man didn't answer, his eyes straying over the ward, his teeth biting down on his lower lip.

'Where am I?' He looked at her, a questioning stare, his face drawn with pain.

'Why, in the accident hospital in Whitechapel,' said Peggy. 'You were hurt in the thigh. If I am not mistook it was a pistol shot.'

The young man winced, raised his head off the pillow and peered under the blanket.

'What's your name?' said Peggy.

'They call me Toiler.' The young man let his head drop

back onto the pillow. 'I come from Hastings.'

'You're a long way from home,' said Peggy. 'What brought you to London?'

He looked at her in silence for a moment, one arm thrown carelessly over his forehead. 'We had some business. Leastways, Surly Will did.'

'Who's Surly Will? A friend of yours?' said Peggy.

'He ain't no friend of mine,' said Toiler, an agitated frown on his face.

Peggy nodded and waited for him to continue. At length he seemed to calm himself.

'They were Frenchies,' he went on.

'Who were?'

'The scrubs what were on the *Mary-Anne* . . .' Toiler ran his tongue over his lips. 'It were Surly Will's idea. He took us across to France. Said he were going to run some silk but when we got there, he shipped these two cullies aboard. When I asked him who they were, he told me to mind me own business and everything would be as right as rain.'

'And was it?'

'Aye, to begin with it were. Mind you, we had a bit of a fright passing the North Foreland, what with all them revenue cutters and the Navy and all. But there weren't no trouble till we reached London.'

'What happened when you got there?'

The boy looked up sharply, as though unsure of how much he should say to her, whether she could be trusted.

'We was bound for one of the wharfs on the south bank, close to London Bridge,' he said, at last. 'Seems Surly knew somebody and we was going to land the Frenchies there. Only we never arrived, on account of the tide turning. The Frenchies weren't none too happy. They went below into the cabin with Surly Will and Bulverhythe.'

'Who is Bulverhythe?'

'A mate of Surly's. He were with us. Anyway, I don't rightly know what happened after that. I went into the hold where me hammock were slung and turned in for the night. But after a while I were woken by a noise. It sounded like someone moving about on deck. I thought it were strange so I got up and looked to see what were going on. It were pitch black but I could just make out two men what were bent over the forward hatch. The next moment I heard a bang like the cover were being dropped into place. Then I hears Surly Will and Bulverhythe shouting from inside the cabin and I knew they were trapped. The Frenchies must have tricked them somehow. Anygate, they couldn't get out.'

'Why would they have wanted to do that?' said Peggy.

'Don't know. I'd not heard them arguing none. At least not since the first time when Surly Will told them we couldn't reach the wharf before the next tide. It didn't make no sense to me.'

'What happened after that?'

'I knew if they had done that to the others, they'd come

after me. I reckon they thought I wouldn't hear them and they could get me while I were asleep.'

'But you did hear them.'

'Aye, so I did,' said Toiler. 'As soon as Surly Will and Bulverhythe started hollering, the two men on the deck turned aft, where I were crouching and one of them came towards me. I were proper afraid. I ran over to the starboard rail, meaning to jump. I nearly made it an' all but I were shot in the leg and fell into the water. Don't reckon he could see me proper, else he'd have got me.'

'D'you know what happened to the others? Your friends?'

'No. And it don't interest me none, neither. If Surly and Bulverhythe's been turned off, I reckoned they had it coming to them after what Surly did.'

'But won't the Frenchmen come looking for you? And what did Surly do that makes you hate him so?' asked Peggy.

'He—'

'Miss Tompkins!'

Peggy turned at the sound of her name. A porter was standing by the door of the ward beckoning to her. She walked over.

'Miss Tompkins, there's two men at the front gate as is wishing to see your patient. I told them as how they couldn't see no patient at this hour but they wouldn't take no for an answer.'

CHAPTER 13

Peggy followed the porter out of the ward and hurried down the stone steps leading to the main lobby. It was curious that Toiler's friends should choose to visit him in the middle of the night. Especially as, she now remembered, they had not taken the trouble to accompany him on his arrival. She slowed her pace, a doubt creeping into her mind. At the main door of the hospital she stopped and looked out across the forecourt. It was too dark to see anything. She picked up a lantern from a table near the entrance and, accompanied by the porter, went out.

It was still raining, puddles forming in the uneven surface of the yard, their shimmering surface reflecting the light of the lantern. She reached the gates, could see the outline of two men. She raised her lantern, allowing the light to fall on their faces. The older of the two she'd seen before. She struggled with the memory. Then the months fell away.

She was working as a children's governess at a house in Mincing Lane, just off Upper Thames Street in the City. It was late on a summer's evening, the high clouds streaked with orange and red and pink from the dying sun, the streets and houses below shrouded in a crepuscular gloom. She was standing by the landing window gazing out over a darkened courtyard to the wrought iron gates that gave onto the lane. There had been few people about at that hour. Even during the day there was nothing to attract the crowds to Mincing Lane, a quiet, tree-lined road bounded on either side by the grand houses of the City merchants.

That was what had so surprised her about the arrival of the stranger. She'd not expected any visitor to her master's house at that hour. She'd watched him pause at the gates, look up and down the street and hurry across the courtyard, turning now and again to look back over his shoulder. He had seemed fearful of being seen.

She stared at him now as he stood outside the gates of her hospital. There was no doubt in her mind that it was the same man despite the alteration in his appearance; more pale and sickly than she remembered.

She glanced at his companion, a short, stocky man in his mid-twenties, his skin a light shade of brown turning deeper around his dark eyes. Even from this distance and in this light he made her feel uncomfortable.

'My name is Miss Tompkins. I am a nurse at this hospital.

You wish, sir, to see a patient here?' She looked at the older man, angling her head, her eyebrows raised. She thought she saw a momentary tightening of the mouth as though he were in pain.

'Indeed, I would.' The man returned her gaze and bowed, a wintry smile crossing his lips. 'His name is Toiler.'

'I regret it extremely, sir,' she said. 'The patient to whom you refer was discharged this morning. Perhaps I should say that he discharged himself since it was against the advice of the physician that he left.'

'Doubtless you are aware of where my friend has gone?' said the man.

'He did not confide in me, sir,' said Peggy. 'He left without saying. But should he return, who shall I say has asked after him?'

'Our names are not important,' said the older man. 'Perhaps you would tell him that his friends were most disappointed to miss him on this occasion.'

Peggy removed her wet cloak and walked back into the ward. She knew Toiler was watching her; she could feel his eyes boring into her. She turned to him and tried to smile. There was a look of fearful apprehension in his eyes. He must have guessed where she'd been. She laid a cool hand on his forehead. His skin was still hot to the touch, his body trembling.

'It were them, weren't it?' he said.

'You're not to worry yourself. It was just two men who wanted to speak to me.'

'About me? Did they ask about me?'

'They've gone now. I told them you had left the hospital.'

Toiler chewed his bottom lip and looked at the door of the ward as though expecting the men to come bursting through.

'They'll be back for sure,' he said, drawing a sheet up under his chin. 'I must leave at once.'

'Where . . .' Peggy hesitated and glanced at the boy's face, drained of colour. She'd not give much for his chance of surviving the fever if he left the hospital now. And yet, if he stayed, he'd be in equal danger. 'Where would you go? You're a long way from home.'

Toiler did not answer immediately. His head resting on the pillow, he looked away from her, out through the window, at the darkness. A frown furrowed his brow and his lips moved as though debating some notion in his mind.

'Bulverhythe told me once who he and Surly Will saw when they came to London. It's a gentleman what owns a warehouse where we was headed in the *Mary-Anne*. I reckon I'd be safe with him until I'm well enough to travel home.'

'Do you know the name of this warehouse?'

Toiler glanced up, a startled look on his face as if he'd not previously considered the point. He thought for a moment. 'I've a notion it's on the south bank. Leastways, that's where we was heading.'

'You don't really know, do you?' said Peggy, gently. 'And what of this man you wish to meet? Do you know him? From what you've told me, Surly's friends are not your friends. What makes you think this gentleman you speak of is going to be any different, even if you were to survive the journey to his warehouse? You are to consider the fever is still with you.'

'Aye, I feel it right enough but what choice do I have?' said Toiler. 'If I stay here, them rogues will come for me for sure. If I go, I've a chance.'

'At least wait for the fever to subside,' said Peggy. 'If you must leave, go in the morning, after you've rested some more.'

He nodded.

Behind her one of the other patients was calling. She moved away, conscious that she'd already spent too long with Toiler. She bent over the new patient, concentrating on what needed doing. She didn't notice Toiler climb from his bed and creep to the door.

CHAPTER 14

Tom Pascoe and Sam Hart walked up Fleet Street, heading east. The noisy crowds of early evening had largely disappeared, the lights fewer in number, an overcast sky adding to the pervasive sense of isolation. The rain had intensified, stinging their faces and hands.

The crack of a whip and the beat of hooves warned of an approaching chaise. Tom looked round. Plenty of room for it to pass. A slight movement to one side of the carriage caught his attention. He stopped. The light of the coach lamp had fallen on a man's face. The next moment the man had sprung out of sight into a doorway.

Tom grabbed hold of Sam's arm and pulled him to the side of the street. 'Reckon we're being followed,' he said, in a low voice.

'Don't see no one, sir,' said Sam.

They waited. No one appeared.

'I'll warrant whoever it were will be long gone by now,

sir,' said Sam. 'Did you recognise him at all?'

'Reckon you're right, Sam,' said Tom turning on his heel. 'And, no, I didn't recognise him. He were too quick for that.'

They pressed on, up past the dark edifice of St Paul's Cathedral and then along Watling Street towards the Tower where they turned towards the Thames.

'This is where I leave you,' said Tom, when they reached the junction with Burr Street, in the Parish of St Catherine. Stopping suddenly, he said, 'Moses Solomon.'

'What of him, sir?' said Sam looking round expectantly.

'Didn't you tell me he saw two men in the vicinity of Pelican Stairs on the night the *Mary-Anne* was sunk?'

'Aye, so I did.'

'I think it's time you spoke to him again.'

'That might be difficult. I ain't seen him since I found him at the synagogue. He's not been back there nor any place else as I know of. I reckon he's too afeared to show his face in these parts – at least for now.'

'Look for him, Sam,' said Tom. 'We need a better descrip tion. From what you've told me it seems clear enough that it wasn't just the lad who came off that lugger. Speaking of whom, didn't you tell me he was injured?'

'I did,' said Sam. 'According to Solomon, he looked as if he'd been shot in the leg.'

'Then best we make some enquiries of the physicians and apothecaries in this area for anybody who might have seen him. Include the accident hospital in Whitechapel in that, will you? If he wasn't involved in the deaths of the other two, then he might be able to tell us who was. Present my compliments to Mr Judge. I believe he's on night duty. Ask him to begin enquiries tonight. We can't wait for morning.'

With that, they parted.

Heading into Burr Street, Tom thought back over the events of the past few days, each detail occupying a part of his consciousness, refusing to leave, like a stubborn and unwelcome parasite. They formed no logical order, coming and going as though to confuse and baffle him; the discovery of the bodies on board the fishing lugger in the Lower Pool, the chance remark by a bystander that had led Tom to the coastal town of Hastings and what he had learned there, the attack on him by Stevy, an image of a hesitant Ruxey on the deck of the *Mary-Anne*, the damage to the lugger's hull, brutal, calculated, efficient. And then there was the old hat-seller who'd seen Toiler coming ashore and, later, two men apparently searching for him.

Tom walked on, oblivious to his surroundings. A great mist continued to hang over the detail of his investigation. He still did not know what the *Mary-Anne* had been doing in London. There was a suggestion that two men, in addition to the original three, may have been on the lugger, but who they were and what they had been doing on the vessel, he did not know.

Suddenly, he heard a muffled scraping sound behind

him. He looked over his shoulder and listened, his pulse quickening. It was too dark to see anything. The only sound was that of the rain beating against the surface of the road.

He reached for his sword, drew it two or three inches, and let it slide back into the scabbard. It ran smoothly. There was no point in taking any unnecessary risks. The wind howled as a gust passed between the houses.

Another scrape, barely audible.

Tom stood still, his eyes sweeping the impenetrable darkness, alive to any movement. Someone was there. He could feel it. He drew his sword. The rain was in his eyes. He wiped it away with the sleeve of his coat and cursed the absence of the moon behind the clouds. Nothing stirred.

He turned and walked slowly towards the house where he had his rooms, his body tense, alert. It was less than fifty yards away. Still there was no sound from behind him, nothing to suggest he was being followed. Perhaps what he'd heard had been a cat or a dog. Ten yards, five. He could see the steps ahead.

The lightest of sounds. So soft he might have missed it in the ordinary course of events. He spun round, saw the flash, a yellow tongue of flame, ten, perhaps fifteen paces distant, the ear-shattering explosion of a pistol shot. He ducked, felt the brush of hot metal against the side of his neck, a sharp, stinging, burning sensation.

*

Toiler walked unsteadily down the stairs of the London Hospital, his hand gripping the rail for support, his legs threatening to give way beneath him. He was shivering despite the heat of his skin and the sweat dribbling down his face. He gritted his teeth and forced himself to keep going. If he gave up now there was no telling when the opportunity to leave would come again. He was lucky that the nurse had been distracted by another patient.

Reaching the ground floor, he paused and looked up and down the long, candlelit central corridor of the hospital, a series of doors leading off to left and right. A woman appeared through one of the doors. She walked towards him, her short, quick steps clattering on the stone-flagged floor. He slipped back into the stairwell and waited for her to pass. He peered out again. The corridor was deserted. He studied each of the doors. They all looked identical.

He heard voices. Soft and quiet. They were getting closer, the talking intermittent, urgent-sounding. He glanced up the stairs and then along the corridor. Several of the candles had blown out. He was sure they'd been alight moments before. Feeling a cold breeze on his cheek, he ran his eye down both sides of the corridor, searching for the cause.

The voices again. Closer. He couldn't see anyone. He stared in the direction of the sound. Two figures loomed out of the darkness seemingly unsure of where they were, their gait slow and cautious. Toiler slid back out of sight. Whoever they were, he didn't want to be sent back to the ward. He looked round. There was a space beneath the steps. He ducked into it.

A moment later, the footsteps turned off the corridor and into the stairwell where he was hiding. Abruptly, they stopped and a man's voice broke the silence. It was a voice he knew. He'd last heard it on the deck of the *Mary-Anne*. His heart raced. He had no illusions about what would happen if the men discovered him.

The area he occupied was small with little headroom and he'd had to crouch to get in. The thigh muscles in his one good leg screamed for some relief and his head throbbed from the effects of his fever. He bit his lip, wondering how much longer he could hold on.

The men stopped talking. Toiler heard their footsteps retreat along the corridor. Soon he could hear them no more. He sat down on the stone floor and carefully stretched first one leg and then the other. Blood was oozing through the bandages covering his thigh. He felt weak, dizzy from the pain. Sweat had soaked through his shirt, cold against his skin. He climbed to his feet and crept back to the corridor. Another candle fluttered and went out. It had to be near an outside door – or an open window. If he could find it, it would offer a way out of the hospital. The corridor was deserted. No sound of movement. He looked at the candles that had gone out. The nearest one was at least thirty paces away. Once he left the stairwell, there would be nowhere to hide if someone else came by. He hesitated, knew he had no option, checked left and right and then hobbled out into the corridor.

He found it not far from the first of the candles that had blown out. The door was ajar and looked as though it had been forced; he wondered if the two Frenchmen were responsible. It led onto some steps down to a garden quadrangle at the back of the hospital. At the far end was what looked like an orchard. A cold, wet gust of wind struck him. Rain, too. He wasn't wearing a coat; had left it behind in the ward. He limped down the steps and looked back. No one had seen him. No alarm at his disappearance had yet been raised.

He breathed a sigh of relief and made his way to the orchard, glad of the comparative shelter that it offered. The pain in his thigh was growing more acute. Blood continued to soak through the bandage. He could barely put any weight on that leg. He leaned back against a trunk of one of the fruit trees and thought about his situation. He'd told the nurse that he planned to see Surly Will's contact at a warehouse on the south bank of the Thames. Not that he had any idea where that was. Doubtless someone would tell him when he reached the river. At least he knew where that was, had seen the silver ribbon of reflected light from the window of his ward – due south from here, straight down New Street to the Ratcliff Highway and then onto Wapping.

He glanced up and watched the rain clouds scudding across the night sky. There didn't seem much prospect of a break in the weather. Slowly, he eased himself away from the shelter of the branches above his head and limped over to the road. He checked both ways. Up towards the junction with the Whitechapel road he could just make out flickering patches of light from the windows of houses lining the highway, but nothing down here. He slipped into the street and, keeping close to the edge of the marsh, began to make his way southwards.

Tom Pascoe could see nothing. The muzzle flash had seen to that. He struggled to regain his night vision, a few precious seconds lost. He could hear running feet receding into the distance. He still couldn't see properly. The footsteps turned into an alley on the right. He stumbled after them, tripped over some rubbish in the roadway, cursed and ran on, losing yet more time. At the far end of the alley, he burst out into King Henry Yard and stopped. Silence. Nothing but the wind, the rain and the sound of his own laboured breath.

Whoever had fired at him could have turned left or right. The bastard couldn't have got far. Certainly not far enough for the sound of his footsteps to be out of earshot. He decided to go right, checking each of the doorways he passed. His vision was improving. On the other side of the street he could see the entrance to another alley. He cursed. Could have done without this further distraction. He decided to ignore it and continued up the street.

Another side street. This one fifteen, perhaps twenty yards ahead on his left. A dog barked. Tom stopped. Something had alarmed the brute. It could have been anything. He moved forward, raising himself onto his toes. No point in making more noise than he needed to. The hound was still barking, the sound coming from the next turning.

'Far enough, cully.'

Tom felt an arm encircling his neck, the sharp edge of a knife pricking the skin, the weight of a man's body pressing against his back.

The Ratcliff Highway lay ahead. Toiler felt dizzy. He stopped and leaned against the trunk of a solitary tree, his sodden garments cold against his body, his waterlogged boots, worn thin, scoring his fevered skin.

Two shadows passed along the road, not five yards from him. The outlines of two people, moving quickly. He could hear their breathing. He waited a minute or two. The silence returned. He moved off. Whoever they were, they'd gone. Probably nothing to have worried about.

He passed a church. It stood on the corner of the highway, its tall, rectangular bell-tower rising into the night sky, a gated path leading to its front door.

He stopped at the junction. Few people were about –

two or three hatless women lounging in doorways, a pair of seamen tottering arm in arm down the centre of the road, some likely bullies eyeing passers-by as a cat might watch a mouse, the sleeves of their shirts rolled to the elbow despite the weather. But not much else.

He had already started to cross when he saw the two Frenchmen. They were standing on the far side of the highway, clearly on the lookout for someone. Toiler shrank back into the shadows and his stomach tightened. There was no doubt in his mind about who they were seeking. He watched them for a minute or two, unsure of his next move. To cross the highway at this point was madness. They were too close. But if he was to reach the Thames he would have to cross somehow.

He remembered the church and its path. There might be another path leading to it directly from the highway. If there was it would offer him the chance of crossing the Ratcliff Highway at a point further east of the two men.

He retraced his steps. The church gate wasn't locked. He opened it and, feeling his way through the darkness, he skirted the south side of the building. At the far end he found what he was looking for and walked down between a row of houses to the highway where he stopped and peered round the corner. The rain had stopped. Shimmering pinpricks of fire were emerging from behind the clouds. The pale disc of a three-quarter moon slipped fleetingly from behind a cloud, disappeared and then came out again.

He glimpsed a tricorn hat. He stared at it as it passed close to a lantern, barely twenty yards from him. It was Moreau. He was moving slowly in his direction his head moving from side to side as though searching. Toiler couldn't see Dubois. He hesitated. If he didn't cross now, he never would but if he was seen he knew he couldn't hope to outpace them – not with his leg in its present condition. He thought of returning to the hospital but what then? Wait to be caught? His face paled as another thought struck him. By this time the *Mary-Anne* would have been found and the bodies of Surly and Bulverhythe discovered. No one would know about the two Frenchmen. Suspicion would fall on him. It didn't much matter who caught him – the Watch or the Runners or the Frenchmen – the result would be the same. Getting back to Hastings, to his home, no longer meant the end of his nightmare. But doing nothing was not an option. He raised the collar of his jacket, ducked his head and scurried at an angle across the road.

He'd reached the halfway point when he glanced back. Moreau was staring straight at him. For a moment the Frenchman didn't move. Then Toiler saw him raise a hand and point in his direction.

Tom Pascoe acted instinctively. He brought his arm back with all the force he could muster and felt his elbow sink into the soft flesh of the man's stomach. There'd been no time for reasoned thought, no time for weighing up a

138

course of action that reason might, in more leisured circumstances, have dictated he should take. He'd learned his lessons the hard way, in the maelstrom of hard-fought battle. He knew that he had taken a risk. It could so easily have failed but he'd done it anyway.

He heard the whoosh of escaping air and spun round to face the man. The cully was bent double, winded, the knife he'd held at Tom's throat falling from his grasp. Tom brought his balled fist up from somewhere close to his knees and connected with the fellow's jaw with a sickening crack. The man fell against the door of a house, blood pouring from his mouth. From inside the building people were shouting. Tom lunged and caught the man by the throat, dragging him to his feet.

'Get up, mister.' Tom was breathing heavily. He noted the empty sleeve of the man's coat. 'I want a word with you. Who the fuck are you? What's your game?'

The man didn't reply. Tom rammed him against the door. 'Your name, cully.'

'Clarke,' mumbled the man, spitting out a mouthful of blood.

'And what's your business with me, Clarke?'

Before the man could speak, the door of the house was wrenched open and two, three, maybe more people rushed out. Tom turned to face them, his attention distracted. He felt a stinging blow to the side of his head. He staggered, fell. Around him people were shouting. He tried to speak, couldn't form the words. He felt dizzy. From somewhere he could hear his name being called. He fought to stay awake, felt his world falling away. Out of the corner of his eye he saw the one-armed man disappearing into the night.

Toiler ignored the pain in his thigh. He pushed past a drunken group of revellers, reached the south side of the Ratcliff Highway and sprinted down a narrow, mud-coated lane that ran south towards the Thames. Ten yards in, he saw an entrance to a court. He dived in, the noise of the highway suddenly far away, the court quiet and deserted. He looked round, searching for somewhere, anywhere, to hide. To his right, at the top of a short flight of steps, a door stood ajar, the house in darkness.

He went towards it. Pushed open the door. The stench of urine and unwashed bodies wafted over him. He thought about retreating, finding somewhere else to hide. He looked out over the courtyard to the lane along which he'd come. There was no sign of his pursuers. He began to descend the steps to the courtyard.

A sudden noise. Not loud, but a noise nevertheless. It had come from the lane. Then a muttered oath followed by silence. Toiler stopped and listened. It had been Dubois's voice. He couldn't be certain but it seemed that way. He turned and ran back up the steps into the house, pushing the door closed behind him. He stood quite still waiting for his eyes to adjust to the gloom. Gradually he was able to make out the faint outline of the fanlight over the front door, a staircase, a doorway leading off the entrance passage. He was aware, too, of a low buzzing sound. It was a moment or two before he realised what it was. He looked down at the floor in front of him but could see nothing. He didn't need to; he'd recognised the grunts and snores of people asleep. He felt around with the toe of his boot. It touched something soft, then another and a third. The smell was becoming easier to bear, his breathing less tortured.

Oddly, he found himself thinking of home – the old fishing lugger, upended on a piece of waste ground behind a house in Fish Lane. His father had dragged it there with the help of some of the other fishermen, years before. Toiler had never known anything better. The revenue boys had cut the vessel in half, straight across her beam; they'd suspected it of carrying run goods and that had been that. A readymade home for those who couldn't afford anything better, the main deck acting as the front wall, into which a door had been cut. The boat was where both he and his sister had been born and where they had lived until his father's death. He and his mother had still been there when his sister had disappeared.

He'd never believed that she'd drowned. If only for his mother's sake he had gone on believing that one day she would return. But as the months turned into years and still she did not appear, his conviction had wavered and, to his shame, he'd thought of her less and less.

Until the rumours involving Surly had begun to circulate.

Toiler had never liked the crab-faced villain, even when they used to play together on the Stade. But it had still come as a shock to hear of what had happened between him and his sister. The news had left him feeling physically sick, convinced that her disappearance had been the direct result of what had occurred that afternoon on the East Hill.

At that moment, revenge had sprung easily into his soul.

For weeks after that, he had brooded on his loss. There seemed to be nothing he could do that might satisfy his thirst for retribution. Then when Bulverhythe approached him and asked him to help slide the *Mary-Anne* down the stone beach to the sea, it seemed that the gods had finally begun to smile on his endeavours. He might, at last, be given the opportunity to settle the score. There was no other reason why he should want to go with Surly and Bulverhythe onto the high seas. He and they shared no common interest. No bond of kinship or affection held them close. But he hadn't killed Surly Will, nor Bulverhythe George either. That had been the work of these men that were now seeking to do the same to him.

A dry, hacking cough in the courtyard roused him from his reverie. He edged away from the front door, feeling his way through the sleeping bodies. Then he heard hurried murmurings, coming from the same direction. He crouched down between two bodies and waited. If he was seen, there would be no escape.

Toiler watched the front door swing slowly open. The squat figure of Dubois stood, silhouetted against the moonlight, the glint of steel in his right hand. Behind him someone was speaking. Toiler recognised Moreau's voice. He saw Dubois pause, look over his shoulder, say something he couldn't quite hear and then step into the passageway. More words were exchanged, sharper than before. The two men seemed to be arguing. He watched Dubois move down the hall towards him. He drew his own knife and blinked the sweat from his eyes.

Suddenly Dubois stumbled.

'Oi, watch what you're doing, cully.' It was an English voice.

The outburst made Toiler jump. Through the door he could hear Moreau's hoarse, querulous whisper, could see the answering, dismissive wave of Dubois's hand. All around him people were stirring, a babble of voices growing louder, angered by the broken sleep. Dubois hesitated, looking down the passage as if deciding whether to go on. Another order from Moreau. Dubois seemed torn. Then he turned and walked back towards the front door. Moments later the only sounds were the curses of those whose rest had been interrupted.

Toiler waited ten minutes. He crept to the front of the house and peeped out. The courtyard was silent and deserted, the rain-washed walls of the buildings opposite bathed in the ghostly light of the moon. Warily he descended the short flight of steps to the mud-covered yard.

He still had to get to the south side of the river, to the warehouse of a man he'd never met.

There he hoped he would be safe.

Tom came to his senses with a blinding headache, vaguely aware of an oval object hovering over his head. He tried to focus on it, but to no account. The object was prating. He knew the voice – but from where? Tom closed his eyes. With any luck it would go away and leave him in peace. Someone shook his shoulder. Reluctantly, he opened his eyes again and found himself gazing up into Sam's anxious features.

'Why, Sam, is that you, old friend?' Tom was aware he was still slurring his words. 'And who are all these people standing round?'

'For all love, sir, you gave me the fright of me life. Thought you were a goner.'

Tom looked from one face to the next of the small crowd of people gathered round him. He looked back at Sam, his eyes suddenly widening.

'Was you able to catch the cant scrub?' he asked.

'If you mean, sir,' said Sam, indignantly, 'the cully what nearly turned you off, I regret I did not. I were more interested in what he'd done to you.'

'I'm sorry, Sam,' said Tom, feeling better by the second. 'I did not mean to criticise. How is it you were able to get here so quickly?'

'I heard the pistol shot. Seemed to me to have come from Burr Street, somewhere near your rooms. But by the time I got there, there was no sign of anything amiss. Then I hears someone running, so I followed. After a while I could hear a noise fit to wake the dead so I knew it must be you in another scrape. The other cully were away on his toes before I could see him proper.'

'I'm glad you're here, Sam,' said Tom, struggling up onto one elbow, 'and these good people, too. Now I must be away and find the villain before he causes any more mischief.'

'You'll do no such thing, sir,' chortled Sam. 'It's the accident hospital for you. Get you patched up by the physician.'

It took a while to reach the London Hospital and a little while longer to persuade the night porter to open the gates and allow them entry. More discussion followed at the main door until, finally, Tom was admitted to the large, dimly lit and almost deserted receiving room at the western end of the building.

'If I'm not sadly mistook, sir, you are Captain Pascoe, late of the Navy and now of the marine police,' said a large, dark-haired man, dressed entirely in black. 'We have met before, sir.'

Tom squinted up at the speaker while he struggled to remember the man's name.

'Dr Hamilton?' Tom had a vague recollection of the physician who had been present at the examination of young Jacob Newman, brother of Gabriel, five months before.

'Ah yes,' murmured the physician as he held a candle close to Tom's forehead and peered at the unsightly gash. After a short pause, he added, 'Damage don't look to be too serious. I think—'

'Tom?' Tom felt a blush of pleasure rising in his cheeks at the sound of Peggy's voice. 'I heard you was here. I did not believe it. Are you hurt bad?'

'A scratch. No more,' said Tom, encouraged by her apparent concern.

'This is becoming a habit, sir,' said Peggy, avoiding his gaze and turning instead to the physician. 'Should you so wish, doctor, I will clean and bind this patient's hurt.'

'Aye, nurse, let it be so,' said Dr Hamilton, arching an astonished eyebrow. 'I must tend to another patient who is making a prodigious fuss over some matter. Call me should you need me.'

'Perhaps, doctor, I might have a word with you as you go,' said Sam, falling in beside the physician and casting a meaningful look at Tom and Peggy.

'What happened to you?' said Peggy when, at last, they

were left alone and she had set to, cleaning the wound with a damp cloth. 'Was you in another fight?'

He glanced at her, conscious of how close she was and aware of the disquiet in her voice.

'Aye, there was a fight, right enough,' he said, deciding there was little point in telling her quite how serious the outcome might have been. 'It were a cove who was following me and Sam.'

'Why would he do that?' said Peggy, picking up a roll of freshly laundered bandage from the table beside her and beginning to wind it round Tom's head.

'I'm not entirely sure. It may have been a man I first saw when I was in Hastings. I thought I saw the cully earlier this evening when I got off the coach. But why he should wish me harm, I've no idea ...' Tom's voice trailed away. 'It matters not.'

Peggy opened her mouth as if to speak, changed her mind and went on with the task of binding his wound. After a short pause, she said, 'Tom, I've been meaning to ... That is, I've wanted to ...'

She stopped and looked at him as though unsure of how to go on, her brow creased into a small frown. Tom waited for her to continue, his pulse quickening. She turned back to the table where she'd placed the dressings.

'I know I have caused you unhappiness,' she said, her back still towards him. 'And no words of mine can possibly redress that but I wanted you to know—'

The door leading to the stairs burst open and Charity Squibb rushed in. 'Thank the Lord I've found you, Miss Tompkins. Matters is all ahoo on the ward and I needs your help.'

Tom sighed as he watched the two of them leave the room. The moment had passed.

CHAPTER 15

André Dubois suppressed his anger. Toiler had been within his grasp. He'd smelt his presence in that house and if Moreau had not been so impatient he would have caught him. As it was, the boy was still missing. If that meant nothing to Moreau, it certainly meant something to him. He'd no intention of getting caught by the English on account of a lack of resolve on his colleague's part.

'I tell you the boy was in that house, *citoyen*,' said Dubois, accusingly. 'Another minute and I would have had him.'

'Did you see him?' Moreau turned to look at him, his eyes rimmed with red, his face filmed with sweat.

'No, but . . .'

'Exactly.'

Dubois clenched his fists and forced himself to remain calm. It was not his natural state. He had never learned to accept criticism in spite of his time spent under the yoke of military discipline. More often than not he found

himself chafing at the restrictions imposed by his prox-
imity to authority. He had always been much happier
working on his own, as he had done for much of his time
on the Italian campaign.

Dubois smiled at the memories of those months spent
in the mountains above Lake Garda. Only a soldier could
know what it was to wage war in the freezing conditions
of winter, to have fought in the mud and snow; to feel the
stiffness of frozen clothing and to walk barefoot because
one's boots had rotted. He recalled the long weeks when
the supply trains failed, usually because of the blockading
activities of the British Navy, and the terrible pangs of
hunger and cold that were the result. Lack of food and
medicine, of boots and warm clothes had been responsible
for the demise of so many.

He shook his head. So far as the food was concerned, he'd
been luckier than most. Catching rats to fill an empty
stomach was not a new experience for him. He'd acquired
the skill as a young man growing up in the slums of Marseille
where hunger had again been his constant companion.

Alleviating the worst effects of the broken supply lines,
he had taken matters into his own hands, conducting one-
man raids on the stores and relieving the quartermaster
of copious quantities of food and any number of boots
intended for the sick and the injured. Eventually caught
and court-martialled, he'd been lucky to escape with his
life.

Yet it was the incidents leading to his court martial, more than any other, that had led to a recognition of his particular talents. On the frequent sorties behind enemy lines that followed his near fatal appearance before his superiors, his ruthless aggression was allowed free rein with, for the French, gratifying results. He had seldom been more content.

'If we are not to search for the boy, where are we going?' said Dubois, dragging his thoughts back to the present.

'To St Saviour's Dock. Just upriver from the London Bridge,' said Moreau. 'There is a tavern there. The Blind Beggar. My contact is waiting for us.'

Dubois watched the older man steady himself against the wall of a house and grip his forehead between finger and thumb. He'd known Moreau was ill but there had always been something more pressing, more urgent and important to deal with. Now he could no longer avoid the reality of Moreau's increasingly delirious state, his dry, hacking cough and the stiffness in his joints.

He backed away, had seen the symptoms too often for there to be any doubt in his mind. Typhus had struck down many a fine man during the campaign in northern Italy.

'You are a sick man, *citoyen*,' he managed. 'You should be in bed.'

'Perhaps you are right, Dubois,' said Moreau. 'Perhaps it is best if you meet with our contact alone. I will wait for you at the warehouse.'

Dubois said nothing. He had already made up his mind to keep his distance from his colleague. He was starting to move away when Moreau gripped him by the arm and pulled him to the side of the street.

'Get behind me,' hissed the older man, flattening himself against a wall. He pointed along Wapping Street. Two figures were approaching. 'I know policemen when I see them. It's best if we are not seen.'

Dubois peered through the darkness at the taller of the approaching figures. The fellow seemed familiar. He waited for them to get closer. Suddenly, he started, his eyes widening in disbelief.

'Captain Pascoe,' he breathed, his fists clenched in a tight ball.

'What?' said Moreau. 'D'you know those men?'

Dubois didn't answer. The memories flooded in. It was a hot, August day in 1795. He was nineteen years of age, aboard the Mistral, a 16-gun sloop, a corsair inherited from his late father less than a month before. They were a hundred miles south-south-west of Marseille when he saw the sail on the starboard quarter, a mere haze of white against the sunlit sea. She'd not looked much to his young and inexperienced eye, an opportunity for a prize. He'd ordered the sloop put about and had set a course to intercept her, deaf to the warnings of his crew.

When the truth had at last dawned, it had been too late to do anything but await the inevitable. The distant speck on the horizon that had promised so much was flying the colours of a British man-of-war.

Dubois had watched, helpless, as the pursuing warship overhauled them, water foaming at her bows. He'd seen the puffs of smoke and heard the boom of her bow-chasers. He'd seen the spouts of water, where the round-shot had ploughed into the sea, getting gradually closer. And all the while the fluttering ensign of the enemy grew ever larger in his sight.

They'd been caught as the sun had touched the western horizon. Ordered to heave to, Dubois had refused, instead firing a broadside that failed to reach its target. The response of the British had been as swift as it was savage. The returning broadside had carried away the *Mistral*'s main mast, the round-shot tearing across the upper deck at head height, killing several of the crew. Still he had refused to surrender, firing broadside after broadside as the enemy fetched alongside. The boarding party, when it came, had been led by a man in an officer's uniform, a single gold epaulette at his shoulder, a tall, well-built man with yellow hair tied at the nape.

In those bloody minutes of hand-to-hand fighting where no quarter was asked for nor given, he had sought out the yellow-haired officer, determined to kill or be killed. Rushing at his enemy, he had brought his cutlass sweeping down on the British captain's head, slicing through the man's flesh close to his right eye, exposing the bone of his cheek. He had thought the man done for, had not been prepared for the pulverising punch to his jaw that had sent him sprawling.

He'd lost his dream that day, his ship and his liberty taken from him. Six months were to pass before he was released as part of an exchange of prisoners, and returned to France.

And the man responsible was walking towards him down a darkened street in Wapping.

Dubois moved towards the junction, his knife already in his hand.

'No,' hissed Moreau, gripping his subordinate and pulling him back. 'Not now.'

Dubois shook himself free and considered ignoring the order, before sliding the knife back into his belt. He watched the two men walk past and continue along Wapping Street.

'Why, *citoyen*?' Dubois struggled to control his anger.

'Do I need to tell you? Isn't it obvious? While I remain in command you will do nothing to compromise what we have been sent here to do. Is that clear?'

Dubois glared but said nothing, following the older man as he stepped out into Wapping Street and turned towards London Bridge. He would, he thought, wait until Moreau was safely deposited at the warehouse. Things would get done a lot quicker once he, Dubois, was on his own.

*

On the south bank of the Thames, Toiler awoke. His thigh was throbbing, his clothes wet from the rain. It was still dark, a keen, northerly wind slicing through his threadbare garments. He shivered and looked around at the unfamiliar surroundings. The wharf was an untidy jumble of barrels stacked one upon the other, their contents spilling onto the cobbled surface. Beyond them, barely visible against the night sky, a line of flat-roofed timber huts, supported on stilts, sat like enlarged sentry posts overlooking the river, their treadmills silent and unmoving. Some distance away he could see a group of men huddled round a brazier. He'd seen them when he'd first arrived, had briefly considered asking if he might warm himself at the fire but had thought it a risk too far.

He drew his jacket about him and clutched it to his throat as the memory of where he was and how he had got here began to form in his befuddled mind – the long, painful walk and the frequent diversions as he sought to find his way through the maze of narrow, unfamiliar streets of the capital. Many times he had considered returning to the hospital in the Whitechapel road, to a warm and comfortable bed where the nature of his hurt could be seen to. But the consequences of capture drove him on, half blinded with the stream of his sweat and the pain of his injury.

Once he thought he'd seen the two Frenchmen and his heart had quickened as he stared through the gloom at some figures close by. He had tried to banish the fear, recognise it for what it was – a figment of his imagination. But it had seemed too real to be dismissed. An encounter with the devil himself.

It was the smell of the river, that peculiar mix of damp wood, hemp, fish and tar, that told him he'd not far to go. He'd drawn strength from that smell and his strides had become more purposeful. Weak with the fever and loss of blood, he'd finally made it across the river. It was only then that he realised he had not the first idea which warehouse, amongst the several dozen that populated the various wharfs on this side of the Thames, he should be heading for. Exhausted, he had lain down to sleep.

He rolled onto his side and levered himself up onto an elbow. The effort left him feeling dizzy. He lay down again and closed his eyes. He'd try again in a minute. He fell asleep.

Something sharp was pressing against his throat. He opened his eyes and stared up at the face a matter of inches from his own, swarthy, dark-eyed and cold as ice. A hand gripped the front of his jacket and pulled him into a sitting position, the knife blade still at his throat.

He tried to wipe his eyes but his hand was brushed roughly aside, the blade of the knife pressed harder against his skin. He dropped his hand, too ill to care.

'We meet again, *Monsieur* Toiler, do we not?' André Dubois's breath smelt of garlic. Behind him was Moreau. 'Get up.'

Toiler scrambled to his feet, wondering how the Frenchmen had managed to find him. He was sure they'd not seen him crossing the river. He looked desperately about him as Dubois caught hold of his arm and dragged him across the wharf's cobbled surface. Out of the corner of his eye he glimpsed a movement. He turned towards it. The face of an old man peered at him from behind a stack of barrels, his features hidden behind a long, grey-white beard, his head covered by the three or four hats he wore. The face disappeared and the image quickly faded from his mind, replaced by thoughts of the terrors to come.

Then he fainted.

CHAPTER 16

The low glimmer of half a dozen candles provided the only source of light in the synagogue in which he found himself. Moses Solomon occupied one of the benches at the back, his upper body rocking gently back and forth, a small skull cap perched on top of his head. On the bench beside him, lay three or four hats, his stock in trade. He'd come here straight from the Wharf.

He was frightened. No more than usual. No more than yesterday or the day before. But frightened, nevertheless. Now that he came to think about it, his entire existence seemed to pass in varying states of fear and tension. Seldom did a day go by when he was not assaulted or otherwise abused by those who considered it their right to do so. There was, therefore, no reason why today should be any different – except that the cause of his fear was for someone other than himself.

It was none of his business. He knew he should steer

clear of it. Indeed, if he had learned anything at all in his long life it was to stay out of the affairs of others. All the same, what he had seen was troubling him greatly; a young man dragged across the cobbled surface of the wharf as one might pull a sack, and with every appearance as to lead him to fear for the boy's life.

To make matters worse – if it were possible to add to the list of his concerns – he knew those involved. Or, more precisely, he had seen them both before, and not so many nights since. That earlier encounter had left him with a dread sense of what they were capable of, particularly the shorter, swarthier of the two.

He turned the matter over in his mind. He couldn't do anything to help. Not at his age. But he knew of a man who might. Perhaps he would mention the episode to Sam Hart when he next saw him.

He looked up at the double row of arched windows that ran down the length of the synagogue. A shaft of silver light pierced the gloom and then faded as the moon passed behind a cloud. He wondered how long he had before the silence of the night was gone. He returned to his thoughts.

Even if he wanted to help, and the Lord God knew that he did, he could not do so today. Not on the Sabbath, with its iron doctrine in the matter of work. He'd known that from his earliest youth when he'd been made to read Exodus and Deuteronomy and much else besides. The Sabbath belonged to the Lord. Even to inform others of what he had seen might be to contravene the ancient tractate of the *Talmud*.

He paused, conscious of an uncomfortable feeling that he was leaving something out of the equation. He was sure that somewhere in Holy Scriptures, there was a requirement to help those in peril, even on the Sabbath. He quickly pushed it aside, his mind made up. He would do nothing until after sunset, then he might seek out Sam Hart.

Mr John Harriot stood to greet his visitor in the magistrate's first floor office at 259, Wapping New Stairs.

'My dear sir, thank you for agreeing to see me at this ungodly hour of the morning.' Richard Ball, the Hastings jurat, extended a well-manicured hand. 'I would have written but time is, I believe, of the essence in the matter about which I wish to speak. I arrived last night but the hour was late and you had already retired for the evening.'

'Always, sir, a pleasure to meet a colleague,' said Harriot. 'You already know Mr Pascoe, do you not?'

'I do, indeed.' Ball eyed the bandage round Tom's head, a concerned look on his face. 'You are well, I hope, Mr Pascoe?'

'You are most kind, sir. A trifle, no more. But how can we be of assistance?'

'Why, sir, I believe I may have some information which might be of benefit to you in connection with your enquiries in Hastings.'

'Pray continue, sir,' said Harriot, waving the stem of his pipe in the direction of a chair.

'Shortly before Mr Pascoe left Hastings yesterday morning to return to London,' said Ball, taking his seat in front of the fire, 'a stranger arrived in the town making enquiries concerning the present whereabouts of a young man called Stevy . . .'

'The lad who died?' asked Tom.

'The very same. It appears the stranger was a friend of the boy. In any event he said he was looking for something that he described as important. The impression was that whatever he was looking for was closely connected to the boy and had probably been in his possession.'

'What, pray, makes you think that, sir?' said Harriot, lighting his pipe from a taper and filling the room with a noxious cloud of smoke.

'I believe, Mr Pascoe, you are acquainted with Harry Fearne, publican of the Cutter?' said Ball, turning to look at Tom.

'Yes. He asked to see me concerning the disappearance of the *Mary-Anne* and a young man called Toiler.'

'Quite so,' said Ball, turning back to Harriot. 'Shortly before the stranger's arrival, Harry Fearne made it his business to visit the place where Stevy had lived. While he was there he found these.'

The jurat reached into a portmanteau, withdrew a bag and emptied its contents of gold coins onto Harriot's desk.

'There is, of course, little to suggest that these coins – and there are three more bags of them here – were what the stranger was referring to, but it seems likely, given their quantity and value.'

'What d'you make of it, Mr Pascoe?' said Harriot, picking up one of the coins and examining it. 'There must be over two hundred here. And French, if I'm not sadly mistook.'

'Aye,' said Tom, picking up another of the hoard. 'They are *louis d'or*. Legal tender in France before the Revolution, but since replaced by the franc. They are now unofficially used in dealings with foreigners who, for understandable reasons, have little confidence in the value of the Revolutionary coin, particularly as it is silver rather than gold.'

'But what the devil would this lad Stevy be doing with such a fortune in his possession?' said Harriot, a puzzled frown on his broad face.

'As to that, I cannot say,' said Tom. 'But, as you say, the value is significant, the *louis d'or* being roughly equivalent to our English guinea. If it was given in payment for a service, then I suggest the service must have been of considerable importance to someone.'

'And you're suggesting ... what, exactly?' said Harriot, his eyebrows arched.

'I am merely thinking aloud, sir,' said Tom. 'You will recall a recent case when a peer of the realm was caught trying to get to France in a fishing boat?'

'Yes, I remember,' said Harriot. 'A very foolhardy thing for him to have done. He was never able to give a satisfactory reason for his actions; was lucky not to hang, escaping the consequences by reason of patronage, if I remember aright.'

'That's the fellow,' said Tom. 'Anyway, he was said to have negotiated a fee of twelve guineas to cross the Channel.'

'And you think the same thing was happening in the opposite direction? Someone in Hastings was paid to bring a Frenchman over to these shores?'

'I mention it for reason of comparison, sir,' said Tom. 'If the going rate for taking a peer of the realm across the Channel is twelve guineas, what will a thousand buy? As I have said, I think the money was intended as payment for a service of considerable value.'

'Perhaps, sir, this might help,' said Ball, reaching into his coat pocket and withdrawing a piece of charred paper. He handed it to Tom. 'It was found at the same location as the French coins.'

Tom placed the scrap onto Harriot's desk, smoothed it out and studied it in silence for a moment.

'I grant it's a poor likeness,' he said. 'But if you hold the paper thus, you'll notice the lines travel down the page before sweeping up to the top and turning left. I believe the drawing may represent the Thames. This downward sweep, here, is Blackwall Reach. And here, the upward stretch appears to be of Limehouse Reach. Look how the lines then go to the left, just here. That, if my analysis is correct, is the Lower and the Upper Pool. And if it is a sketch of the Thames, then just off the page, where the paper has been burned, is London Bridge.'

'What d'you suppose that cross is for?' said Harriot. 'A meeting point of some kind?'

'It's possible,' said Tom. 'I'd say it certainly marks a location of interest to the person who drew that map. Its position would put it just downriver of the Bridge and on the Southwark side.'

'Not far from where the *Mary-Anne* went down,' said Harriot.

'Quite so,' said Tom. 'We already know that Stevy was friendly with the men whose bodies were found on that lugger. What we don't yet know is what they were doing in London. It's entirely possible that their final destination was the point marked on the paper but that still doesn't tell us why they were here.'

'I suppose the money could have been in payment for goods smuggled into the country – rather than people?' said Harriot.

'You are, sir, to consider,' said Tom, 'that those engaged in running goods must pay the supplier and not the other way round. In this case, it is, if I am right in my assumption, the smuggler who is being paid and therefore the English who are supplying the service.'

'Yes, yes. Of course,' said Harriot. 'I was not thinking clearly. But where does this leave us? Stevy's possession of a large amount of money is not, of itself, a criminal offence.'

'But it is, sir, indicative of one,' said Tom, looking at the magistrate. 'It was discovered in the possession of a man known to have close links with two others whose bodies were found not far from here. With the money – French money – was found a plan which I believe to be of the Thames. Does that not suggest to you an operation involving the French; an operation of very considerable value to them?'

'It may do, but . . .' said Harriot.

'Clearly, the sum involved is of such a magnitude as to suggest an operation of some size and importance. It is certainly more than would be necessary to pay for conveying two or three bottles of wine or an agent or three across the Channel. I think it is much more than that, and may also go some way to explaining why Stevy should have tried to kill me.'

'What have you got in mind, Mr Pascoe?'

'If we assume, for the moment, that the *Mary-Anne* was carrying something of considerable value when she arrived in the Lower Pool and that the mark on this map was the intended destination, we at least have a starting point for our investigation. What we have no way of knowing, at this stage, is exactly what was being transported and with what intent. Nor, for that matter, do we have a motive for the deaths of the crew.'

'And if it was agents, what then?' said the Hastings jurat.

'As I have already indicated, the sum of money found is

too great simply to have paid for the transfer of two or three men,' said Tom. 'I've a notion, gentlemen, that we may be facing a serious threat to life and property in the capital.'

'How long d'you think we've got, sir?' asked Ball, a little nervously.

'I only wish I knew,' said Tom. 'By the by, you mentioned a stranger who was making enquiries of the lad Stevy. Pray, what did he look like?'

André Dubois felt his colleague's eyes boring into him as he entered the first-floor room of the warehouse on Hay's Wharf.

'You made sure the boy will not escape?'

Dubois didn't answer. He walked to the window, reluctant to approach the other man. He looked out over the mud-brown Thames where the pale rays of the early morning sun was glinting off the water and onto the hulls of ships moored three and four abreast. On the wharf, lumpers had already begun the day's work, their shouts mingling with the rhythmic chant of the men in the tread-mills working the lighters tied at the edge of the quay.

Moreau's question hung in the air. He thought of the boy – funny that he should think of Toiler as a boy, a lad less than two years his junior – lying on the floor of the room below. No, he wouldn't escape. But was that a sufficient answer? Or should he tell Moreau the boy was still alive but only just, that he had tried to snuff out the life of someone who, so long as he lived, posed a threat to their own existence? He shook his head. Perhaps not. Moreau was dying; might not last the day. There was little to be gained by telling him the truth. He turned to face the sick man. He would deal with Toiler after Moreau's death.

'The boy will not escape, *citoyen*. I have made sure of that,' he muttered.

Moreau's head slumped forward, resting on his arms. He mumbled something that Dubois didn't catch.

'What was that, *citoyen*? I could not hear you.'

'Tonight I want you to go and meet our contact.' Moreau spoke with difficulty, his voice hoarse. 'You'll find him at the Blind Beggar tavern, close to St Saviour's Dock. You are to confirm with him that everything is ready.'

'Ready for what, *citoyen*, and how will I know him?' said Dubois, remaining by the window.

'You don't want to catch what I have,' nodded Moreau, a weak smile crossing his lips. 'I can't say I blame you. I know I am dying.' He paused to draw breath, then continued, 'I will tell you the nature of the operation before you go. When you reach the tavern, you are to make yourself known to the publican. The words you use and his reply are quite specific. I will tell you what they are before you leave.'

'What then?' said Dubois.

'He will point out the man you are to meet. He is expecting me so he will doubtless wish to ensure you are who you say you are. Show him this.' Moreau took a silver snuffbox from his coat pocket and handed it over. It was inscribed with his colleague's name. 'He has seen it many times.'

'And he has made the arrangements for this operation, the details of which I do not know?'

'Yes.' Moreau broke into a fit of violent coughing. When he again spoke, his voice had assumed a wheezing quality. 'Half the necessary funds were handed to a man named Stevy, about two weeks since. The rest, which I have here, will be paid once the operation has been completed.'

Moreau removed a cloth pouch from a bag at his side and passed it over.

'*Louis d'or*?' murmured Dubois, eyeing the head of the late King embossed on the face.

'Yes.' Moreau closed his eyes. 'It's quite normal. No one outside France will accept anything else.'

'And there is enough left to get us back to France?'

'Naturally. Four of these pouches are to pay for the operation,' said Moreau, putting his hand back into the black leather bag. 'The fifth is to cover the cost of our return to France.'

A worried frown suddenly creased his brow.

'Is there something wrong, *citoyen*?' said Dubois, forgetting his concerns and walking quickly across the room.

The older man leaned his back against the wall and looked up.

'It seems the remaining four bags are still in the fishing vessel that brought us here. I placed them in a safe place in the hold where we slept. After that business with Toiler and the other two, I must have left them behind.'

'Then I'll return to the boat and search for them,' said Dubois.

'Not now,' said Moreau. 'The money is safely hidden and there are too many people about at this hour. You'll be caught. Leave it until night falls.'

Dubois hid his irritation. The old man had clearly lost his senses.

For how long he remained unconscious, Toiler had no idea. When he awoke it was to find himself lying on a bare wooden floor wedged between piles of empty sacks. He tried to wipe away the dust and the grime around his mouth and eyes, but couldn't. His hands were bound tightly behind his back and a rag had been shoved into his mouth, making it difficult for him to breathe. There was a stinging sensation around his neck and his throat was sore. Slowly, the memory of what had happened returned. He recalled coming to his senses as he was being dragged across to the warehouse, his captors taking care to avoid the night-watchmen. He'd been dumped into this room, bound and gagged. Then . . . Toiler felt his stomach somersault. Then something had happened. He had the dimmest of memories of a cord being placed round his neck, of his difficulty in breathing, a sense in which his eyes had been forced from their sockets.

He peered up at a small window high on one wall through which he could see a patch of blue sky, streaked with smoke. He wondered where Moreau and Dubois had gone and how long it would be before they returned. He tried to think of something else, of the possibility of rescue. He'd told the nurse in the accident hospital about his plan. She would know what to do.

His sense of relief was short-lived as he remembered that he'd not said exactly where the warehouse was. He'd not known himself. And even if he had known and had told her, it was extremely unlikely anyone would think to search for him. He had, after all, discharged himself from the hospital.

An image dropped into his mind's eye. It was that of an elderly man, his thin face deeply lined, his long, white beard streaked with yellow. Toiler tried to remember where he'd seen it and why he should have thought of him at this moment. The image faded. He attempted to bring it back but couldn't. Perhaps it was nothing.

His thoughts drifted to his home. He imagined himself standing on the cliffs of the East Hill gazing down onto the rooftops of Hastings, could see the tiny figures of the fishermen moving between the boats drawn up onto the stone beach far below. Others were tramping up towards Fisher Street, their heads bowed. They'd be exhausted at the end of a night or more at sea. He could smell the wood fires and see the thin grey curls of smoke rising from the chimneys as meals were prepared for the returning menfolk. On the far side of the valley the sunlight was tracking down the slopes towards the town, catching first one house and then another in its burnished glare. He smiled to himself. Soon it would reach the net shops on the Stade and after them the houses on Fisher Street behind which he lived. His mother would be up and about. He frowned. She'd be worrying about him.

Through the window of his personal prison wafted the sounds of the port coming to life, the shouts of the gangsmen and lightermen and the rumbling squeal of cart-wheels on the cobbled surface of the wharf. He would have shouted for help if he'd been able. But he doubted anyone would have heard him even if he had had the strength to raise his voice. He felt better than he had done over the last day or so, the worst of the fever now behind him, but he was still weak. He'd be no match for the Frenchmen when they came back. He turned his attention to the ropes binding him. One of them was not as tight as the others.

CHAPTER 17

Tom left the meeting with Harriot and Richard Ball, and made his way to the police office in Bow Street. Arriving there, he mounted the steps and went inside.

'Hello, Tom.'

Tom grinned as he saw his friend Nathaniel Morgan of the Bow Street Runners waving at him. The two had met in the early days of the formation of the marine police when Nathaniel had proved an invaluable source of help and information to him. Now Tom was hoping that his friend's vast experience would again help.

'Nathaniel! The very man. If you is at leisure, there is a matter on which I wish to speak.'

Ten minutes later the two men were ensconced in one of several boxes at the White Hart on Drury Lane.

'You've been a runner a fair while, Nathaniel. What can you tell me about a one-armed scrub called Clarke what's making a nuisance of himself on my beat?'

'Big cully, aged about forty, shoulders like a barn-door?'

'Sounds about right,' said Tom. 'What's his game?'

'His first name is Jim.' Nathaniel frowned and shook his head. 'A right bully boy is that one and slippery as an eel. Spent some time in the army in France and, later, in Ireland. I heard he lost his arm in a disagreement with some Irishmen with a cannon and were kicked out of the dragoons. He weren't too happy about that, though you wouldn't know it from listening to him.'

A knock on the door of the box interrupted them and a waiter bustled in to take their orders.

'What did you mean, just now?' said Tom, as soon as the man had left them. 'When you said he was as slippery as an eel?'

'He's right clever when he wants to be,' said Nathaniel. 'A bully boy one minute and a charmer the next – that's our Jim. In course, we didn't know nothing about him to begin with. Then we started hearing stories of coaches being held up to the west of town, out beyond Hyde Park. All we knew was it were a cully with one arm as could ride a horse like he were born to it. Most of the time he got what he wanted with his charm and the sight of his pistol. But once or twice, folk who should have known better tried to take him on and were cut down with no mercy.'

'Was he never caught?' asked Tom, watching the froth settle on his mug of Whitbread.

'No, it would have been a dance at the end of a rope if we had,' said Nathaniel, with a knowing jerk of the head.

'So he went on plundering?'

'No. Leastways, we didn't hear on him for a while. Then he pops up round Southwark way.'

'Doing what, pray?'

'That's the interesting thing,' said Nathaniel. 'We're not sure. There've been no tales of robbery that we've been able to tie down to him but the sightings keep coming. I warrant he's up to something. The lads from Customs reckon they've seen him once or twice out there. They suspect he's responsible for the deaths of at least two of the five officers they've lost down that way in recent months.'

Another knock on the door of their box and the waiter returned with plates laden with a selection of meats, oysters, crab and thick slices of white bread. Leaving them, he returned a moment later with a fresh jug of ale.

'Please,' said Tom, waving at the feast. 'Do start.'

They attacked the food in silence for a few minutes before Tom said, 'You were saying the Customs boys suspected Clarke of murdering two of their men.'

'Aye, so I did.'

'Why? Because they think him involved with the smugglers?'

'You might have thought so,' said Nathaniel, spooning

174

a liberal portion of oysters onto his plate. 'It's where most of the goods coming up from Sussex and Kent end up. But there was never any evidence that he had anything to do with that. Thought they had him when they saw him with a young cully up from the coast. They stopped the boy but there weren't nothing on him, so they let him go.'

'Did they get his name?' said Tom, looking up from his plate.

'I believe it were Stevy something.'

Tom threaded the police galley up through a cluster of lighters in the Upper Pool waiting their turn to be unloaded at the legal quays, the swelling chorus of shouts and oaths mingling uneasily with the clatter of the tread-mills and the rumble of carts on the cobbled surface of the wharfs.

He kept well in towards the bank, away from the main force of the tide, his eyes moving rapidly from vessel to vessel searching for any sign that something might be amiss amongst the bustle of humanity, a too-casual glance, a determined avoidance of eye contact, a bulging pocket. There was something indefinable in the behaviour of a man bent on plunder that radiated his guilt as surely as a hilltop beacon.

He was sure that Jim Clarke, the man who'd followed and shot at him last night, was the same man he'd seen in Hastings. He wondered if the attack had simply been in revenge for the death of the boy Stevy although it didn't seem likely. Not after the discovery of the hoard of *louis d'or* and Clarke's probable connection to it. It seemed to Tom more likely that the scrub suspected him of taking the coins and had sought to get them back in the only way he knew how.

Tom hauled his thoughts back to the present and caught sight of Joe Ruxey, the newest member of his crew. It reminded him that he still had not spoken to the boy, had not got to know him properly. He would do so as soon as they got back to Wapping.

'Stand by to go about.' Tom eyed the vast bulk of London Bridge and the constant stream of vessels passing down through its arches, on their way to the sea. He pulled hard on the larboard guy and watched the galley curve round to face the Southwark shore, the sleek hull slicing through the water, the crew's backs arching and straightening in perfect unison as they bent to their oars.

'Easy all,' he said when the galley had reached the south bank and was gliding gently downstream, close beneath a tier of coal blackened colliers, great palls of choking dust hanging like formless clouds over their upper yards. It had been his life, once, long ago, before he'd joined the King's Navy. He let the memory go as the colliers dropped astern. He cast a cautionary glance over the side, acutely aware of the falling tide and the danger of running aground. Getting stranded on an ebb tide ranked, in terms of embarrassment, alongside falling out of the galley.

Cotton's Wharf came and went. Hay's Wharf lay ahead. Tom watched the gangs of barefooted men swarming over the lighters tied alongside, their faces streaked with sweat, their ragged clothing covered with the sheen of grease.

'Something we should know about, sir?' said Sam.

'What's that, Sam? Oh, that. No, I was just watching them lumpers and wondering how much of that cargo will ever see the inside of the owner's warehouse.'

He already knew the answer to his question. Very little. He couldn't say he was surprised. The men were seldom paid for their labours. They were expected to take the sweepings of sugar and coffee and the like in place of money. The practice had been going on for so long that the men had come to regard a portion of the cargo as their lawful perquisite, their payment for a day's work.

'What the devil . . .'

'What was you looking at, sir?' inquired Sam, turning to look over his shoulder.

'Over there, on Hay's Wharf. D'you see him? Short fellow. Swarthy face. There, by them hogsheads.'

'Now I see him. What of him?'

'Seen him before, somewhere,' said Tom, thinking hard. 'He knows me, too. Took one look at us and was away on his toes.'

177

Suddenly his face cleared and his fingers traced the outline of an old vertical scar, close to his right eye.

'André Dubois,' he murmured as an image formed in his mind and his memory went back to an encounter with a French corsair on a clear summer's day in 1795, a hundred miles off the south coast of France.

Tom watched the figure of the Frenchman disappear amongst the crowds on the wharf as the police galley swept down to Battle Bridge Stairs and glided to a halt at the eastern end of the wharf.

'Sam and Ruxey. You two come with me. Kemp, stay with the boat,' said Tom, leaping ashore and racing up the stairs.

'You, Ruxey, cut along Hay's Wharf to the end and then make your way up to Tooley Street. Know what you're looking for?'

'Aye, sir.'

'Good. Best you get going. Sam and I will look for the scrub up Mill Lane. We'll meet you in Tooley Street. If you see the cully, don't approach him on your own. Is that clear?' Tom's eyes scanned the crowded wharf.

'Aye, clear enough, sir,' said Ruxey touching his forehead and peeling away.

Tom watched him go before setting off, closely followed by Sam, along the lane that led south, away from the Thames. As with the wharf, Mill Lane was pestered with a constant procession of men and women, each seemingly intent on outdoing his neighbour in the noise that could be generated. Horse-drawn carts jostled for space with porters, food sellers with pedlars, prostitutes with ballad singers, in a shifting, amorphous mass.

'Morning, Mr Pascoe.' A tall, thin woman of about forty, her scalp visible through her thinning hair, leered at Tom.

'Morning, Maggie,' said Tom. 'What are you doing this side of the water?'

'Business, Mr Pascoe, sir.' The woman's eyes flitted from one passer-by to the next. 'A better class of customer over 'ere.'

'Seen a bully boy come this way, have you?' said Tom, his tone friendly, conversational. 'Foreign-looking, early twenties.'

'Ain't seen nothing, your honour, and that's the honest truth.' The woman's eyes narrowed. 'What you want to know for, anygate?'

'Just a chat, Maggie. Just a chat.'

He turned as Sam touched his elbow, his eyebrows raised in a silent question. His friend was looking at a cluster of broken-nosed men on the corner of County Row.

'You know them?'

'Aye, they're crimps,' said Sam, exchanging a nod of recognition with one of the group. 'Don't usually see them up this way. Work out of Deptford. I reckon if your friend had come this way, they'd have swifted him aboard a ship afore he knew what hit him.'

'In that case we'll not waste time looking for the bracket-faced scrub here,' said Tom. 'Time we met up with Ruxey. See if he's had any luck.'

They pushed through the crowds up the lane and turned right into Tooley Street, making their way to the junction where they had agreed to meet Ruxey. There was no sign of him.

'Must still be on the wharf,' said Tom turning down an alley that led back towards the river. At the bottom they separated and Tom walked along a short, rubbish-strewn path, at the end of which he saw a group of people drawn into a tight circle apparently looking at something at its centre. He felt a small knot form in the pit of his stomach. The circle parted as he approached. John Kemp was crouching over a body.

'What's happened?'

'It's young Ruxey, sir.' Kemp glanced up, his large face sombre. 'Been stabbed. Looks to 'ave lost a fair amount of blood.'

Dubois turned off Hay's Wharf and ran up the steep incline into Borough High Street, thankful for the heavy press of people and the cover they provided.

At the top of Tooley Street he turned left, stopped, changed his mind and, keeping his head below the level of the parapet, sprinted onto London Bridge. Carefully, he raised his head and peered over the edge.

The police galley was still tied up at the foot of Battle

Bridge Stairs. There was no one on board. His gaze shifted to the western end of the wharf. It was crowded, his view obscured by the line of treadmill huts perched on top of their thick timber supports. There was no sign of Pascoe. For a while longer his eyes swept back and forth over the crowd in what seemed a futile attempt to find him. He realised he was shaking.

Suddenly he saw him, pushing his way through the crowd. Behind him, two others were carrying a third person, almost certainly the lad he'd stabbed. He watched the group's slow progress, a mixture of fear and loathing welling within. He looked down at his trembling hands. He clenched his fists and forced them against his thighs as if the tension would somehow still them. It wasn't the first time he'd experienced the almost physical pain of fear. He would never admit to it – could never do so. He'd spent a lifetime burying the shame beneath a mask of violence directed towards anyone foolish enough to suggest he did not possess nerves of steel. Driven by the fear of fear itself, Dubois invariably responded to any perceived slight with all the vigour at his disposal. It was how he was.

Pascoe and his little group had now reached the galley and were placing the injured crewman on board. Dubois hardly noticed, his eyes fixed on the man wearing a grubby coat and breeches that had once signified an officer in the English Navy.

'You will pay for what you did.' Dubois's thick, stubby fingers wound themselves round the hilt of his knife.

The problem with the lad had made things more difficult. After the boy had seen him, there had been no going back. He had done what he had done a hundred times before, his hand sliding to the hilt of the knife, the blade leaping from its hiding place to pierce the soft skin of the boy's stomach.

He watched the galley draw away from the bank and head out into the centre of the channel between the tiers of brigs and barques, each one surrounded by its fussing flotilla of smaller craft. He waited until the galley was lost to sight and then turned to leave the bridge, crossing Borough High Street and turning down a footpath by the church that Moreau had told him about. Yes, the incident with the boy had certainly complicated matters.

'Follow the path to the end and then turn right,' Moreau had said. 'You will see the Blind Beggar tavern ahead of you.'

He was early. He knew that, but he wanted to get the meeting with their contact over and done with. After that he'd return to the *Mary-Anne* and search for the missing coins. He'd wanted to ask Moreau where he'd hidden the pouch but knew the *commissaire* would have refused to tell him – at least until he considered it safe for Dubois to go.

He stood in the doorway of a derelict house in Church Street, Southwark, its windows and doors gone, its roof collapsed. It seemed the fate of most of the houses in the street. There was no one about, the place devoid of life. Further along the street, at the point where it bent away to the left, he could see the tavern he'd been looking for.

The Blind Beggar was a peculiar building, part brick and part timber, which grew outwards as it rose so that its upper floors were everywhere larger than those below. On its right side, the wall leaned to such an alarming extent as to appear on the point of collapsing, requiring a series of stout, twisted timbers to be placed against the offending wall. The result, apart from preventing the collapse of the tavern, was to partially block the narrow path leading to the dock.

Dubois stood and watched the front door. His instructions had been to go into the premises and make himself known to the publican. Moreau had told him the landlord would, at some point, comment on the weather. Dubois was then to reply in the exact words Moreau had given him. After that he would be taken to meet the contact.

Cautiously, he approached the tavern, no light coming from its windows. He tried the door. It opened and he stepped across the threshold.

The room in which he now found himself was a cramped, low-ceilinged affair with black timber beams supporting the upper floors. Such daylight as was left seeped through a single mullioned window. A solitary candle burned in its sconce on the bar in the corner. Behind this was another door, presumably leading to the rest of the house. Most of the remaining space was taken up by a long deal table presently occupied by half a dozen carousing sailors. At the far end, a dirty grey blanket hung from a rope dividing the room in two.

'Makes a change to see the sun, don't it?' Dubois spun round, crouching low, his knife jumping to his hand. A man had appeared in the doorway behind the bar. Dubois cursed his lack of attention and walked over.

The man had said something. He struggled to recall the words but nothing came to mind; nothing that made any sense. He remembered the two phrases that Moreau had told him about, the first that would be given in greeting and the second that he was to use in reply. He stared at the short, womanish fellow standing a few feet from him.

The man was expecting a reply. Dubois decided to risk it.

'But it always shines in the winter.' He was relieved to see the man gesture towards the other end of the room and lead the way through a gap in the blanket. Here the publican stopped and pointed to a table in the corner.

Dubois could see nothing, his view obscured by a heavy pall of tobacco smoke. He waited for it to clear, his fingers resting on the hilt of his knife. Gradually, the outline of a man came into view, his back to the wall, a pipe clenched between his teeth.

'Where is Moreau?' There was no preamble. No introductory pleasantries. It reminded Dubois of his *chef de brigade*, except that this cully was bigger and fitter-looking.

He noticed one sleeve of the man's coat was empty and had been pinned across his chest.

Jim Clarke wore a look of faint alarm as he watched the publican of the Blind Beggar usher the stranger in. He'd been expecting Pierre Moreau, a man he'd met and done business with on several occasions in the last few months. If the stranger was here in his stead, it was going to be difficult – not to say dangerous – explaining the loss of a thousand *louis d'or.*

Clarke had thought of little else since going to Stevy's shack on the hill outside Hastings to find that both the lad and the money were missing. Not even the news of Stevy's death had succeeded in pushing the matter from his mind. He knew it was wrong, knew that what he should be feeling was grief at the loss of his only son.

But he'd felt nothing beyond the initial shock of the unexpected, a raging anger directed at the man responsible for his death. What had exercised his mind was the growing realisation of the consequences that the loss of the money would bring.

What had begun as a vastly profitable enterprise was now threatening to overwhelm him. A simple task had become a crushing weight. He'd made a promise he could no longer fulfil. He'd borrowed against the promise of rich returns in the future. And he knew, better than most, the price of failure.

But the day of his reckoning had not yet arrived, despite the increasingly strident demands being made by his debtors for his promises of payment to be made good. He had, at best, another two or three days' grace in which to escape their wrath. Time enough to consider what needed to be done.

The train of his thoughts led him, inevitably, to the cause of his present difficulties. That Pascoe had taken the money was, to his mind, a given. He'd followed him from the Bolt-in-Tun to Burr Street with the intention of killing him and recovering the missing *louis d'or*. But he'd under-estimated his opponent, had been lucky to escape capture.

'Who are you?' Clarke leaned forward and eyed the stocky newcomer as the latter sauntered towards him.

'I've come to check the arrangements,' said the stranger, ignoring the question.

'I don't know what you're talking about, mate,' said Clarke with an attempt at an air of bafflement. 'Who are you?'

'You were expecting Pierre Moreau. He is not well. I've come in his place.'

'How do I know that?'

'My friend asked me to show you this.' The man reached into his pocket and handed over a snuffbox.

Clarke glanced at the item and nodded. There was no doubt it belonged to Moreau. He'd seen it several times when the two of them had had occasion to meet. He nodded.

'What's your name?'

'André Dubois. Does anyone know of this meeting?'

'No. Why should they?'

'I was recognised on my way here,' said Dubois, cocking his head on one side as the sound of carousing on the other side of the curtain stopped abruptly. 'A man I once knew. I believe he is one of your police.'

'For the love of God,' said Clarke. 'Who?'

'I know him as Captain Pascoe.'

'Pascoe? Again?' Clarke jumped to his feet and ran to the window, his eyes scouring the street outside. It was deserted. 'Where did you see him?'

'By the river. He'll try to find me.'

'You, too?' Clarke slumped back in his chair. 'It seems we have something in common – you and me. I were—'

'We have no time for this,' snapped Dubois. 'Show me the arrangements that have been made. After that we might talk.'

Clarke's jaw muscles flexed. He didn't like the Frenchman's attitude, and would not, under normal circumstances, have put up with it. In time he remembered the missing cash. This was not the time for an argument.

'This way,' he said, sweeping the blanket to one side and heading for the door. 'You can see for yourself what's been done.'

CHAPTER 18

Peggy's eyes flitted across the noisy confines of the receiving room. Afternoons were always hectic and this one was no exception. Behind her, the door squeaked open.

'Miss Tompkins?' Peggy felt the colour rising in her cheeks at the sound of the familiar voice. She turned to see Tom. He was with two other men.

'It's one of my crew,' said Tom, gesturing to the figure being carried on the stretcher. 'He's been stabbed.'

'Take him over there.' Peggy pointed to one of the three small consulting rooms leading off the main area. She followed them in. 'What happened?'

'We were searching for a suspect,' said Tom, looking down at his injured crewman. 'We think Ruxey here found him and got stabbed.'

Peggy bent over the young man's unconscious form and folded back the blood-soaked shirt from around the injury to the stomach. His face was deathly pale, almost grey. She turned to one of the porters outside the door and said, 'Please ask the duty physician to come directly.'

She turned back to her patient, acutely aware of Tom's closeness, recalling the last time they had been in each other's company, the lost opportunity for making amends for the past. She was, of late, conscious of a thaw in those feelings of mistrust that had characterised her attitude towards him, a man wholly innocent of any offence against her. She had begun, at last, to separate the activities of the man responsible for her hurt from those of men in general, and Tom in particular, and dared to hope that the trust with which she had once regarded him was returning.

She looked round for the duty physician. There was no sign of him. Nor could she see the apothecary. She beckoned the porter from his place by the door.

'Is the duty physician informed?'

'I sent word, miss,' he said. 'Seems he's engaged with an object what's been hurt bad. He might be delayed for some time.'

'This patient cannot wait,' she said. 'Be so good as to take him to Harrison Ward on the instant. He can be examined there when the physician is at leisure.'

She waited as Ruxey was lifted onto a stretcher and carried towards the stairwell. She knew she had taken a chance admitting the boy without the necessary authority but there had been nothing for it. It was that or risk the boy losing his life for want of care. He'd likely be seen more quickly on the ward.

She turned to Tom. 'Should you wish to see the young man, I dare say he will be able to receive a visitor later this evening.'

'Will you be there?'

'I . . .' Peggy hesitated, felt the heat return to her cheeks. 'I'm sure of it.'

'Until then, dear Peggy.'

She watched him stride away, a slow smile of pleasure crossing her lips.

Tom stretched his legs out in front of him and cupped his hands behind his head, feeling the heat of the fire beginning to warm him. Outside the rain had set up a fierce patter against the windowpanes. He could still see Peggy, a surprised and delighted expression flitting across her face as she had turned to see him entering the receiving room. He had, at that moment, felt a surge of hope for the future, a hope that the months of separation might soon be at an end.

'How is young Ruxey?' John Harriot's voice cut across his thoughts. Tom looked away from the fire. The resident magistrate had helped himself to a toasted muffin and was spreading it with a generous quantity of butter.

'Too early to tell,' said Tom. 'But he's in good hands. I hope to see him this evening. By then we should know more.'

'Any idea of who might have been responsible?' said Harriot returning to his desk and sitting down to eat. 'Do help yourself to the muffins, won't you?'

'Aye, thank you, sir,' said Tom. 'I believe it's a man I've had previous dealings with. It was a long time ago, mind, when I was still in the Navy. His name is André Dubois, a Frenchman. It's possible he might be one of the two men who were on the *Mary-Anne*.'

'Speaking of which, have you any more thoughts on this?' Harriot picked up the charred scrap of paper given to him by the Hastings jurat.

'I'm still of the same view,' said Tom. 'I think the position of the cross indicates a place of interest to whoever drew this. When I saw Dubois, he was on Hay's Wharf. I can't help wondering if the position of the cross on this paper and the position of Hay's Wharf aren't identical.'

'There is nothing of interest there,' said Harriot, leaning back in his chair and gazing at the ceiling, his muffin temporarily forgotten. 'At least, nothing of interest to the enemy.'

'Perhaps, but something is happening in that area,' said Tom. 'What of Lord Portland? Did he mention anything when you saw him last night?'

'The Secretary of State? No, just the usual litany of complaints. Mainly talked about the rising national debt as a result of the war. Apparently, the administration is finding it difficult to raise the necessary funds from the financial markets and is being forced to pay ever increasing interest rates on those loans that *can* be obtained. It's all having an adverse effect on the war effort.'

'Did he say anything else?'

'Said something about the arrival of the West India fleet.'

Tom's head snapped up.

'When, sir, is it due?'

'Why, I believe the first vessels are due this evening or perhaps tomorrow morning,' said Harriot. 'By the end of tomorrow we should have the whole fleet at anchor. Why the interest, sir?'

'And the ships currently in the port?' Tom waved an impatient hand. 'When are they expected to leave?'

'According to the harbour master, not for two or three days.'

'So for one, possibly two days, there'll scarcely be room to move for the press of ships?'

'Yes. What of it, Mr Pascoe?' Harriot was beginning to sound irritated.

'Who else, sir, knows about this?' said Tom.

'Well, the movement of all merchant ships is published by Lloyd's,' said Harriot. 'It's a simple matter to discover the estimated time of each vessel's arrival at its destination.'

'So the French would also know?'

'Without a doubt, sir,' said Harriot. 'The French receive copies of all the English newspapers and I've no doubt they will also receive the Lloyd's List.'

'It could be,' muttered Tom, staring at the floor.

'It could be, what?' said Harriot.

'We believe that the *Mary-Anne* was carrying French agents at the time she was sunk,' said Tom. 'Those agents will have been sent for a specific purpose, the nature of which we don't yet know. But given the amount of money involved, it's likely to be something big. We now know that a sizeable fleet is due to arrive in the Port of London, some days before the ships already here are ready to leave. The port, already overcrowded, will be intolerable once the additional ships arrive. No one will be able to move. And all this information is readily available to the enemy.'

'So you think the agents are here to attack the port?' said Harriot. 'How?'

'You were, I believe, a naval officer, were you not?' said Tom.

'Aye, so I was,' said Harriot.

'And when the enemy's fleet was discovered in port, how did you attack it?'

'Why, by the use of—' Harriot stopped in mid-sentence and stared at Tom.

'Precisely,' said Tom. 'A fireship or three. The idea has been practised for as long as there have been wars at sea. Send a burning hulk into a port pestered with shipping and let nature do the rest. In the case of the Port of London, there will be so many ships here, they'll be unable to manoeuvre out of harm's way.'

'Destroying the Port of London and our merchant fleet could be decisive for the war.' Harriot locked his hands behind his head and whistled. 'Now that you mention it, Portland told me something else. He said the government was pinning its hopes on raising an additional five million pounds. But that was dependent on the continuing rise in the value of the goods crossing the King's Beam. If the port was destroyed, that would put an end to overseas trade and effectively put us out of the war.'

The two men lapsed into silence. A catastrophic fire in the port would not only destroy the merchant fleet on which the country depended but could quickly spread ashore through the narrow streets and crowded buildings of the capital.

'How d'you suppose we're going to find these fellows in the next day or two?' asked Harriot.

'I don't think it'll come to that,' said Tom, pouring himself some coffee. 'The wind's in the wrong direction for anyone coming up the tideway. As long as it stays there, we won't be seeing any fresh arrivals. In the meantime I think we should concentrate our efforts on finding the potential fireship. The most crowded part of the port is the Upper and Lower Pool. It's not only crowded but it's close to the City, meaning that a fire here will cause the most mischief. It's most likely that any attack would begin above London Bridge and the vessel be brought down on an ebb tide. If that is the case it will, even now, be moored in some backwater between London and Blackfriars bridges.'

'Then best we begin, Mr Pascoe,' said a grim-faced Harriot.

Dubois and Clarke left the Blind Beggar and turned down the narrow path beside the leaning wall and its twisted timber supports. In front of them lay a cone-shaped stretch of water about a hundred and fifty yards long and, at its junction with the Thames, about fifty yards wide. If it had ever enjoyed any pretensions as a shipyard there was now little evidence of this. The place was deserted but for the presence of perhaps twenty or thirty hulks. No movement, no sound, save that of seagulls, disturbed the peace. The two men took the right-hand fork and walked past a line of ancient brigs and barquentines, stripped of their rigging, their masts and all else that had once been an essential part of their being.

'This is the one.' Clarke stopped opposite a hulk, older, dirtier and more battered than the rest, her once gleaming paintwork blistered and peeling, her decks littered with rope-ends, strips of canvas, bent nails, old rags and offcuts of timber. Like her neighbours, her masts had been removed and she appeared abandoned and forgotten.

'What's that for?' said Dubois, pointing to a pair of davits curving out over the taffrail and fitted with blocks and tackle.

The question caught Clarke unawares, his mind still on

the missing money. It was going to be difficult, not to say impossible, keeping the loss from Dubois. And then what? How would the Frenchman react? He'd not even the money to pay for the half-dozen men needed to take the ship through the Bridge. He began to sweat. There was no way out for him.

'The davits?' Clarke struggled to concentrate. Somebody had suggested putting them there. How the hell was he supposed to know what for? He caught sight of an upended skiff. Now he remembered. 'They's for a boat to get us all ashore once this 'ere hulk's through the Bridge.'

Dubois nodded again and two men walked up one of several gangplanks positioned on the quay and onto the brig's upper deck.

'You're limping,' said Dubois. 'Did something happen to you?'

'Ran across Pascoe. It's nothing.'

'What d'you mean, you ran across him? Is he looking for you, too?'

'No. He doesn't know me but he soon will. I've a score to settle with him.'

Dubois spun round, a finger pointing at Clarke's face. 'You'll do nothing until this operation is finished. Whatever your personal quarrel, it has nothing to do with what needs to be done here. You understand?'

Clarke controlled his temper with difficulty.

'Where are the masts? asked the Frenchman. 'How the devil do we sail without masts?'

'You ain't got no masts 'cos the bleedin' bridge is in the way,' said Clarke, his temper flaring up again. 'How d'you think we'd get through with them things on top? You're going to have to do whatever every other bleeder does and let the tide take her down.'

Clarke ducked below the fo'c'sle break and climbed down the companion ladder, through the lower decks to the orlop. He unhooked a lantern that had been hanging on a nail close to the bottom of the ladder and gave it to Dubois.

'Light this,' he said. 'The flint's on the beam behind you.'

The lantern flared into life, casting a golden glow over its surroundings. There were bales of straw stacked into every available space, leaving only narrow corridors to separate one section from another. Interspersed amongst them were little piles of faggots coated in tar.

'Those corridors let the air feed the flames,' said Clarke, seeing the questioning look in Dubois's eyes. 'Without them, the fire wouldn't take hold. Leastways not for a long time.'

'Tell me what you know of Pascoe,' said Dubois, his interest in the fireship seemingly on the wane.

'Not much,' said Clarke, scowling. 'Saw him for the first time down in Hastings. The bastard killed my son, Stevy. I wanted to kill him but ...'

'Is that why you had a fight with him?'

Clarke glanced across, nervously. 'Aye, you could say that. Next time there won't be no mistake.'

'There'll not be a next time,' snapped Dubois. 'I've told you, the operation comes first. Now tell me, what do you know of him?'

'They say he were in the Navy.'

'I know. What else?'

Clarke thought for a while.

'I thought the first time I'd seen him were in Hastings. But it weren't. I recall now. I saw him once before. I were at the infirmary. The one up in Whitechapel. One of the nurses were seeing to me when Pascoe walks in. Course, I didn't know his name then, but it were him. I could see right away she were a friend of Pascoe. A most particular friend.'

'What was her name?'

'Miss Tompkins, as I recall.'

Dubois turned towards the companion ladder and seemed on the point of leaving. As though an afterthought, he looked back at Clarke.

'What of the crew? Where are they?'

Clarke felt his stomach sink. He thought quickly. None of the gangmasters he'd approached for a crew had been prepared to help without an offer of immediate payment – except one. Silas Grant had hesitated, his greedy eyes had shone at the prospect of the sort of money most men on the river could only dream about. The problem was that he'd neither agreed nor disagreed, had wanted to keep his options open. Clarke had known better than to push. He had meant to try again, perhaps after he'd got the money back from Pascoe, but it hadn't happened. He still had no crew to help get the hulk down through London Bridge and in amongst the ships in the Pool.

He remembered Moreau telling him, when the idea of attacking the port was first mentioned, that half the agreed amount of money would be retained until after the operation had been completed. If that were the case, he might still be able to persuade Silas Grant to provide a crew and pay them after the operation was over. He decided to risk it.

'Silas Grant's taking care of them.'

'Who?'

'He's a gangmaster. He'll be here when I give him the nod, like. Saw him only the other day. In the Nag's Head.'

'Then we go tonight.'

A long pause. Clarke needed more time. He had to see Silas Grant. Things were moving too quickly for his comfort. He remembered hearing something about the West Indies fleet being delayed. Relief flooded through his brain. A chance to postpone matters.

'Don't make no sense to go tonight. What with the trouble an' all.'

'What trouble? What are you talking about?'

'The West India convoy what you was expecting,' said Clarke. 'It's stuck fast at the Nore. Wind's in the wrong direction. Leastways, that's what I hears.'

'*Mon dieu*. How long before they get here?'

'How would I know?' said Clarke, shrugging his shoulders. 'Don't make no difference, anygate.'

'What do you mean, it makes no difference?'

'Nothing.' Clarke bit his lip, realised he'd said too much.

'You said it didn't make any difference. What did you mean?'

Clarke stared at the Frenchman and weighed up his chances of being able to thrash him. They were not good. The scrub was half his age and had the use of both arms.

'The money's gone.'

Dubois looked at him in stunned silence.

'The money's gone? All of it? How?'

Clarke gave a dismissive wave of the hand. 'I went to get it – from Hastings, like – and it were gone; stolen, plundered – call it what you like. It weren't there no more.'

Dubois's eyes narrowed into a cold stare. 'Find it, my friend – you have until tonight. If you fail, there will be consequences.'

'You threatening me, Frog?' said Clarke, leaning close to Dubois's face. 'I'd be very careful what I said if I were you. The money's gone. Taken. It ain't got nothing to do with me.'

'Find it, *monsieur*, or you will suffer,' said Dubois, letting his hand slide towards his coat pocket.

'It ain't me what'll suffer, mate.' Clarke turned away with a derisive laugh. 'In this country we hang people what spy on us, if you get my meaning. I've only to say and it'll be all over for you.'

'You think so?' said Dubois.

'Yes, cock, I do.' Clarke moved towards the companion ladder. Behind him he heard a light scuffle of feet. He began to turn. It was too late. He saw something dropping over his head, across his eyes and down towards his mouth. Instinctively, he raised his hand to swat it away. Missed it. A wave of fear swept through him. He brought his hand up again, his fingers clawing at what felt like a length of cord about his throat. It was too tight. He leaned back, trying to relieve the pressure. Was struggling to breathe. A knee was being pressed into the small of his back, the string round his neck tighter. His eyes were hurting. He couldn't focus. He tried to cry out. Could hear nothing but a soft gurgle from within him. He'd lost his balance, his legs kicked from under him, was lying on his stomach, Dubois was on his back, pulling hard on the cord. He was oddly aware of his arm and both legs thrashing the air. He felt weak, his movements were slower.

Clarke's body had become limp. There was no sound coming from his mouth. Dubois released his hold on one end of the garrotte and watched the head fall silently to the deck. He climbed off the body and placed an index finger close underneath the man's nostrils. Clarke was no longer breathing.

He got to his feet. Far above him, through the forward hatch, he could see the sky had begun to darken.

CHAPTER 19

Peggy Tompkins looked anxiously at the pale weather-beaten face on the pillow. She glanced at the door. There was still no sign of the duty physician and she really had no business being away from her post in the receiving room.

'How are you feeling? Ruxey, isn't it?' said Peggy, smiling as the young man opened his eyes. 'The doctor should be here any minute to have a look at you.'

'Thankee, miss,' said Ruxey, resting an arm across his forehead and closing his eyes. 'Is Mr Pascoe still here?'

'No, I regret he had to leave. Doubtless he'll be back to see you before long.'

Ruxey seemed not to hear her, his face contorting with pain.

'What happened to you?' said Peggy.

'We was on patrol in the Upper Pool.' Ruxey turned

towards her. 'Mr Pascoe sees some cully on Hay's Wharf what he wants a word with, so we went ashore.'

A bout of coughing made him stop. He bit his lip and went on, 'There were a fair press of folk on the wharf and it were some time afore I sees somebody crouched behind a pile of sacks. I reckoned he were doing a bit of thieving but when I got to him, he jumped me. But I ain't been at sea these eighteen months since without learning a thing or two about scrapping. Anygate, he soon starts cussing and swearing in froggie language and draws his knife . . .'

'You say he spoke French?' said Peggy, remembering the two foreign-sounding men who'd come to the hospital looking for Toiler.

'Aye, it sounded that way to me,' said Ruxey, wiping the sweat from his brow with the flat of his hand. 'Then, quick as a flash he stabbed me good and proper.'

'What did he look like, this man?' said Peggy.

'He were a swarthy bugger, that's for sure, and quick as a hare in March.'

'And you've not seen him before?'

'No. Why is it you ask?' said Ruxey.

'Just curious,' Peggy replied, momentarily caught off guard. She looked again at the pale face on the pillow. There seemed an air of vulnerability about the lad that, for all his bluster, he could not altogether hide. She let the feeling pass. 'You've not been with Captain . . . Mr Pascoe, long?'

'No,' said Ruxey. 'I were with the East India Company. Served five years, mostly between Bombay and Macau on the Pearl River. I left when we reached Blackwall a month or two since and signed on with this new mob what's at Wapping.'

'What made you change?' Peggy glanced at the door of the ward, hoping for the physician. 'Did you not like your life at sea?'

'Aye, I liked it well enough, but I'd done me bit.'

Peggy looked back at her patient. She was aware of that same hint of vulnerability in Ruxey's voice she thought she'd detected a short while previously. What had caused it and what it might mean, she had, for the present, no means of telling. Perhaps, as with her own life, there were aspects that he wished to remain hidden from public scrutiny. Whatever its cause there seemed little doubt that something was amiss.

Her thoughts were interrupted by the sound of the ward door opening and a group of young men pushing their way in. They were quickly followed by the principal physician.

'Good day to you, Miss Tompkins.' Dr William Hamilton smiled at Peggy and looked along the double row of beds. He caught sight of Ruxey. His smile faded.

'Who is this, Miss Tompkins? I do not recall seeing him before.'

'If you please, sir, this object is a waterman constable

with the marine police and is the victim of a stabbing. I thought to bring him immediately to your attention.'

'Hmm. This is most irregular, Miss Tompkins. However, since he's here, I shall examine him.'

He turned back to an anxious-looking Ruxey and, placing the back of his hand on the boy's forehead, said, 'How, sir, do you feel? Good. Excellent. Keep it up.'

Then, looking down, he peeled away the bloodied shirt and exposed the wound to the stomach. Suddenly he stopped, a look of intense surprise in his eyes.

'I think, Miss Tompkins, I will need to speak to you after we have completed our work here.'

'Yes, sir,' said Peggy, feeling the heat rise up her neck. Why the physician should want to speak to her was a puzzle. Perhaps it was to chastise her for admitting the object to the ward without the necessary authority. She edged away from the side of the bed, embarrassed by the affair, fretting over the likely consequences. She wished she'd waited in the receiving room for the duty physician's arrival.

'Now, gentlemen,' said Hamilton, turning to face the noisy gaggle of young men around him, 'if any of you is at leisure, perhaps you would care to pay attention. Here we have an object who, we are told, has been stabbed. You will doubtless recall that the healing process consists of two stages. In order to survive, the object must success-fully pass through both. If the treatment and care is improper, death is the likely outcome. Perhaps someone could tell me what is the first of these two stages?'

This invitation was followed by a great deal of coughing and shuffling of feet, but no audible answer – at least none that Peggy could hear.

'Inflammation, gentlemen,' said an exasperated Hamilton. 'And this is followed by the second, which is . . . ?'

'Digestion, sir,' squeaked a young voice from the rear of the group.

'Very good, Mr Smythe,' said Hamilton. 'Kindly note that neither of these stages is yet apparent in this case, indicating a hurt of recent origin. Should the object exhibit signs of suffering, the pain can be controlled through the use of opium together with the application of a poultice.'

He again bent to his task and a minute or so later, looked up. Gazing round at the group of students, he said, 'Fortunately for this young person, the blade does not appear to have penetrated the body cavity and our task is, therefore, comparatively simple. What is our next task, Mr Johnston?'

'Suturing, sir?'

'Don't answer a question with a question, man. What's it to be? Suturing or not?'

'Suturing, sir, with the use of cotton thread or sinew, sir.'

'Very good. Let it be so.' Dr Hamilton glanced at an assistant and was handed a needle, already threaded with sinew.

Dipping the tip into a dish of oil, he looked at Ruxey. 'I regret this might cause you some discomfort, but it is for the best. Should you wish for a little opium? No? Very well.'

It was soon done. As he turned to leave, Dr Hamilton beckoned Peggy over to a corner of the ward where they could not be overheard.

'Perhaps, Miss Tompkins, you would be good enough to explain what that object is doing in this ward?'

'I beg pardon, sir,' said Peggy. 'I thought it an emergency and—'

'No doubt you did, Miss Tompkins,' said Dr Hamilton, raising a hand to silence her. 'But why this ward? It is, I believe, for the exclusive use of male patients, is it not?'

'I regret I don't understand, sir,' said Peggy.

'The patient, Miss Tompkins, is a female.'

CHAPTER 20

Ruxey lay quite still as the two nurses on the females' surgical ward passed from bed to bed, tending to the other patients. She had been moved from the men's ward within minutes of Dr Hamilton's round.

'I need to know,' said Peggy, standing at the foot of the bed, her arms folded. 'I may lose my position at this hospital for what I did. Who are you? Why are you dressed as a man?'

'I hardly think of myself as a woman, Miss Tompkins,' said Ruxey. 'I have lived and worked as a man in a man's world these five years since, first as a seaman on the East India run and now as a waterman constable with His Honour, Mr Pascoe.'

'That may be so,' said Peggy. 'But you are not a man.'

'Becoming a man were the only way as I knows of to keep from going into the workhouse,' said Ruxey. 'That, or working as a doxey, the plaything of every drunk in Wapping.'

'What of your family? Could they not have helped you?'

Ruxey flinched. Until the last few days she'd seldom thought of her family; it had been too painful. She'd found it easier to concentrate on the day-to-day routine of a ship at sea, endlessly repeated. Her life had taken on an unconscious normality that had allowed her to perform the functions required of her without determined thought. The cumulative effect was to create a sense and belief in her assumed persona to the point when she had all but forgotten her real gender.

'Aye, I have a family, right enough, though my father is dead and my mother has little enough with which to feed herself. All she has is . . .'

Ruxey stopped, her eyes welling with tears.

'All she has is – what?' coaxed Peggy.

'My brother, Toiler,' said Ruxey. 'But now there are those what think him guilty of murder.'

'Toiler is your brother?' said Peggy, surprised.

'Aye. D'you know of him?'

'He was here, in this hospital, not a day since,' said Peggy. 'I regret it extremely but he left without telling anyone where he was going.'

'Why? Why did he leave?' Ruxey struggled to sit up but collapsed back onto the bed.

'Some men – Frenchmen – came to the hospital asking for him,' said Peggy. 'I remembered your brother told me he and two of his friends had brought some Frenchmen across the Channel so I thought they were the same ones. I went out to see them and when I returned I could see that your brother was very frightened. He told me that the men had tried to kill him as they had killed his friends and would, doubtless, try again. He must have slipped out when my back was turned.'

'And you have no notion where he might have gone?' asked Ruxey, biting her lip.

'He spoke of a wharf on the south bank of the Thames for which he and his friends had been bound,' said Peggy. 'He said he would seek help from the man who owned a warehouse there.'

'Did he say which wharf?' said Ruxey.

'Alas, he didn't know.'

'Then I must go,' said Ruxey, making another attempt to get up. 'He'll be needing my help.'

'You are in no fit state to do anything but rest,' said Peggy, restraining her. 'You are to consider that you are too weak, and anygate, you don't know which of the warehouses he's gone to. How would you find him?'

'Then what am I to do?'

'I will send word to . . .' Peggy stopped, unsure of her intended course. 'I will send word to Mr Pascoe. He will know what is to be done.'

'No,' said Ruxey. 'Not him. If he finds Toiler he'll send him to the gallows.'

'Why don't you tell me the story from the beginning. Then we can decide what's best.'

'I scarce know where to start.' Ruxey clasped her hands to her chest, her fingers twisting in on themselves. After a while, she said, 'We lived by the sea. In Hastings. When me brother and me were little, we used to spend our time around the fishermen, helping them carry things to and from the boats. When we weren't doing that we'd be putting down the trows so the luggers could be slid down the beach. There were other children there too. Among them were two boys, Will Sutton and George Dighton, who used to play with us. About five years ago when I were fifteen, I saw that the two boys seemed to be sweet on me ...'

Ruxey laughed awkwardly. Then she went on.

'George Dighton were the quiet one. Sort of shy. He never pushed. But Will Sutton wouldn't take no for an answer. I fancy I were quite taken with his attention and his flattery. I knew he and George were up to no good, running goods from France, but that made it all the more exciting for me. Everyone on the Stade knew what they were doing but nobody stopped them on account of every one of the fishermen were in the same game.'

'Running?' said Peggy, arching her eyebrows.

'Aye, you know. Free traders, smugglers, running anything and everything past the Revenue. Anygate, in the early days Will – the men called him Surly Will – were kind towards me and I thought I were in love with him.

But it weren't long afore he began to turn and he'd get angry and would beat me. The least thing would set him off and he'd cuff me or box me ears.'

'Did you not tell anyone about what he was doing?' said Peggy.

'I were too afraid to tell anyone. I knew if I told George or Toiler there'd be a terrible scrap and I didn't want that to happen, so I kept me mouth shut and decided not to see him no more. Then, one day in late summer, I were on the East Hill overlooking the sea. It were a beautiful afternoon what with the sun sparkling on the surface of the water and the seagulls crying and swooping to catch the fish thrown from the fishing boats. I didn't think nothing could spoil the day.'

Ruxey stopped talking. She seemed to be reliving what had happened. When she spoke again, her voice had quietened.

'It were then I saw Will Sutton coming towards me. He said he wanted to talk to me. To begin with it were all right but then he started to get familiar and wanted to ... well, you know. I didn't want nothing to do with that so I told him to stop, but he wouldn't.'

Peggy stretched out and caught hold of Ruxey's hand, as though remembering her own, more recent, ordeal at the hands of a man. For a minute or two neither of them spoke.

'What did you do?' said Peggy, at last.

'There was no one I could tell. Not even me mother or me brother. I thought they would think me a trollop, so I made up me mind to leave. I'd never been out of Hastings in all me life, but one of the men I knew who lived over the hill in Ore said he'd take me to London the next time he were going. The next week he said he were on a run and I joined him and left.'

'Is that when you joined the East India Company?'

Ruxey nodded. In other circumstances she might have talked about the years she'd spent at sea, of how she had managed to hide her womanhood and do all the things expected of her male shipmates. She would have enjoyed telling of the battles she'd been involved in. Like the time when her ship, the *Earl Talbot*, was attacked by French corsairs, or better still, the occasion in the Indian Ocean when her convoy had outmanoeuvred a French squadron of men-of-war, and escaped.

She might have done. But not now. Not while Toiler was out there, alone and in need of her help.

'Why did you leave the sea?' said Peggy.

'Why?' Ruxey gazed out of one of the open windows of the ward, at a grey, overcast sky that was threatening rain. 'Because there's a difference between doing something because there's nothing else and doing something because you want to. I didn't want to go to sea. I was – I am – a woman. I wanted, and continue to want, to do those things that all women like doing. I got no pleasure from drinking and smoking and cussing and fighting that my shipmates seemed to revel in doing. I could make no friends amongst them for fear they might discover my secret. It was, for me, a lonely and frightening life and, at the back of my mind, there were the constant threat of the Press. All seamen dread it and do what they can to avoid it. I were lucky. Twice we was boarded and twice I were left behind. I wanted no further part of that life and when the *Earl Talbot* reached Blackwall, a few months since, I left her and bade farewell to my shipmates.'

'And then you discovered that your brother was in London.'

'Not at first,' said Ruxey. 'I'd been with Mr Pascoe for close on three weeks afore we was ordered to investigate a sunken lugger in the Pool. As soon as I saw her, I knew she were the *Mary-Anne*. I never sailed in her but I knew her just as well. She were Will Sutton's boat and his father's before him. It were terrible to see the boat like that and think that men you knows could be dead inside her. No, it were only when Mr Pascoe returned from Hastings that I heard Toiler had been on the *Mary-Anne* and were suspected of murdering Surly Will and Bulverhythe George.'

'But your brother could not have known of what happened between you and Will unless . . .'

'Unless someone told him,' said Ruxey, finishing Peggy's sentence for her. 'Will Sutton could never keep his mouth shut. He would have told Bulverhythe George sooner or later what passed between us – what he'd done, like.'

'We must tell Mr Pascoe everything we know.' Peggy's voice was firm. 'It's the only way to clear your brother's name.'

'No,' said Ruxey, chewing her knuckles.

'We must,' said Peggy. 'Toiler's only hope is for me to tell Mr Pascoe what I know; what your brother told me, and what I saw of the two men here in this hospital.'

'Why would he believe you?' asked an anxious Ruxey. 'Do you know Mr Pascoe?'

'Yes,' said Peggy. 'I know him. He is a fine man. He will listen to what we both have to say.'

It was later that afternoon when Sam Hart awoke from his slumbers. He stretched, turned over onto his back and allowed his mind to drift. He thought of his mother. He'd last seen her at the feast of the Passover when they and a few neighbours had shared the traditional meal of lamb and bitter herbs. He smiled. Some things never changed. Before their guests arrived, she'd sent him round the room in search of hidden pieces of leavened bread – a tradition born out of the Jews' flight from Egypt, two thousand years before the birth of Jesus and still observed. As a child, Sam had done it every year on the night before the Passover. It had always been the high point of the evening.

He stared at the ceiling of his room, a nagging feeling

at the back of his mind that there was something he'd forgotten to do. The image of the *Mary-Anne* popped into his head and, just as quickly, disappeared again.

Then the realisation struck him. He'd forgotten to carry out the search of the wreck. Tom Pascoe had told him to do it but the tide had come in too soon. He'd intended to go back and finish the task but the matter had somehow slipped his mind.

He swept the blanket aside and let his legs drape over the edge of the bed while he untied the string securing his boots to the bedstead. He was always faintly surprised to find they hadn't been stolen while he was asleep. He let himself out of the house and walked rapidly down Coleman Street towards the Thames as the low winter sun dipped towards the rooftops of the City. He wondered if there was anything to be gained by doing the search now. It was a week since the lugger had sunk. Whatever might have been left behind on the night she went down was surely gone by now. The scavengers who combed the river bed at every low tide would have picked their way over the wreck and taken everything of even the most paltry value. Yet it was possible they'd missed something.

He reached the junction with Wapping Wall and pushed his way through a jostling mass of bodies to the south side of the highway where he turned right by the Devil's Tavern and arrived at Pelican Stairs. He stopped beneath the rusting arch from which was suspended a lantern, and looked out over an expanse of blackened mud to the wreck of the *Mary-Anne*.

She was a forlorn sight, stripped of her sails and rigging, her masts and hatch covers plundered, her anchors gone. The hole in her starboard side, that he'd first seen on the morning when they had lifted out the bodies of the crew, had been enlarged. It was obvious she'd been visited in the days in between. His doubts about finding anything of interest resurfaced.

He tensed. Somebody was moving inside the lugger's hold, the top of his scalp just visible above the hatch coaming. Most probably it was a scavenger. He watched for a moment. It was a man, his hair looking brushed and tolerably clean – not at all like a scavenger. Sam stood back against the side wall of the passage and waited for the head to disappear.

Descending the stairs, he crossed the black, glutinous mud of the foreshore, taking care to keep the lugger's hull between him and what he suspected was the point of entry for the intruder. On reaching the vessel's overhanging stern, he stopped to listen. From inside came a scraping, bumping noise. He edged down the port side hoping he might see a ladder, anything with which he might climb to the deck. He wanted to avoid taking the obvious route through the damaged hull, maintain the element of surprise. The noise inside the hold stopped. Sam froze. He looked up, half expecting to see a face peering at him from above. There was nothing.

He reached the bows and looked along the starboard hull to where the strakes had been damaged. The hole did seem considerably larger. Fleetingly, he wondered if it had been struck by a passing vessel. He looked again; decided the damage was too low down to have been caused by a collision.

The scraping noise started again. It sounded close. Sam pressed himself against the hull. A shoe appeared through the hole, followed by a stockinged leg. Whoever it belonged to was no scavenger – too well-dressed for that. A head protruded, quickly followed by a neck and shoulders. Sam recognised him. It was the man Tom had called Dubois, the same cully they'd seen on Hay's Wharf; the one suspected of knifing Ruxey.

Dubois turned. His eyes widened a fraction.

'In the King's name,' growled Sam, 'stand fast, cully.'

The man ducked back inside the lugger, catching his shoulder on a protruding length of a strake. For a moment, he could not move. Sam leapt towards him, grabbing him by the front of his coat, his foot slipping as he did so. They both fell.

Dubois was up before Sam, a knife in his hand, its blade weaving a pattern in the air as he came towards him. Sam scrambled to his feet and watched his approach, the man's slate-grey eyes blazing, saw the blade scythe towards him, ducked and, balling his fist, hit the man in the crotch.

Dubois bellowed in pain but seemed to recover quickly.

He came at Sam a second time, his torso bent forward, his right hand outstretched, still holding the knife.

Sam waited, his fist stinging from the force of his initial punch. He grinned to himself in spite of the danger. If his fist was hurting he could only imagine what the other fellow was going through. He raised an eyebrow in mocking surprise as the man lunged at him, the blade of his knife curving upwards towards his stomach.

Sam chose his moment with care. He stepped back and smashed the heel of his hand against the extended wrist of his opponent before following through with a battering ram of a punch to the man's chest. This time it was Sam's turn to be surprised as the stranger, half turning, rode the punch.

Someone was shouting from the bank. He couldn't hear the words. His eyes were fixed on the knife blade coming in for another attack. He jumped aside, misjudged the moment and slipped. He put out a hand to steady himself but it was too late and he fell for a second time.

He felt a cord loop over his head and around his neck. It tightened. A knee was pressing down between his shoulder blades. He struggled to free himself, tried to insert a finger between the cord and his neck. The cord was too tight. He felt giddy, tried to cry out but no sound was possible. The weight on his back increased, the upward pressure on his neck inexorable.

Voices. Several of them. People were shouting, the sounds

far away, a blur of noise. Suddenly the pressure on his neck was no more, the weight from his back removed. Sam gulped greedily and coughed. A dry, retching convulsion. He let his head fall onto the mud, felt its coolness on his cheek.

More noise. Feet pounding on the foreshore. There seemed to be hundreds of them. Or maybe two or three. Sam didn't care. His ears were ringing, his neck was on fire.

'Sam?' The voice was muted. Sam rolled his eyes and peered at the speaker. He recognised him. A waterman constable from one of the other crews. Didn't know him that well. Isaac Wells. That was his name. Sam struggled to sit up. He must have lost consciousness. The man put a hand on his shoulder. Supported him.

'It's a wonder you're still breathing, mate. Yon scrub were doing his best to turn you off.'

'I'll be all right,' said Sam, his voice hoarse. 'There's no damage, thanks to you. Did you see where the arse-faced villain went?'

'That way.' Isaac Wells pointed in the direction of the City. 'Will you be wanting the apothecary?'

'No, I've something I must do,' said Sam, climbing carefully to his feet. 'Was you able to assist, I'd be grateful.'

'Anything.'

The two of them walked the few paces to the Mary-Anne,

the rising tide already lapping at her outer keels. Ducking their heads, they climbed through the damaged hull and into the hold, the air musky with the smell of damp wood and fish.

'Who was he, Sam?' said Isaac. 'The cully what got you.'

Sam closed his eyes as a throbbing pain passed through the back of his head. He bent down, resting his hands on his knees, waiting for the pain to lessen before he spoke.

'A Frenchman by the name of Dubois,' he said. 'Seems Mr Pascoe knows him from years ago. We reckon he arrived over here in this lugger. Must have been looking for something he's lost.'

They went in. The hold was about forty feet long and about ten feet wide, most of which was enclosed by the overhead decking. Sam waited for his eyes to become accustomed to the change in light before looking around him. It was empty, devoid of all clutter. He might have been surprised had he not already known the vessel had lain here for days.

He thought for a moment. No one, with the possible exception of the man who had just attacked him, would have come to the wreck with the expectation of finding anything of real value. The only question was whether Dubois had succeeded in finding something which others before him had missed. There was, he thought, only one way to find out.

Beginning at the stern, Sam felt his way along the ceiling

boards looking for evidence that any of them might have been disturbed. Then he checked behind each of the head ledges, hatchway carlings, half beams and deck stanchions. There was nothing. He pinched his forehead between thumb and forefinger as another bout of pain hammered the inside of his skull. This was hopeless. He didn't even know what he was looking for. He knew only that he would recognise it when – and if – he found it.

He started again. It was beginning to get dark and the tide was rising. He would have to stop soon and return tomorrow. He still hadn't searched the crew's cabin.

He leaned a hand against a deck beam, his eye travelling to its furthest end where it rested against the larboard strakes of the hull. Below it was the huge shape of the knee whose job was to support the beam and hold it in place. He looked away and then, almost immediately, looked back, aware he was missing something. He stared stupidly at the roughly hewn triangular shape of timber. If it was trying to tell him something, it wasn't doing very well.

From beyond the wooden walls that surrounded him, Sam could hear the dull roar of the port. Not as loud as it had been earlier in the day but still there. He looked up through the hatchway. The light had almost all gone. Work would finish soon, and with it would go the hammering sounds of the shipyards, the calls of the bumboat men, the coal-heavers and the watermen. And the nearby streets of Shadwell would fill instead with pimps, prostitutes, bully boys, and sailors with pockets full of money – at least for the next hour or so. At the sound of lapping water, he looked down. The incoming tide had reached the ceiling boards and was sloshing around the soles of his boots.

'We'll have to leave shortly,' said Isaac Wells.

Sam didn't answer. He ran a hand over the oak beam closest to him, his fingers trailing down onto the knee, feeling the gap between the two pieces of timber. He drew his knife and worked the blade into the crack. The oak had hardened, was difficult to work on, but not impossible.

He moved to the next beam and studied the joinery. It was much the same as the first, the gap irregular. He looked for any indication that someone had worked on it in recent days but could see nothing at this knee or any of the others in the hold. He decided to leave. The rising tide had reached his ankles. He ducked his head and, in doing so, caught sight of a sliver of wood sitting proud of its surroundings. It was no more than three inches wide and perhaps twelve inches in length. He waded towards it and pushed it with his forefinger. It didn't move. He inserted the tip of his knife blade at one edge and twisted. The sliver fell into the water, exposing a large hole dug into the oak.

Sam put his hand up and felt inside, his fingers prodding the seasoned timber. He felt something soft and pulled it out. It was a small cotton sack, heavy for its size, tied at the neck with a length of twine. He put his hand back into the hole. There was another bag, then another. Finally a fourth made its appearance. He opened one. It contained *louis d'or* coins. He took one out and examined it.

'*Ay yay yay!*' Sam leaned back against the hull and stared at it, his hands trembling. He opened the neck of a second and then a third of the bags. All full of coin. He remembered Tom telling him about similar bags found in Hastings and of his conviction that they were connected to French agents who'd been brought across in the *Mary-Anne*.

'Isaac,' he managed, 'bear a hand, and take these bags back to the police office. I want to look round and see if I can find the scrub what gave me a flogging.'

CHAPTER 21

André Dubois pressed against the wall of a house on Wapping Wall and watched the two men emerge from the wreck of the *Mary-Anne*. The older of the two appeared to be carrying something. He was too far away, and the light too dim, to see what. But he could guess. He waited for them to climb the river stairs. He knew there was but one route back to the police office. He'd wait for them and retrieve the money. The older man would present few difficulties but the other one . . . he hesitated. The other one was a handful. Sometime, somewhere, the scrub had been taught how to fight. He made his way through the yard where he'd been keeping watch, down the side of the house and out into the street.

The early evening crowds had begun to form. He watched a group of sailors make their unsteady way along the street, their efforts aided by hatless girls whistling their strident invitations, their skirts hitched above their knees. He hung back. Despite the comparative darkness, there remained a chance he'd again be challenged.

He slid into a doorway and waited. The minutes ticked by. Now and again he would lever himself away from the door to watch people approaching from the direction of Pelican Stairs. Then he would sink back out of sight, disappointed. Perhaps he'd been wrong about the route they would take. Or possibly he'd missed them in the crowd. He thought about running to a point closer to the police office and waiting for them there – just in case he had missed them. People were beginning to notice him. One or two had stared at him. He would go if nothing happened in the next minute or so.

He looked round the corner of the door for the umpteenth time. A man was walking towards him. There was nothing particular about him, nothing that in the ordinary course of life would have merited a second glance. He was aged about fifty, slightly stooped, a sailor from the way he was dressed. Yet there was something that drew Dubois's attention. The man was weaving in and out of the crowd, his eyes sweeping from side to side, seeming to observe everything, to miss nothing. Dubois recognised the behaviour. The fellow was nervous, was holding something heavy in, or perhaps under, his coat.

The man got closer. Dubois could see him clearly. He couldn't be sure, but it looked to be the older of the two men he'd seen coming out of the wreck of the *Mary-Anne*.

Dubois searched for the second man. He wasn't there. He looked back. The fellow was almost upon him.

He waited until he'd passed and then dropped in behind him – not so close as to be obvious but close enough to ensure he didn't lose him in the crowd.

A hundred yards further on and the crush began to thin out. Another fifty and there was barely a soul in sight. Just the odd vagrant shambling his way along in the gathering gloom of evening.

Dubois looked over his shoulder. There was no one following. A little way ahead he could see a gap in the houses. There were some ships' masts visible above the rooftops. He walked faster.

New Gravel Dock quickly came up on his left. Dubois broke into a run. The man in front seemed to hear him for the first time, and half turned.

The man went down without a sound, the garrotte round his neck pulled taut, Dubois's face contorted with the effort as he watched his victim struggle for his life. Then, as quickly, the body went limp, the head fell forward and the shoulders sagged.

Dubois dragged the body into the dock and out of sight. Dropping to one knee, he searched the man's pockets. There were four bags, each tied at the neck with a length of twine. And heavy. Dubois didn't open them. He knew what they contained, had seen a similar bag in Moreau's hand.

He checked to make sure he'd not been seen and then tipped the body over the edge of the dock, listening for the splash. It wouldn't be found until the morning. Perhaps not for several days.

He emerged back into Wapping Wall and walked to the junction with Wapping Street where he rejoined the crowds. Five minutes later he was approaching the police office. He looked up at one of the first floor windows where a candle was burning.

And his heart jumped.

Tom stood at the window of the first floor of the Wapping Police Office, staring down at the ebb and flow of a crowded Wapping Street, the lanterns above the doors of the shops and brothels shining down onto the faces of passers-by. A man was looking up at the window. For a second, their eyes met. Tom began to turn away, his mind elsewhere. Suddenly, he realised who it was. He looked back, his eyes searching the crowd, forehead pressed against the glass. He knew he was too late. Dubois had already gone, disappeared. With an effort of will, Tom stopped himself from running to the door and out onto the street. There was no point. The scrub wouldn't wait to be caught. Reluctantly, he turned to face the rounded shape of Charity Squibb standing by the door.

'Did Miss Tompkins say what she wanted to speak with me about?' He tried to think.

'She ain't confided in me, sir.' Charity's guttural tones could be painfully loud at the best of times. 'She mentioned a lad called Ruxey and said you'd know what she meant.'

'I see,' said Tom, his mind still on Dubois. 'I shall come directly. Perhaps you would be good enough to wait for me?'

She waddled away, closing the door behind her. Tom turned back to the window, deep in thought. The wreck of the *Mary-Anne* lay in the direction from which Dubois had been walking. But why would the Frenchman have been there? He walked towards the door. He'd ask Sam if he'd managed to search the lugger. But first he would see Peggy and find out what she wanted.

It was after seven o'clock by the time Tom arrived in the Whitechapel road. A keen north wind nipped at his ears and the tips of his fingers as he and Charity turned in through the gates of the London Hospital and mounted the front steps to the main entrance. He'd found it hard to believe the story Charity had been unable to resist telling him as they made their slow progress north from the Thames. Ruxey, a woman? And, moreover, the sister of a young man he wanted to question in connection with a double murder?

'Where's Toiler now?' asked Tom when he, Peggy and Charity were standing together, at the foot of Ruxey's bed.

'I don't know,' said Peggy. 'All he said to me was that

he was going to try and reach the man who owns a warehouse on the south bank.'

'Nothing more?' Tom ran a hand over the top of his head.

'No, nothing.'

'And the Frenchmen. You say they're trying to find Toiler?'

'Yes,' said Peggy. 'They came to the hospital making enquiries about him.'

Tom looked across at Ruxey. She – he'd have to start getting used to the idea that he was a she – looked pale. It was little wonder, after what she'd been through. Yet he suspected the pallor was, at least in part, the result of concern for her brother.

Tom's thoughts returned to the two men Peggy had described. There was little doubt one of them was Dubois. He looked at Ruxey.

'Would you recognise the man who stabbed you?'

'I regret, sir, I would not.'

'Pity. Did you see where he went after he released you?'

'He ran back towards Hay's Wharf.'

'Did you see him go into any of the warehouses?'

'No, sir. All I sees is him disappearing through the alley what leads from Bridge Yard to the wharf.'

Tom stared at the foot of the bed increasingly convinced that Hay's Wharf, the place where he'd first seen Dubois and the place where Ruxey had been stabbed by someone answering Dubois's description, held the answer to many questions. He remembered the map on the scrap of paper with its cross. Now he was being told that Toiler might be heading for the same location.

'It's possible,' he said, looking at Ruxey, 'that the wharf your brother is heading for is the same one the Frenchmen have been using for their base. If that's the case, I think we have to be prepared for the fact that Toiler may already have been caught by them.'

Ruxey's eyes widened, her hand flying to her mouth. She looked at Peggy and then back at Tom. 'Can we not rescue him?'

'Assuming he is already in the hands of the French, the task is well nigh impossible without endangering his life,' said Tom. 'Even if I am right and the French have him in a warehouse on Hay's Wharf, you are to consider that there are any number of warehouses on the wharf, all of which would need to be searched. If your brother is a prisoner and his captors were to hear of our approach, I would fear for him. It is imperative that we discover the exact building where he is being held before we blunder in.'

'Tom, there is something else you should know,' said Peggy. 'I believe one of the Frenchmen I saw at the hospital may be ill.'

'Is it serious?'

'I believe so. If I am not mistook, he has typhus.'

*

'What are the chances of the Frenchman surviving?' asked Tom a few minutes later when he and Peggy had left the ward and were standing on the landing outside.

'He may live. But it would be better for him were he to see a physician.'

'If he doesn't, what then?'

'He will infect others. It has happened before.'

'Including Toiler, if he is with them?'

'I'm afraid so.'

Tom paused. 'What about Ruxey's injury?'

'She was seen earlier today by the principal physician,' said Peggy, smiling at him. 'Dr Hamilton is of the opinion that she was extremely fortunate and will make a full recovery.'

'But she is to remain in the hospital?'

'Just for a few hours. Dr Hamilton will see her in the morning but it's unlikely he will wish to keep her longer than is absolutely necessary.' Peggy paused and, lowering her voice, said, 'You do know, do you not, that as far as she is concerned you still suspect her brother of murder and intend to arrest him?'

'I *did* suspect him,' said Tom. 'But that's no longer the case. I may need to ask him some questions but I am as sure as I can be that the two fishermen on the *Mary-Anne* were murdered by the Frenchmen.'

'Tom . . .' Peggy stopped and looked at the floor of the lobby.

'Yes?'

'What will happen to Ruxey? When she leaves the hospital, I mean. Will she be removed from the police?'

'I haven't given the matter any thought,' said Tom. 'We had a few women on board Navy ships but they weren't supposed to be there. Usually they ended up helping the ship's surgeon or the cook. I've even heard of one or two who, like Ruxey, dressed as men and served the guns but they only lasted as long as no one knew about them. Amongst the merchantmen it was more common but still unusual. She's been a useful member of my crew despite my initial reservations. And yet, I warrant, this is no work for a woman.'

'Perhaps you would consider leaving your decision at least until she has found her brother.'

'That could be some time,' said Tom. 'And we've all got to hope that we find him before some harm befalls him.'

CHAPTER 22

André Dubois slept badly and awoke well before dawn the following morning, conscious of a heavy weight of anxiety in the pit of his stomach. The events of the day before were playing on his mind. He'd gone too far to expect any mercy from the English if he were to fall into their hands.

He tried to rationalise the fear, compare it with the greater dangers and privations he'd suffered on a daily basis while he'd been in the army. It didn't work.

He looked around him. He was on the orlop deck of the hulk in St Saviour's Dock; had not thought it safe to return to Hay's Wharf – not after he'd been seen there by Pascoe.

The deck was crammed with the bales of straw and faggots that would feed the inferno soon to be released within the port. The sight added to his sense of being trapped in a situation from which there was no escape. This was not familiar territory. He was, at heart, an opportunist, a thief, a man who avoided, or at least minimised risk in the pursuit of his self-interest. His enjoyment of violence had always been tempered by the overriding requirement of self-preservation.

Now he felt exposed. He had no knowledge of ships beyond his all too brief career on his father's corsair. With Moreau sick, the weight of responsibility for the success of the present operation had fallen on his shoulders. At least he had some money. It was sufficient to pay for his passage back to France and would cover the immediate costs of the operation. He took one of the bags from his pocket and tipped the contents onto the deck. Two hundred and fifty *louis d'or*. With the other three bags, more than enough to persuade half a dozen men to help him get the hulk down through the Bridge. As for the others, those who'd supplied the ship and the hay and the explosives, they would be looking for Clarke, and Clarke was dead.

It was small consolation. Pascoe knew he was around, would know that it was him who'd stabbed the boy on the wharf and tried to strangle his friend down by the *Mary-Anne*. He clenched his fists, cursing the luck which had twice placed him in a position where he might have been caught. He wondered if it was pure coincidence that Pascoe had seen him or whether someone had told him of his and Moreau's arrival in London.

He remembered the old Jew. He, along with Toiler, was the only person who could place them close to the scene of the murders of the crew of the *Mary-Anne*. His presence at the stairs where they had come ashore might explain how he and Moreau had been found so soon. He should have disposed of the old man when he'd had the chance.

He slumped onto a straw bale. There were more pressing matters that needed to be addressed, including his colleague's worsening state of health. He realised he'd not seen Moreau since yesterday morning and, if truth be known, had no wish to do so. The livid red spots, vomiting and high fever all pointed to the same thing. He'd witnessed the disease carrying away too many of his comrades in the mountains around Laono. He considered calling a physician but thought better of it. Even if something could be done for Moreau, the risk of betrayal was too great.

He made his way to a companion ladder and climbed to the upper deck. It was still dark outside. He could hear footsteps on the quay and ducked out of sight, waiting for the sounds to fade. Soon it was quiet again. Probably a nightwatchman from further along the dock.

He hurried down the gangplank and made his way past the Blind Beggar into Church Street. Ten minutes later he had reached the junction with Tooley Street where he turned down towards Hay's Wharf. Few people were about as he reached the quay. A small group of watchmen – he counted six – were gathered round a brazier, talking quietly. He waited. He'd seen them before. He doubted they would do or say anything even if they saw him. He crept past, staying outside the ring of firelight, and stepped through the door of the warehouse. On the first floor he approached the room he'd left the morning before. He pushed open the door. The room was in darkness.

'*Citoyen* Moreau,' he called, softly.

There was no reply. He closed the door and made his way across to the corner of the room where he'd last seen his colleague lying.

'*Citoyen le commissaire.*' He bent down and shook Moreau's shoulder. It felt stiff to the touch. He went to the table in the middle of the room where he knew there was a candle and tinderbox. A moment later he was back, the flickering candlelight held close to Moreau's face. The man's mouth hung open, his eyes were closed and his face pallid. Dubois touched the forehead. The skin was cold and wax-like. The commissaire was dead.

Dubois blew out the candle and thought quickly. He'd been expecting this, had known Moreau was likely to die sooner or later. His first task had to be the disposal of the body. The fewer people who knew about their presence in London, the better. He thought of searching the body but he didn't want to come into any more contact with him than he had to – he had seen what happened to others who'd made that mistake.

He lit the candle again and looked around. There was a small pile of sacks in the corner of the room. He collected a few and pulled the first one down over Moreau's head and shoulders. The second, he drew up over his legs. They overlapped. Fastening them both with a length of twine, he sat back on his haunches and considered his next move.

Moreau had never been a big man. His weight would present few problems if he were to be carried down the stairs and across the wharf. There were still, apart from the nightwatchmen, few people about. All the same, he would need to be careful. He couldn't afford to be caught with a dead body, even one that had died of natural causes. He knelt down beside the stiffening corpse and hefted it onto his shoulder. It was lighter than he could have hoped. He carried it to the door, stopped and listened for any sign of movement. There was nothing. Easing his way onto the landing, he made his unsteady way down the stairs to the front door. Again he stopped and listened. He could hear the murmur of voices, caught the scent of a coal fire. He opened the door a crack and counted the men sitting round the brazier. Six. They were all there, all accounted for.

He slipped out onto the wharf, keeping close to the building line. He knew from experience that the men would see nothing beyond the light of their own fire, their eyes accustomed to the glare of the flames. He reached the edge of the wharf, the gurgle of the ebbing tide absurdly loud. He peered over. The water level had dropped. But how much was left covering the mud, he could not tell. He couldn't risk throwing the body into the river without knowing how deep it was. Too shallow and Moreau would lie on the mud of the foreshore, in full view, until the next flood tide.

He remembered the river stairs a few yards downstream. From there it would be easier to judge the depth of the water. He looked back at the circle of watchmen. One or two of them had got up, were walking about, their magnified shadows thrown against the wall of the warehouses. Bending low, he headed for the stairs, the weight on his shoulders growing heavier. It took longer than he'd anticipated to reach the water-line. Carefully, he pulled the body after him and, on reaching the bottom step, slipped the cadaver into the tideway.

For a minute or so he watched the bundle float away, a small flicker of regret at the man's death. The mood soon passed, pressed from his mind by the crush of events. He still had to deal with Toiler.

He looked across the wharf. The watchmen had settled down again.

Toiler held his breath and listened. Three or four minutes had passed since he'd heard footsteps descending the stairs outside the door of the storeroom, the clumping noise heavy and uneven as though someone had been carrying a heavy load. He guessed it was one of the Frenchmen. Since then, all had been quiet.

He twisted his wrists, feeling the knots of the rope begin to loosen. He tried again, stifling a cry of pain as the rope bit into his raw flesh. He was under no illusions about his chances of survival if he failed to get away. His stomach somersaulted at the thought. He wondered what was delaying the two Frenchmen.

Some lengths of twine caught his eye, draped over what appeared to be a nail hammered into the wall. It was of no interest to him, unless ...

He looked at the nail with greater attention. It was old and rusting, secured at about waist height. He shuffled over to it on his rump, turned his back to the wall and levered himself into the standing position, searching for the nail with his fingers. It was still out of his reach. He bent forward and strained his arms upwards, his fingers just grasping the nail. It didn't move.

He heard voices. They seemed to come from the front of the building. He froze. The voices faded. He finally managed to loop the rope binding his wrists over the nail, a wrist on either side, and began to saw against the nail's sharp, irregular edges. He lost track of how long he worked, his wrists beyond the point of pain, his flesh torn and bleeding, the muscles in his arms screaming for relief. Then, with a suddenness that surprised him, the rope parted.

He would have liked to rest, to allow the pain to fall away but he knew that was never going to be an option. He slipped down the wall and sat on the floor where he removed the gag and began to untie the knots around his ankles. His fingers, numb with the effort of the past five minutes, failed to work properly. Again and again he worked at the knots, slowly loosening them. At one point he thought he heard people moving about, men talking. He stopped and listened, realised they were the night-watchmen he'd seen on the first night, then carried on.

He lost track of time but it couldn't have been long. Then he was free. Walking quickly to the door of the store-room, he tried the handle. It wasn't locked. He pressed his ear to the panel. From what seemed like far away, he could hear the same voices as before. He opened the door a fraction and looked out into the lobby area.

To his left was the entrance to the wharf, a matter of three or four paces away. Close to it was a pile of empty sacks reaching almost to the ceiling together with some old brooms and a hogshead or two. In front of him were the stairs leading to the upper levels. Toiler inched towards the warehouse door, his ears straining to hear the sounds of anyone approaching.

He was about to put his hand on the handle when he saw it move. He started back, his heart racing. He looked round, saw the sacks and sprinted for them, pressing himself into the gap between them and the wall.

A moment later the door creaked open and footsteps walked across the lobby towards the stairs. Suddenly, they stopped, turned and strode to the room from which he had so recently escaped.

CHAPTER 23

From his hiding place behind the sacks, Toiler watched Dubois enter the storeroom. A moment later, the Frenchman re-emerged, and ran to the main door. Toiler watched him stare out onto the still darkened wharf. For a moment there was utter silence, broken only by the man's heavy breathing and his muttered oaths. Toiler remained quite still, gulping air through his mouth, reducing sound to the minimum. Dubois moved out of his sight. A stair board creaked, followed by another, then a third. Toiler peered round the edge of the pile of sacking. Dubois's attention was focused on the floor above. He waited for him to reach the landing, saw him move to one of the doors, open it and go inside.

He waited for a second or two, listening to the tread of footsteps in the room above his head. Then he slid out from behind the sacks, his eyes fixed on the upper landing. He heard another footstep, somewhere above his head. He moved closer to the door leading to the wharf. A broom lay propped against the wall behind him. He failed to see it and touched it with his foot. It started to fall, scraping noisily against one of the hogsheads. Toiler tried to grab it. He was too late. It clattered to the floor. He yanked open the door and ran out onto the wharf. From upstairs another door crashed open.

Dubois ran to the top of the stairs and looked down into the lobby. He was in time to see the main door to the warehouse swinging on its hinges. He drew his knife, half expecting to see Pascoe racing up the stairs towards him. There was no one. For a second or two Dubois stood staring at the empty hallway and the entrance beyond.

He sprinted back into the room, to the window overlooking the wharf. All was dark, except for the half-dozen watchmen sitting round their fire. There was no sign of Pascoe. Then, out of the corner of his eye, he saw a flicker of movement. It was at the very edge of the circle of light thrown out by the watchmen's fire. He thought he'd imagined it, then he saw it again. Someone was out there. He thought of Toiler.

He ran down the stairs and out onto the wharf. The men round the fire had stopped talking and were staring at him. He sped to the edge of the quay. Looked along its length, could see nothing of the boy, nothing of anything. He looked up at the nearest of the treadmills, ran up its stairs, opened the door at the top and checked inside. It was empty. He looked inside the others. Still no sign of anyone.

He could hear the watchmen stirring. He glanced in their direction. They were on their feet, walking towards him, black figures against the light of their fire. It was time to go.

Tom Pascoe watched the silver orb of the moon disappear behind a cloud as he brought the police galley round into the tide to begin its approach to the police stairs at Wapping. He and the rest of the crew – in fact the crews of all three duty boats – had spent most of the night searching for their missing colleague, Waterman Constable Isaac Wells.

'It were my fault, your honour,' Sam had said when he'd eventually returned to the police office and discovered that Wells had failed to arrive with the bags of *louis d'or*. 'I should never have left him on his own.'

'You weren't to know, Sam,' said Tom.

They had eventually found him, lying face down in the filthy waters of New Gravel Dock. The angry red marks around his neck had not escaped Tom's notice. Regrettably, no one had seen anything and, with the pressing need to find the suspected fireship, the search for witnesses in the Isaac Wells case had quickly been wound down.

'Easy all. Stand by to ship oars.' Tom drew down on the

larboard tiller-guy and canted the galley at a slight angle to the tide. The twenty-eight foot craft glided gently alongside the pontoon, her way finely judged. 'Ship oars. Make fast fore and aft.'

He climbed out and walked up the stairs towards the office closely followed by Sam and the huge bulk of John Kemp.

'You really think they'll try and set fire to the port?' asked Sam.

'I'm damned if I can think what else they could be up to,' answered Tom. 'But what's worrying me almost as much is Toiler. We've got to try and find him before he gets himself killed.'

'Yes, but as you've said yourself, your honour, it's too big an area to search,' said Sam. 'By the time we got to the right warehouse, Toiler would be dead and the Frenchmen gone.'

'The thought had not escaped me. We'll—'

'Forgive me, good sirs.' Tom looked up to see an elderly white-bearded man with an assortment of hats on his head, standing in the passage by the main entrance to the police office. 'Permit me a moment of your time.'

Tom looked at the old man before turning to Sam, a quizzical expression on his face.

'Why, if it ain't Moses Solomon,' said Sam. He turned to Tom. 'This is the man who saw Toiler and the other two men coming ashore from the *Mary-Anne*.'

'I remember you, now,' said Tom, his face clearing. 'We met some months since. If I'm not sadly mistook, you were having a little difficulty with some bully boys, were you not?'

'Aye, so I was, your honour.' The old man's diction had not improved, his English spoken with a heavy Polish inflection. He touched his forehead with the knuckle of one finger. '*Yasher koach.*'

'How can we be of assistance?' asked Tom.

'If you will permit me, sir, I wish to speak on a matter which is troubling me.'

'Then let us talk,' said Tom, leading the way through the building, down a flight of steps and into an enclosed yard on the eastern side of the building. At the bottom, he turned left and entered a large, square room, bare but for the presence of a deal table and four chairs. He didn't like the place but it was the only room where they could talk in private. It was the smell that put him off. The room next door – not really a room, more an open area below the main building that was open on the river side – was where the cadavers were kept until they could be identified or removed to the local dead-house. Inevitably, the stench permeated the whole area.

'What is it you wanted to talk to us about?' said Tom, lighting a candle and waving the old man to a chair, while he perched himself on one corner of the table.

'You came to see me some days since,' said Solomon,

glancing in Sam's direction. 'You asked me if I'd seen a lad come ashore from the river.'

'I remember it well,' said Sam.

'I seen the boy again.'

'Where?' said Tom, getting to his feet.

'It were at first light. He were on Hay's Wharf on t'other side of the tideway. He were held fast by two men, the same two men what were asking after him on that night by the Pelican Stairs. They took him into a warehouse.'

'And this was this morning, you say?'

'Not this morning, your honour. It were yesterday morning.'

'Yesterday?' said Tom, suppressing his anger. 'Why didn't you tell us sooner?'

Solomon rocked back in his seat and stared anxiously at Tom. 'It were on account of the Sabbath, your honour.'

'The what? Men's lives may have been lost on account of your idleness!' He felt a touch on his arm and turned to see Sam shaking his head.

'We've no time for this now, sir. Let me talk to him and I'll explain it to you later.'

Tom glowered at his friend. He stalked to the window and gazed out at the blackness. Behind him, he could hear Sam's soothing voice.

'You did right in coming. We are both very grateful. Did you see which warehouse the lad was taken to?'

'Aye, I saw. I don't know its name.' The old man's voice shook as he spoke. 'Only what it looks like.'

CHAPTER 24

Toiler stifled a cry of pain as he tried to move. He opened his eyes and stared up at the sky, visible through the open hatch of the lighter. His whole body ached. Yet it was as nothing compared to the throbbing pain of his thigh. He lifted his head and looked at the torn fabric of his trousers, where the surgeon had cleared it away from the wound. For an absurd moment he thought of trying to find something to mend the fabric. He let his head fall back onto the ceiling boards and closed his eyes. His escape had been a close-run affair. He'd barely reached the edge of the quay when he'd heard the door of the warehouse open and slam shut and known it could only be his captors – one or both of them. It made no difference to him how many or how few caught up with him. He'd not be in any condition to resist them.

He'd grabbed the chain pennant of a lighter moored alongside the edge of the quay and swung down into the river, pressing himself into the darkness of the river wall. Mercifully, the force of the tide was almost spent, the water tolerably shallow. Moments later, he'd heard someone creeping up and down the edge of the quay and seen a head peering over the edge. But he'd not been discovered and soon the sounds had faded.

Exhaustion had eventually persuaded him of the need to find some other hiding place and he'd climbed into the hold of one of the lighters to try and get some sleep. Now, cold beyond the telling of it, he attempted to rub some life back into his limbs before getting to his feet and peering over the hatch coaming. The nightwatchmen were still there. One of them was on his feet, throwing some coal into the brazier and sending a shower of sparks into the air. Toiler's eyes swept the wharf. It was too dark to be sure but it seemed Dubois had gone.

He ducked down below the coaming. He couldn't stay where he was. In an hour or two work would begin and he'd be discovered. He checked the state of the tide. It had gone out. He lowered himself to the foreshore and made his way to the river stairs he seen a few yards away.

Peering over the top step he realised he couldn't reach the road without the risk of being seen by someone in the warehouse. Nor was he convinced that Dubois was not still looking for him on the wharf. If he was seen, he couldn't run – not with his injured thigh.

It started to rain. He caught sight of the row of treadmills standing on their high stilts and, hobbling over to the nearest one, he climbed the steps and went inside. By morning, if he wasn't seen first, he'd be gone.

A fine curtain of rain drifted across the Thames, drenching the men in the galley as they waited at the foot of the Wapping police stairs.

'All present and correct, sir, including Ruxey,' said Sam, as Tom came down the police stairs and took his seat on the arms' box. 'I've told her she ain't in no condition to do no rowing. Nor Moses Solomon neither. I've taken a second oar in her place.'

Tom glanced at the old hat-seller sitting next to him before peering down the galley to the slender figure of Ruxey at bow thwart. She and the others all knew where they were going and what was expected of them. He'd made sure that she, especially, knew the risks involved in searching a building which might be occupied by armed men. He'd tried all his powers of persuasion, short of an order, to stop her coming, but she'd been adamant to the point of insubordination. He couldn't help admiring her courage.

'Cast off. Give way together.' The galley curved round in a tight arc, her bow facing upriver and, a few minutes later, was gliding in towards Battle Bridge Stairs at the eastern end of Hay's Wharf.

'If we come across the French,' said Tom, opening the

arms' chest and handing Kemp and Hart a cutlass and pistol apiece, 'we'll try to take them alive unless they make that impossible. Dubois is a dangerous cully as Ruxey and Sam can tell you. The other scrub I know nothing about, but there's every chance he may be sick with typhus. Don't get too close to him. Is that clear?'

'Clear, sir,' said Sam and Ruxey, simultaneously.

'Aye, clear, your honour,' said Kemp.

'Ruxey, I don't want you near any fighting. You're to look after Solomon. As soon as he's identified the warehouse, get him out of the way and then wait for us by the front door. Kemp, you and Sam are to come with me. We'll do this quietly. I don't want the whole of Southwark to know what we're about.'

Tom moved up the steps, and looked across the rainwashed wharf to the dull outline of the warehouses barely visible but for the light of a fire around which several men were sitting. The old Jew had told him about them.

'Which building is it?' said Tom, looking at him. He noticed the old man was trembling.

'I regret, my eyes are not so good, your honour,' said Solomon, his lower jaw moving rapidly from side to side.

'Then best we get closer.'

'That's the one,' said Solomon a few moments later, his gnarled finger pointing to a tall, narrow stone warehouse on three floors. Above the main door and on each of the floors above it was a hinged platform onto which sacks, barrels and other goods could be landed and taken into the building. At roof height, a solid timber beam extended outwards, and from this was suspended a block and tackle. On either side of the platforms windows fanned out to left and right.

'Thankee, Solomon. Go with Ruxey here. She'll take you to a safe place.' Tom turned away and caught sight of the circle of watchmen huddled around their brazier. The men had stopped talking and were staring apprehensively at the new arrivals. 'Ruxey!'

'Aye, sir.'

'When you get back, cut along to them watchmen and put their minds at rest.'

Tom watched her go and then turned to the others.

'Let's go,' he said.

Toiler listened to the soft voices. At first he thought they were those of the watchmen sitting round the brazier. He opened one of the shutters of the treadmill and looked out. The voices quietened. Suddenly there was a movement. Someone was passing behind the brazier, followed by two others, their shadows magnified on the wall of the warehouse. Behind them, he could see another two figures, moving in the opposite direction. Why would they be there unless they were looking for him? He swallowed hard. There was nothing he could do but wait. Escape was out of the question.

The first group was walking towards the door of the warehouse where he'd been held. The way they moved reminded him of the only time he'd seen customs officers preparing to seize some of the Hastings lads coming ashore from a run. They didn't seem at all concerned about being seen. It was as if they had a right to be there. They entered the warehouse. He couldn't see what had happened to the other two.

Christ, his leg hurt. He closed his eyes and gripped his thigh. The pain subsided. He pushed open the shutter. Someone was approaching the brazier, talking to the nightwatchmen. He couldn't hear what was being said but guessed it was one the two figures that hadn't gone into the warehouse.

He saw one of the nightwatchmen get up and throw fresh coal onto the fire. It blazed up, lighting the faces of those gathered round it. The newcomer looked familiar. The face was harder, thinner and older than the one he remembered, the skin the colour of nutmeg, the hair swept back and tied at the nape – but nevertheless familiar.

He pressed his face to the shutter. The light from the fire had faded. He couldn't be sure of what he'd seen. He continued to stare at the newcomer, the face no longer visible. What if he were wrong? What if it was not the person he had imagined it to be? Years had passed. Much had changed. He struggled to make up his mind, frightened of the consequences of any mistake.

He wondered what the rest of the group were doing, those who'd gone into the warehouse. If they were looking for him, which side were they on? His heartbeat quickened.

He moved away from the shutter. He'd wait until they left and then be on his way. The risk of doing anything else was too great.

Tom stood inside the door of the warehouse, the darkness impenetrable. He opened the gate of the lantern he was carrying and let the light spill out. In front of him was a staircase while to one side of the main door was a large pile of empty sacks. Further down the lobby he could see a second door. He looked at Sam and pointed. The two of them crept towards it.

It was empty except for more sacks scattered on the floor. Tom raised the lantern above his head and inspected the room more thoroughly. He noticed a rusty nail driven into the wall. Several strands of twine were looped over it. He was about to turn away when he noticed a few black smears on the wall adjacent to the nail. They had the appearance of blood.

He squatted, his eyes moving slowly over the area of the floor immediately below. There were some strands of twine similar to those he'd seen looped over the nail. He went on searching. A few feet into the room he saw what he'd expected to find. Several lengths of thick cord lay in a heap amongst some sacking. He picked them up and examined them under the lantern light. Two of them had frayed ends and were stained with red marks. He picked them up and put them into his pocket.

'Your honour?'

He turned to see Sam jutting his chin at the ceiling. 'Someone up there?' He asked.

'I'll not be certain,' said Sam, quietly. 'Heard a noise, though.'

They made for the stairs, Tom's eyes fixed on the upper landing, his feet planted on the outer edges of each tread. He didn't want a creaking timber giving them away.

They reached the landing and looked round. The first floor consisted almost entirely of a large storage area with a loading door and several windows facing the wharf. At one end were three internal doors, presumably leading to smaller rooms. Shuffling noises were coming from behind the door furthest from the river. Someone was moving about. Tom put a finger to his lips, cocked his pistol and crept forward. The door was not substantial. With a sudden, savage kick, he knocked it off its hinges and burst in.

The room was in semi-darkness, the thin, grey light of dawn struggling through the layers of accumulated dust on the window, the room half-filled with sacks of coffee, their rich aroma filling the air. There was a sudden movement to his right. The barrel of his pistol swivelled round. It was an old man. Tom lowered his gun in time to hear the metallic click of another pistol being cocked.

'No!' he roared.

Sam lowered his gun.

'He's not armed.' Tom held up the storm lantern and looked back at the old man. 'Who are you?'

The man remained silent, a pair of frightened eyes staring back at Tom.

'What are you doing in here?' Tom tried to keep the aggression out of his voice.

'It's sick that I am, sir. I ain't been home for close on a week. If I go home, I'll not be paid.'

'D'you know him?' Tom glanced at his friend.

Sam peered at the man from a safe distance. 'Aye, now that I sees him, I reckon I do. He's a watchman. I've seen him in Wapping once or twice. But mainly he stays south of the river. No harm to him as I knows of.'

Tom turned his attention back to the old man. 'Seen a young lad in here, have you?'

'Can't say as I 'ave.'

'Anyone else?'

'I seen two foreign-looking cullies as has been in and out these last days . . .'

'Sir.' Tom felt, rather than saw, Kemp's bulk hovering over him.

'Yes, Kemp. What is it?'

'Begging your pardon, sir, but I think you ought to see what's across in one of the other rooms.'

From his place inside the treadmill hut, Toiler heard a door close. He struggled up onto one elbow and looked out. Someone had come out of the warehouse and was approaching the watchmen. The face came into the circle of light, the same face that had earlier seemed so familiar to him. This time he was sure.

There'd been no warning, the day his sister Josephine had gone. She'd simply vanished. The effect on their mother had been devastating. He'd watched the steady, downward spiral of her health, looked on helplessly as she mourned the loss of her daughter. Month had followed month and year had followed year in ceaseless yearning that she might one day return. There had been no respite, even when Bulverhythe George had told him the truth about why she had disappeared. He had not dared tell his mother. Had lived in hope that he would one day find her, alive and well.

He thought again of the day Bulverhythe had approached him. He'd been surprised to see him that afternoon. The two of them had seldom found reason to speak to one another since the days of their childhood. He remembered the odd expression on Bulverhythe's face as he had approached him – half smiling, half sneering as though relishing the prospect of imparting some unpleasant news.

It was, of course, long after the event. But no less shocking for that. Knowing what Surly had done to his sister had reopened the old wounds and sorrows and added new ones. He'd brooded for days on what he'd been told, a determination to exact revenge on the man responsible, gathering strength in his mind. What shape this would take, he had not the slightest idea. He had got no further in his plan than to try and obtain for himself a berth on the *Mary-Anne* and see what opportunities presented themselves.

Yet achieving even this objective had been difficult. Surly had long enjoyed a reputation for – well – surliness. He was naturally suspicious and apt to keep people at arm's length, even those he had known all his life. That Toiler was able to achieve his initial objective at all was largely due to the influence of Bulverhythe who, for reasons that had become obvious to Toiler, had offered to help persuade the reluctant Surly to allow him on board the *Mary-Anne*.

For a long moment he continued to stare out through the hatch. The face at the fireside was leaving. Toiler started to get up. A sharp pain shot up his thigh. He stifled a cry and fell back. He tried again, determined to reach the ladder that would take him down to the wharfside. He felt giddy, unsure of where he was or what he was supposed to be doing.

The inside of the treadmill began to spin.

Kemp led the way out into the main storage area of the warehouse and through another door. The room was larger than the one they'd just left. A table and a chair stood at its centre. In one corner was a scattering of empty sacks. The thick layer of dust covering the floor had been recently disturbed.

'Here, sir.' Kemp walked over to the sacks and pointed to what appeared to be a handkerchief protruding from under one of them.

Tom bent down and picked it up.

'Silk,' he said, passing it to Sam Hart. 'I'll warrant, not something your average lumper or nightwatchman would possess.'

'You thinking it belonged to one of the Frogs, sir?' said Kemp.

'It's possible,' said Tom. Suddenly, he stopped and sniffed the air. 'Can you smell anything?'

'Now that you mention it, pea soup, sir.'

'Yes, ever smelt it before, have you?'

'Why, yes, sir.' Kemp grinned. 'It's me favourite, sir.'

'The last time I smelt that smell outside of a kitchen, a cully was dying of the typhus,' said Tom. 'His shit smelt that way.'

Tom paused. Peggy must have been right about one of the Frenchmen suffering from the disease. 'Wouldn't surprise me if he were already dead,' he muttered.

'What of Toiler?' said Kemp. 'You reckon he's dead, too?'

'No.' Tom reached into his pocket and took out the frayed rope ends. 'I think Toiler's escaped. I think he managed to cut through this rope and get out.'

'Still leaves us with one of the French,' said Sam. 'Moses Solomon reckons he saw two of them come in here with Toiler.'

Tom squatted down beside the hessian sacks, his elbows on his knees, and stared at the floor.

'D'you see where those sacks have been disturbed?' he said, pointing. 'And look here. These marks in the dust. Looks like someone has been busy. If I'm right about the typhus, then I think the person who died was wrapped in some of those sacks and taken out of here. Probably got thrown into the Thames. His body will wash up somewhere in a week or two. Whether it will ever be identified or not is another matter. Likely it'll have no skin left or if it has, it'll be black and unrecognisable. We'd probably have caught them if the old Jew had thought to tell us what he knew sooner.'

'You know why he didn't, sir.' Sam's tone was reproachful. 'It were on account of it were the Sabbath. He wouldn't have understood your anger. But even if he had, it would have made no difference. It is our Sunday, only more so.'

'I appreciate you telling me, Sam, but it goes against the grain to put someone in harm's way because of your beliefs. We . . .' Tom stopped. 'Has anyone seen Ruxey?'

'She should be here by the front door, sir. Where you told her to be,' said Kemp.

'But she's not,' snapped a worried Tom. Ruxey was hardly fit enough to be allowed out of hospital let alone be involved

261

in something as potentially violent as this operation. It was entirely his fault. He should never have allowed her to come. His mind raced. One of the two Frenchmen was still on the loose and capable of almost anything. It was possible that Ruxey had seen him and gone after him as she'd already done once before. It had ended badly for her on that occasion. He dared not think what might happen if she came across him again.

CHAPTER 25

Half a mile away, Dubois had spent a fitful hour on the derelict brig in St Saviour's Dock, alternating between sleeping and waking. He was annoyed by Toiler's escape but it wasn't the most pressing matter he had to deal with. The boy could not have got far with his injured leg. He would find him sooner or later. Nor did he have any concerns about the disposal of Jim Clarke's body. When the ship eventually went up in flames, the body would go up with it. The real problem was that Clarke's death had deprived him of the means of obtaining a crew for the fireship. He knew no one in London. No one to whom he could turn for help.

He wondered what Moreau would have done in the circumstances. For all the irritation he'd felt at the restrictions imposed on him by the older man, there'd been a certain comfort in knowing that the responsibility for any decision rested on someone clse's shoulders. Whether consciously or otherwise, Dubois had always felt able to criticise his superior, safe in the knowledge that his own judgement would have no consequences.

He surveyed the tightly packed bales of hay on the orlop deck with an unseeing eye. He wasn't afraid. Not in the ordinary meaning of the word. He'd confronted greater dangers in the winter campaign in the Dolomites and, for that matter, when he'd faced a broadside from Pascoe's ship. But this was different. Perhaps the apprehension he now felt was a product of his growing older. Perhaps it was because, in the Dolomites, he had not been alone. There had been others facing the same dangers, under-going the same privations. The prospect of death had always been present yet he had rarely given it a moment's thought. Now the decisions and the dangers were his and his alone. He would eventually have to justify everything that he did to his superiors in Paris. The thought depressed him, as though preparing him for the demands that were about to be placed on his shoulders. It was the same feeling that he had experienced in the moments after he had killed a man for the first time.

He leaned against a bulkhead and closed his eyes. The act itself – the taking of a man's life – had not bothered him. Not, anyway, at the moment of its performance. It had been afterwards, in the seconds and the minutes after the man had fallen at his feet, a knife through his heart, his bloody hands clutching the place where the blade had entered, his eyes still open in astonishment.

It was then that he had begun to comprehend the finality of his act and he had begun to shake, sweat forming across his brow and running down his face, ice cold against the heat of his skin. He'd stared down at the bloodied knife in his hands as though it, and not he, was responsible for what had occurred, a searing feeling of remorse overtaking him.

For weeks after that he had lain awake at night, thinking about what had happened, his sense of contrition almost physical in its manifestation. The experience had led, perhaps unconsciously, to a preference for the use of the garrotte over the knife in the settling of scores. With the passage of time, his feeling of guilt had lessened with each successive killing.

His mind returned to the present and the practical difficulties he now faced. He had to find a crew. He got to his feet and walked to the foot of the brig's companion ladder, listening to the drumbeat of rain on the upper deck, the low whistle of the wind. Slowly, he climbed the ladder and peered out at the rain-soaked sky. A thin streak of grey was forming over the eastern horizon.

He walked down the gangplank onto the quay and made his way along the narrow passage by the side of the Blind Beggar. Candles had been lit in the taproom, the light glowing through the thick glass of the windowpanes. At another time he might have considered going in for some breakfast, but not now. There were bound to be questions asked about Jim Clarke and his whereabouts, questions that he'd rather not have to deal with.

He emerged into Borough High Street. The first of the early morning traffic was already trundling its way towards London Bridge and the markets that lay beyond. Dubois joined them. He would use the early morning daylight to search Hay's Wharf for Toiler. He turned down Tooley Street. He could smell the Thames. He'd be on the wharf in less than a minute.

He remembered something Jim Clarke had once told him, the name of a man who was to have supplied him with a crew for the hulk, and the tavern where he habitually drank. Silas Grant. That was him. Dubois's smile of relief faded. The name was worthless without the name of the tavern, a name he couldn't remember.

He felt a rising sense of panic. Time was not on his side. Pascoe was aware of his presence in London and that he'd already tried to kill two of his men. It was possible he also suspected him of the murder of the man in New Gravel Dock.

He shivered. He knew Pascoe as well as a prisoner ever knows his captor, knew that the man who'd taken his corsair would be relentless in his pursuit of him. He had to find Silas Grant and finish the task he'd been sent to do. After that he would go after Pascoe. Even the score.

He recalled something else that Jim Clarke had told him. He said he'd first seen Pascoe at the London Hospital. The germ of an idea formed in his mind.

Tom emerged from the warehouse and onto Hay's Wharf. Toiler's continuing absence was worrying. There was no doubt he'd been in the building at some point in the recent past. Moses Solomon had been quite clear on that score; had seen him being dragged in there by the two Frenchmen. It was equally certain that he had now disappeared. But under what circumstances? The frayed lengths of rope offered some hope that he might have escaped but he was far from certain in spite of what he'd said to the others.

'Ruxey's here, sir.' Kemp's voice interrupted his thoughts. 'Says she's sorry if she caused you any distress but she heard something and went to have a look.'

'Where the devil have you been, Ruxey?' said Tom, his anger spilling out. 'I thought I told you to stay by the door and not move.'

'It's begging your pardon, sir, but I heard a noise, sir,' she said. 'Over there, by the edge of the wharf. Sounded like something heavy falling over. I were on my way to see what it was when I heard you coming.'

'Very well, we'll take a look.'

The four of them walked to the edge of the quay and stood beneath the line of silent treadmills, the river slapping gently against the quay, the usual rush of the tide stilled for a moment. Out on the reach, the light of a revenue cutter moved slowly up towards London Bridge, turned and slid by on its return journey, the splash of its oars loud in the surrounding silence.

'Nothing here,' said Tom. 'Perhaps the noise was from further out. A watchman on one of those brigs.'

'Don't think so, sir,' said Ruxey, glancing up at one of the treadmills towering above her head. 'It were a bit closer than that. If it's all the same to you, sir, I'll be looking inside them things. See what's in there, like.'

Tom watched her climb the ladder and pass in through the door.

'Sir, help me.' The cry of her voice was muffled, urgent.

Tom raced up the steps into the cabin. Ruxey was bending over the figure of a young man, cradling his head in her arms. He was shivering, his white face contorted, one hand gripping his left thigh. Blood was oozing through his trousers.

'It's Toiler, sir.'

'Sam, light along there,' shouted Tom, leaning out of the treadmill door. 'It's Toiler. The lad's in a sorry state. Fetch the galley alongside. We've not a moment to lose.'

André Dubois turned into Mill Lane and headed down the slope to Hay's Wharf, wondering how long it would take for Moreau's body to be discovered. With luck, it would be many days before it floated to the surface. He reached the bottom of the incline and peered round the corner onto the wharf. It was beginning to fill up with lumpers, porters and warehousemen. If Toiler was still hiding there he would soon have to show himself.

He looked for the nightwatchmen. They had gone, their brazier removed. Beyond where they had been sitting, he could see a small group of men carrying what looked like a young man. They were close to the edge of the quay, under one of the treadmills and seemed to be making for Battle Bridge Stairs. Dubois crouched and ran to the shelter of a solitary barrel not far from the stairs. He peeped out. One of the group looked like Pascoe.

He waited for the party to get closer. A lantern was raised and the light fell on the young man being carried. It was Toiler. He must, as he had suspected, been on the wharf all the while. Dubois cursed roundly and continuously. Whatever else happened, he needed to silence the boy before he had a chance to talk.

The party halted at the steps. A boat was there, a man already in it. Toiler was lifted into the boat and placed in the stern sheets. Dubois drew his pistol. Aimed it at Pascoe. The man was a matter of yards away. He lowered the barrel. One against four. Even if he killed Pascoe, the others would get him. He watched the galley draw away from the river bank and disappear into the early morning mist.

He couldn't pretend to know London but he did know the locations of the hospitals. He and Moreau had been to them all in their search for Toiler. It would take a while to cover them again but it would be worth it to silence Toiler. He would start in the Whitechapel road, at the London Hospital.

CHAPTER 26

John Harriot put down his coffee and looked at Tom over the top of his spectacles. A warming fire burned in the grate of his room on the first floor of the police office in Wapping. Outside, the rain of early morning had ceased and a low mist hung over the Thames.

'You say you've placed a guard on the boy?'

'Yes, sir,' said Tom. 'The matron saw us as we arrived and told us that someone had been in making enquiries about the lad. Apparently the caller spoke with a foreign accent. She told him she had no knowledge of such a patient currently in the hospital. I'm sure, from the description she gave me, that it was Dubois. As soon as Toiler is better I'll be asking him a few questions about what he knows of all this.'

'Good,' said Harriot. 'In the meantime there's something else you ought to know. I've had a report of the body of a local apothecary being found in his home in

Pillory Lane. Seems he was strangled. Not normally a case we would have got involved in but the local magistrate appears to think we might be interested. Seems two men were seen in the vicinity of the apothecary's house shortly before the body was discovered by the victim's wife. The same two men were again seen at some distance from the house and spoken to by the Watch. One of the men refused to speak to him while the other spoke with a strong French accent. Both men then made off in something of a hurry. It was only after the body of the apothecary was found that the Watch reported his encounter with the suspects.'

'Did anyone see the killing?'

'It appears not. The victim's wife was in bed when all this happened. Seems that she heard a knock of the door and her husband talking to a couple of men in the hall. It was only after her husband failed to come to bed that she went out and discovered him. Apparently they had been talking about a patient that her husband had been treating in the last day or so. The visitors were anxious to know where the person had gone.'

'Two men, probably French, looking for an ill or injured person and who thought the matter so serious they were prepared to kill? The patient's name wasn't Toiler, by any chance?'

'She didn't mention any names but the Shadwell magistrate examined the apothecary's treatment book and this

confirmed the attendance of one Robert Thwaites, known
to his friends as Toiler, on the day before the murder.'

Leaving Harriot's office, Tom walked down the police stairs
at Wapping and paused before the waiting galley. He needed
time to think.

There seemed little doubt that the Frenchmen had
based themselves in the warehouse on Hay's Wharf. But
why there? Unless, of course, it was close to their intended
seat of operations. But what was that operation? He had
told Harriot he thought it almost certain that the intended
target was the Port of London. But where was the
evidence? The large number of *louis d'or*? The money could
have been in payment for anything. The crowded conditions in the port? Mere coincidence. The map? A pure
guess. He needed something more substantial if he were
not to waste time on a line of enquiry that would get
him nowhere.

Any operation of any size required preparations and
preparations were hard to keep secret. Since the two
Frenchmen had chosen to base themselves in Southwark,
it seemed reasonable to concentrate his enquiries in that
area. And he knew just who to speak to.

Harriot had been somewhat sceptical.

What makes you think they'll know anything?

Will they talk?

Can you trust them?

The two Bream brothers had been a fixture in Southwark for years and little happened in the area without them knowing. Introduced to him by his friend, the Bow Street Runner Nathaniel Morgan, they had been a valuable, if somewhat reluctant, source of information ever since.

'We're going to Tooley Stairs,' he said as he stepped into the galley. 'There's two cullies I need to find in a hurry.'

Tom walked up Tooley Street towards the southern end of London Bridge. The mist had largely cleared, replaced by driving rain and the gathering gloom of late afternoon.

His feet hurt. He'd been walking for hours and still not found the men he was looking for. He stepped back into a doorway as a coach-and-four raced by, the thrashing hooves spewing mud from the pitted road surface, the foul-smelling mixture of earth and excrement narrowly missing him. He walked on, zigzagging his way through the stream of porters, drovers and market gardeners, necks buried low into their collars as they attempted to avoid the worst of the weather.

More taverns. The White House, the Drover, the Ship, the King's Head. He went into each of them, was growing weary of the task. Still no sign of them. A few yards short of the Marshalsea Prison, he turned through a narrow overhead archway from which hung a signboard painted with the effigy of a horse's head.

The yard of the Nag's Head Inn was little different from

those of the other coaching inns in Borough High Street. From its narrow opening, the extended cobblestone driveway widened out to a spacious area, presently cluttered with an assortment of abandoned carts and wagons. A newly arrived coach was busy disgorging its passengers at the front door of the inn while a ragbag assortment of nimble young urchins scrambled noisily over the roof, handing down boxes of this and cases of that.

Tom skirted the bustling scene and passed below the inn's galleried landing into a low-beamed parlour whose mullioned windows looked out onto the yard. A dozen or so men were seated on high-backed benches that formed a semicircle in front of a log fire. Some way apart from this group sat another two men seemingly deep in conversation. They looked up as Tom approached.

'Awight guv'nor?' Zak Bream was a slightly built man of about fifty, his high cheekbones and long nose accentuating the narrowness of his face. 'Don't see you too often this side of the river.'

'Why, if it isn't the Bream brothers. Been looking for you lads.' Tom slid onto the bench opposite the two men. 'Fancy a drink?'

'What's this all about then, guv'nor?' said Thomas, the younger of the two, after the refreshments had arrived. Broader in the face than his brother, he had a ready smile to him. 'I'll warrant you ain't crossed the bleedin' river to 'ave a chit-chat wiv the likes of us.'

Tom rubbed the tiredness from his eyes. He was in no mood for idle talk. 'I need some information.'

The brothers exchanged knowing glances.

'What sort of information?' Zak ran a finger round the rim of his drinking mug.

'There's a French cully who's planning some mischief,' said Tom. 'I think it may be connected with the port but I'm not entirely sure. If it's what I think it is, then a lot of people will die. He can't do it all on his own and will need men to help him. What I want to know is whether there has been anyone offering work to the lads in the last few days.'

'Don't know nothing about no Frenchman.' Thomas Bream looked around the room as though to make sure he'd not be overheard. 'But there's a cully by the name of Silas what's been in here two or three times offering the lads some work. He never said what exactly but I heard some talk that it were to lade a ship. Later someone said it were to be laded with straw. It made no sense to me.'

Twenty minutes later, Tom headed back along Borough High Street in the direction of the river, his suspicions about the nature of the attack on the port confirmed. And while neither Zak nor Thomas had been able to say exactly where the fireship was being prepared, what they had said had narrowed the area that needed to be searched. *The job were somewhere above the Bridge, your honour.*

And there had been something else the brothers had told

him. The men, originally happy to accept the invitation to work, had, in the absence of any pay, refused to return.

'Ol' clo', ol' clo'.' The thin reedy voice rose above the general hubbub of noise. The voice was vaguely familiar. He glanced across the street and caught sight of the old Jewish hat-seller tottering along in the opposite direction.

He smiled and went on his way, his mind turning to the man Zak had called Silas Grant. It meant nothing to Tom. He made a mental note to ask Sam if he knew him.

CHAPTER 27

Moses Solomon did not miss much. In his game he couldn't afford to. It wasn't just a question of losing a potential sale – although that was important enough – it was also a question of personal survival. He had long developed an ability to sift the ordinary and the unthreatening events of daily life from those that held the promise of trouble. He would seldom, if ever, initiate a conversation or offer a greeting. In that way he could be reasonably sure of not causing offence to fellow members of the human race.

In the adherence to this practice, he did nothing to acknowledge the passing of His Honour Mr Pascoe on the other side of the Borough High Street. If his honour had wanted to speak to him on any matter, Solomon would have been happy to oblige – but he had not.

The old man shivered. The rain had penetrated the thin fabric of his coat and seeped through to his skin. He noticed the cold more these days. It wouldn't be long before he would have to give up the peddling game. He wasn't looking forward to it. It would mean relying on the synagogue, as he had done years ago before coming to England. He cringed at the memory of those days, when he'd sought sanctuary in Germany and found he was no more welcome there than he had been in his native Poland. He didn't blame the Germans – not really. He was enough of a realist to recognise that they could not be expected to absorb the large numbers of his co-religious who had travelled from the east and sought charity from the local synagogues. Solomon tutted. There was fault on both sides but it still rankled to be regarded as a *Bettlejuden* – one of a band, permanently on the road, making mischief.

He looked up, had the curious sensation that he was being watched. At first he saw nothing beyond a sea of anonymous faces, each one seemingly oblivious to the presence of anyone else.

Then he saw him.

The fellow was standing at the entrance to the footpath leading to St Saviour's church, his head turned towards him. Even from a distance of perhaps thirty yards, there was no doubting who the cully was looking at. Solomon stared at the ground. He'd recognised the squat, broad-shouldered figure, the somewhat flattened face and slate-hard eyes that he'd first encountered a few nights since, not far from Pelican Stairs, on Wapping Wall.

*

Tom had reached the junction with Tooley Street when he heard the scream. It was the sound of a terrified human being, a keening wail, separate and distinct from the bellow of the mob or the cries of street vendors. He raced back, careless of the speeding coaches and thundering hooves of the horses, pushing his way through the crowd that seemed oblivious to the yelps of pain coming from its midst.

He found Moses Solomon lying on the footpath alongside St Saviour's church, barely conscious, an angry red mark encircling his neck.

'It were him,' said Solomon, as Tom cradled his head in his arms. He was shaking and his speech was slurred. 'It were the same one what I saw the night the boy swam ashore.'

'Don't try and talk now,' said Tom. He looked up at the circle of onlookers. 'Anyone see who did this?'

There was no reply, the crowd thinning, people falling away. Tom shook his head. It was always the way. He looked back at Solomon. The old man had lost consciousness. Tom pointed at the nearest of the onlookers.

'You. Hail a cab for me before this man dies for want of attention,' he ordered. The man hurried away.

Tom left the hat-seller in the care of the duty physician at St Thomas's Hospital and walked out into the street, more angry than he had ever been. The marks around Solomon's neck had told their own story, banishing whatever doubts he might have entertained about which of the two Frenchmen had survived.

But why the old man? Why him? He recalled the hat-seller's words. *It were the same one what I saw the night the boy swam ashore.* That was why. Solomon was one of only two people able to place Dubois close to the *Mary-Anne* on the night of the murders. It was reason enough for him to be killed.

The police galley pulled against the last of the ebb tide and edged through London Bridge. A jumble of barges, skiffs and luggers in varying states of disrepair festooned the exposed and sloping banks on either side, and an acrid stench like that of rotting eggs rose from the black mud.

He glanced at the dozen or so scavengers moving ponderously through the glutinous foreshore, each one carrying a sack in one hand and a short stick in the other, head bowed, eyes staring at the dark grey of the river bed. They were what Mr Colquhoun, the superintending magistrate at the police office, was pleased to call scuffle hunters, spending their time on the foreshore, searching for anything that might bring the price of a meal. He doubted anyone knew the foreshore as well as they did. He made a mental note to speak to them, see if they could help in any way.

He let his eyes move on. It was quieter on this side of the Bridge, the rush and the hurry of the port left behind, the movement of vessels slower and more measured. In a sense Tom was a stranger here, beyond the limits of his authority as a constable. He smiled, wanly. He wasn't entirely sure of his legal status anywhere on the Thames. Harriot had made it clear that while he, Harriot, was authorised to act as a magistrate, the legal position of the new police was a little more hazy. They were, in every sense, a private organisation, largely paid for by the West India Merchants and Planters Committee for the protection of their own ships and the cargoes they carried. His own authority, such as it was, was drawn directly from Harriot and not from any Act of Parliament.

The arrangements were a political expedient. With the country at war and no money available to fund the new organisation, the choice had been a simple one. The new force had to be funded by the West India merchants or not at all. The government would only pay the salaries of the two magistrates and the rent for the police office.

Tom's thoughts turned back to the threat facing Toiler and the attack on the port. The boy was under guard and was, for the time being, safe. The port was not. He wondered how long he had. It probably depended on whether or not Dubois knew of the delay to the arrival of the West India fleet. If he found out, he might consider an immediate assault before any more ships could leave the port. There were, after all, still something like a thousand to fourteen hundred vessels of one kind or another left in the Pool. More than enough for the French to achieve their ends.

Tom swung the galley over to the north shore and scrutinised a collection of vessels in a more than usual state of decay. They were all ideal for use as fireships. But so were the last thirty or forty hulks he'd seen since he'd come through the Bridge and been prevented from taking a close look at by the state of the tide. There wasn't enough water under his keel. And there wouldn't be until after dark this evening.

A barge drifted by on the last of the tide, its cargo of sawn timber stacked high above the coaming, a boy sitting on top, his shrill cries guiding the lighterman on his way. It was followed by another, then a third. Tom continued his patrol, the wharfs of the north shore slowly passing astern – Dyers Hall and Red Bull, then the wharf at Dowgate with the dock of the same name next door. He reached Queen's Hithe Stairs and put the galley about, crossing to the Southwark side and heading back towards the Bridge. Slack water. Another ten, perhaps fifteen minutes and the flood tide would begin. He needed to be through London Bridge before the current became too great to allow him to pass. He watched the dark mouth of St Saviour's Dock come up on his starboard bow. As with the other docks in the reach it had its fair share of once proud ships waiting to be broken up, their sound timbers reused, their rigging transferred to other ships. The dock was wider and longer than the others. He stared along its length. The light was fading. It would be dark in an hour, well before the rising tide would allow him to get in.

He thought of the scuffle hunters he had seen earlier. They would be able to tell him of any suspicious activity. He searched for them. They'd gone. Would not be back until the next low tide. He'd come back tomorrow and speak to them – if it wasn't too late. He steered the galley through London Bridge and glanced at Tooley Stairs. They reminded him of Moses Solomon. It had been where he rejoined the police galley after taking the old man to the hospital.

'Sam,' he said, 'as soon as we land, I'd be glad should you cut along to St Thomas's and see how our friend is getting along.'

'I were thinking the same thing, sir. By the by, where did you find him?'

'In the path beside St Saviour's church,' said Tom. 'The one leading to ...'

Tom turned and stared back up the Thames.

'What is it you're thinking, sir?'

'Not sure, Sam. Not sure at all.'

'You reckon they might come tonight? Them Frogs with the fireship?'

'I doubt they'll do anything tonight,' said Tom, remembering what Zak Bream had told him about the men not being paid for loading a ship upriver from London Bridge.

He glanced across as the galley approached the police pontoon. 'Easy all. Make fast fore and aft.'

'Mr Pascoe?' Tom turned to see the waterside constable hurrying down the steps towards him. 'Mr Harriot wishes to see you if you is at leisure, sir.'

'Thankee, Timms,' said Tom. 'Sam. Finish up here, and dismiss the men, will you? After that, see whether Solomon can tell you anything more about what happened to him.'

CHAPTER 28

Sam Hart was conscious of a gnawing sensation in the pit of his stomach, a concern he couldn't quite understand. While he had known the old man since boyhood, had seen him walking the streets of Wapping and Shadwell, carrying to sell whatever he could lay his hands on – beads, trinkets, old clothes, he could never have described him as anything other than an acquaintance, an Ashkenazi Jew like himself. He was known as a petty thief and receiver of stolen goods. Serious enough for him to be hanged if he were ever caught, but harmless enough.

They had spoken for the first time last summer, a hot and humid afternoon on the Ratcliff Highway. A jeering crowd had gathered round some spectacle of general amusement. At its centre, Solomon had been receiving a gratuitous flogging at the hands of bully boys that had left him dazed and bloodied. It might have been worse but for Sam's and – by chance – Tom's presence. Their intervention had probably saved the old man's life.

In the months that followed, Sam had only spoken to him on perhaps a dozen occasions, always in connection with the need for information. The relationship was never destined to be anything other than one based on a realisation of the value that each could bring to the other. Their relative positions – Sam as a waterman constable, Solomon as a pedlar and sometime thief – made sure of that. Despite their shared cultural values, the gulf was too wide to cross.

Not for the first time Sam found himself wondering how it was possible to see so much and know so little, how the lives of those with whom he came into contact could progress in such isolation from his own. It was as if he and the old man shared nothing in common.

Yet there had been something about Solomon that had touched Sam, reminded him of the Judaic faith he'd left behind. He hadn't thought about it until now. Solomon had never alluded to their shared heritage. Perhaps if he had it wouldn't have had the impact on him that his silence had achieved.

He reached London Bridge and turned to cross, the lights from the Southwark shore shimmering across the water, their sparkling beauty at odds with the grim reality of the foul-smelling slums of the south bank.

'Spare us a penny, your honour.' The voice made him

jump. He looked down to see a bedraggled woman of about twenty sitting in the roadway, her back propped against the stone balustrade of the bridge.

For a fleeting, stifling moment he stared at the empty eyes looking up at him from a skeletal face, the skin pitted with open sores, a shawl wound tightly about her head. His mind spiralled back to the spring of last year when he had seen another, once beautiful face gazing at him from the side of some nameless alley, the face of the woman he had loved.

Hannah Pinkerton had worn a shawl like this one, had suffered like this and been left to die. He looked away as a bony arm stretched out towards him, the palm of the hand held like an upwards-facing claw. He reached into his coat pocket, withdrew a coin and gave it to her. He didn't wait to be thanked.

It had not been much, the money barely enough for some bread, a slice of mutton, perhaps a dish of tea. He hurried on, the brief encounter troubling him. Was it simply that the woman had brought back memories of Hannah?

He realised it was more complicated than that, reminding him of how it was to be ignored as a human being, to have one's contribution trivialised and dismissed. He thought of Moses Solomon, attacked and reviled with no more thought than might be given to an insect, in much the same way that Hannah had been.

He turned into the courtyard of St Thomas's Hospital and

steered his way round a line of half-starved horses backed between the shafts of cabs, their heads hung low, their ears twitching. Behind them, willing hands were helping people to the ground and escorting them to the receiving room of the hospital. Sam passed through a gap in the two wings of the building and entered a second courtyard.

'Moses Solomon?' asked a harassed-looking nurse when Sam had reached a ward on the first floor. 'Last bed on the left. You mustn't stay long. He's quite poorly.'

Sam thanked her and made his way along the room, dimly aware of the chorus of low groans coming from either side of him, of the rustle of skirts and the rapid footsteps of the nurses moving amongst their patients. He reached the last bed. A mop of long white hair peeped above the blanket, bony fingers grasping the edge. Neither the head nor the hands moved.

'Moses? Are you asleep?'

Sam gently drew the blanket clear of the old hat-seller's bruised and ashen face, small red spots around both eyes and around his ears that he'd not seen before.

'Moses?' said Sam. Solomon opened his eyes and stared vacantly at his visitor. 'It's Sam. D'you remember me?'

A slow nod of the head.

'How d'you feel?'

Sam thought he saw the old man shrug his shoulders; a resigned gesture of despair. He knelt down on the floor next to the bed, a hand resting on Solomon's clenched fist.

'Do you want to talk about what happened?' He felt anger welling inside him, something close to the desire for revenge. He let the mood pass. It had never achieved anything. Slowly, the anger ebbed away. He looked up. A weak smile inhabited the old man's face.

'You are angry on my account.' Solomon's voice was hoarse, his eyes closed. 'Do not be. I am an old man. My passing is of no consequence. Except to God.'

'Tell me what happened.' Sam tightened his grip on the old man's hand; felt it growing weaker. 'Moses?'

'I hear you,' said Solomon turning towards Sam and opening his watery eyes, rimmed with red. 'What is done is done.'

'Just like that? You would forgive the man who did this to you?'

'One day you, too, will learn how heavy is the burden for those who do not forgive.' Solomon smiled again, a tear falling onto the sheet below his head, the circle of damp spreading outwards. 'For me, my life is at an end. For you, it has barely begun.'

Solomon seemed to slump, his facial muscles slackened. Sam looked over his shoulder and beckoned one of the nurses. When he looked back, Solomon's eyes were closed and his mouth had dropped open. The nurse shook her head and drew the curtains round the bed.

Tom followed Harriot up the path from the river and across Whitehall to the grey stone frontage of Melbourne House, its portico and supporting stone pillars arranged in the style of Ancient Rome. The door was answered by a liveried footman who took them through a domed and marble-pillared rotunda, up a flight of steps into a circular waiting area.

'The Secretary of State has asked me to let him have a briefing on the current state of your investigation. He wants us both to go and see him,' Harriot had said to him earlier. 'He's attending a dinner at the home of Lord Melbourne. Wants to see us there.'

Tom looked about him. It was not a particularly large space. Probably no more than about thirty feet across with a high, ornate, plaster ceiling, the walls hung with portraits of the 1st Viscount Melbourne and his wife, the Lady Elizabeth. Facing them were three gleaming hardwood doors from behind one of which came the hum of convivial conversation, the tinkle of female laughter.

A minute or two later, the footman returned and showed them through one of the other doors into a large room, richly hung with tapestries, mirrors and paintings. At the far end, two arched windows looked out onto a darkened Horse Guards Parade, the panes of glass reflecting the four dozen or so candles placed on tables and the marble mantel-piece. A fire burnt in the grate.

Tom turned at the sound of a door opening behind him.

'My dear Harriot, how very good of you to come.' His Grace, the Duke of Portland, Secretary of State for the

Home Department and former First Lord of the Treasury, entered the room, his broad face showing the effects of a glass or two of red wine. 'And this must be Mr Pascoe. I've heard a great deal about you, sir.'

'Thank you, your grace.' Tom bowed.

'Now then, Harriot, what's this I hear about a couple of enemy agents on the loose?'

The Duke of Portland listened in silence as Harriot recounted what was known about the arrival and subsequent activities of the Frenchmen, and their intended target.

'You say you have not yet been able to find these men or the vessel you suspect they may want to use as a fireship?'

'Not yet, your grace,' said Harriot. He turned to look at Tom. 'Mr Pascoe may be able to assist you further.'

Portland nodded and looked enquiringly at Tom.

'In normal circumstances,' said Tom, 'it would be usual for an attack to be timed for the period of greatest congestion in the port. Those conditions were expected to be present now as a fleet from the West Indies was due to arrive in an already congested port. Fortunately, the new arrivals have been delayed off the North Foreland and are not expected in London for another two to three weeks.'

'Are you saying, Mr Pascoe, that we no longer have anything to fear?'

'I wish, sir, that were the case. What is more likely is

that the enemy agents will make an assessment based on what they know of ship movements. I doubt they will wait two or three weeks. The risk of detection is too great. On the other hand there is no certainty about the weather. The wind direction may change overnight, in which case the convoy may begin arriving as early as tomorrow morning. My assessment is that the earliest we can expect an attack is about two hours after high water, tonight. At the latest, three nights from now. After that, high water at London Bridge occurs after dawn, too late to launch a surprise attack.'

'What are the prospects of finding this ship before that happens?' said a grim-faced Portland.

'I regret it extremely, sir, but if it is launched tonight, then almost none at all.'

Portland walked to the fireplace and looked down into the flames. Without turning round, he said, 'I think it might be useful if I were to give you some background on the likely impact of such an attack.'

He paused as if to gather his thoughts.

'War is an expensive business. In this case, doubly so since the Russians and the Austrians have sought funds from us in order to pay for a substantial portion of their armies. It is likely that we may, in the future, have to subsidise the Prussians as well. Despite these payments there appears to be little that we have been able to do to keep Napoleon in check – at least on land, where he carries all before him. Fortunately the defeat of his fleet off the coast of Alexandria in the autumn, and the resulting entrapment of his army over there, mean that his position is now vulnerable.

'But, as I have said, war is expensive and the government has had to devise new ways of raising the necessary funds, including the new income tax introduced by the minister, in December. Unfortunately, the hoped-for revenue from this new tax has failed to materialise – mainly due to evasion by people who ought to know better. In consequence, we have had to place greater reliance on the tax on goods passing through our ports. And here I come to the point. This revenue is entirely contingent on the ability of this country to trade successfully with others. Last year there was a twenty per cent increase in the value of exports, and a huge surplus over imports. Should that trade be cut off, or even substantially interfered with, it could have a fatal impact on our ability to prosecute the war.'

Portland stepped away from the fire and looked at his two visitors over the top of his iron-framed spectacles.

'That, gentlemen, is exactly what an attack on our ships in the Port of London may lead to. The situation is extremely serious. As much as we cannot afford the loss of our ships, it is as nothing compared to the loss of the facilities offered by the Port of London. It is absolutely imperative that you stop this attack.'

For a moment, there was silence in the room. Tom was the first to speak.

'As I indicated a moment ago, the earliest that any attack could be launched would be about two hours after high water tonight – approximately six hours from now. Two hours after that, the danger would begin to recede as the force of the current increased to the point where it would be too strong to permit a proper navigation of the vessel. She would, sir, be likely to hit the Bridge, and get no further.'

'Six hours should, sir, give you enough time to find what you're looking for, should it not?'

'Patrols are already engaged in the search, sir,' said Tom. 'But there are two problems. The present state of the tide means the patrols cannot get close to the banks of the river and that is where it is likely the hulk is being prepared. They could make their way ashore and search from the land side, but that involves more time than we have available.'

'I see,' said Portland. 'And the second problem?'

'There is nothing to tell a fireship from any other hulk, even in daylight, and we'll be searching at night. On top of that, every dock and warehouse has its fair share of hulks of one kind or another. Searching every potential site would take weeks.'

'Can a hulk be stopped once the fire has been lit?' said Portland.

'The usual way is to try and sink it before it reaches its

target. I've only ever dealt with one before and on that occasion we fired at it with our twelve-pounders. That's not something we could do on the Thames. If it's an old hulk the hull could be rotten and it might be possible to put an axe through it and sink her that way. Much depends on how far advanced the fire is.'

'Let me be frank with you, Mr Pascoe,' said Portland, tucking his hands under the tail of his coat and gazing up at the ornate ceiling. 'If you and your colleagues should fail to find this ship and, as a result, serious harm is done to the port, there will undoubtedly be consequences for both of us.'

'Your grace, I am fully aware of the gravity of the situation,' said Tom.

'Good. Let me know the moment you have any news. Meanwhile I have deserted my host for quite long enough. I bid you good night, gentlemen.'

CHAPTER 29

Sam made his way back along Borough High Street, mindful of the formalities to be observed in the death of a Jew. He doubted anyone in the Christian hospital where Solomon now lay would know what they were. Sam was not at all sure he knew what they were himself, the doctrine a distant memory, the notion of a swift burial equally indistinct. He remembered his father's death, the shroud, the plain wooden coffin – dust to dust. He remembered his mother sitting on a low stool at home, receiving the condolences of friends and family for the seven days. The *shiva* was a solemn requirement. There was so much of his faith he had forgotten.

A cold wind caught him unawares as he left the relative protection of Borough High Street and ventured out onto London Bridge. He glanced up into the night sky, its vast expanse lit by the tiny lights of other worlds, a full moon low down in the east.

He remembered the young beggar-woman he'd seen earlier and his eyes strayed to the place where she'd been. She was gone, her place taken by another. He walked on.

On the other side of the Thames, he passed below the arch of St Magnus the Martyr and turned east along Lower Thames Street. The place was busy with the usual crowds working the legal quays and the market at Billingsgate, the rush of heavy-burdened porters and the ribald shrieks of the fishwives hard to ignore. Soon he was climbing the steep incline of Tower Hill, the walls of the Norman tower black against the blinking sky.

Tomorrow he would see the rabbi at Duke's Place and ask him what needed to be done for Moses Solomon. For the moment he had other things on his mind. Tom Pascoe needed to know of the old man's death.

He crossed the wooden bridge at Hermitage Dock, the street ahead of him deserted but for the occasional passer-by, its empty surface bathed in the cold light of the moon. He left the bridge and walked down the centre of the street away from the shadows of the houses. It was safer that way. There was nothing to be gained by taking unnecessary risks. Not here. Not in Wapping or Shadwell or up round the Ratcliff Highway. His eyes searched the empty doorways, the narrow alleys and the dark mouths of the courts leading off the street. Once, a figure moved and a deep-throated female voice offered comfort from whatever cares he might have. He smiled and kept walking.

He turned in towards the police office and stopped. Something had moved in the periphery of his vision. He looked round, his eyes searching the street. Thirty yards away a man and a woman were walking towards him down the middle of the highway, talking quietly. In the opposite direction a drunk was leaning against the wall of a house, crooning a sea shanty. Sam shook his head. He'd imagined it. He stepped into the passage that would take him to the front door of the office.

Out on the reach, he heard a barked command and the splash of oars. He walked to the head of the stairs. A police galley was fetching alongside, light from the twin lanterns on the pontoon falling on the faces of the two men in the stern. Seconds later John Harriot and Tom Pascoe had climbed ashore.

On the other side of Wapping Street, in an alley that runs down the side of the Pichard Brewery, Dubois was growing impatient. According to his expensively purchased information, Pascoe should have left the police office some considerable time ago, at the end of his tour of duty. But there had been no sign of him. He looked up Wapping Street at the sound of approaching footsteps and recognised Sam Hart's loping gait. He melted back into the shadows.

The fellow strode by and bounded up the couple of steps into the passageway opposite where he stopped. Dubois felt his stomach tighten as Hart turned and looked up and down the street. He could feel the other man's stare sweep over him; was sure there was a slight hesitation when the eyes reached him. His hand slipped to his knife. The moment passed. He released a lungful of air as Sam turned away and disappeared along the passage.

It was time he left. He'd have to deal with Pascoe later. He swore, quietly. He didn't like unfinished business but if he didn't leave now there was a serious risk that the men he'd hired would depart before he got back to the hulk. And he wasn't prepared to take that chance, not after the trouble he'd had getting them there in the first place. He wanted everything to be ready for tomorrow night.

He grimaced. Most of this morning had been spent searching the streets of Southwark for a tavern where he might find the gangmaster Jim Clarke had referred to, the man Silas Grant. By chance, when searching Borough High Street he'd spotted the signboard of the Nag's Head and remembered it as the tavern Clarke had mentioned.

'Silas?' The pot-boy was busy, disinclined to answer the stranger's question. It had taken the weight of two pennies in the palm of his hand to kindle his interest. 'Aye, he comes in most days. Not here just now, though.'

A further two hours passed before Dubois got a nod from the pot-boy and a knowing look directed at the door of the taproom.

Silas Grant was, he supposed, about forty-five years of

age, his face a mass of weeping sores framed by straggling shoulder-length hair, his back hunched.

But ill-looking though he was, he had driven a hard bargain, insisting on a half-payment as the price of his agreement to supply the required number of men at the time and place stipulated by Dubois. The crabby misfit of a fellow had initially wanted the full amount, only changing his mind when he'd been shown a few *louis d'or* and threatened with losing the business altogether.

Dubois took one last look across Wapping Street at the passage opposite. It was a pity he'd missed Pascoe. But there was always the alternative he'd been thinking about for some time. He might have to do that. He'd think about it.

Tom Pascoe stared at the brig's sails, clearly visible in the dawn light of the following morning. There was no doubt it was moving upriver towards London.

'Have we had any word from the harbour master about the fleet that was stuck off the North Foreland, Sam?' said Tom, looking thoughtful.

'Are you thinking yon brig might be part of the West Indies convoy, your honour?' Sam craned his neck to look across the Isle of Dogs.

'Something like that,' said Tom. 'Give way together,' he barked. 'Handsomely now. The sooner we talk to the master of that ship, the sooner we'll know where she's from.'

The long, clinker-built galley surged forward, her fine

bow slicing through the rippled surface of the water, spray whipping back, stinging Tom's face and hands. He glanced again at the brig a little way south of Blackwall Point, hoping he was wrong. If the brig was part of the fleet they had all thought marooned in the estuary, the others would not be far behind.

And sailing straight into a trap.

At the bottom of Limehouse Reach, Tom swung the galley clear of the sloping mud-banks jutting out into river and passed close beneath the massive black and yellow hulls of a couple of first-rate men-of-war anchored off Deptford Creek. Then they turned north, leaving behind them the green dome of the Royal Hill and the Greenwich observatory at its summit. Tom raised himself an inch or two off the arms' chest and looked down the broad stretch of Blackwall Reach that lay ahead, banks of tall reeds stretching away on either side into the distance. The brig he'd seen earlier was clubbing down towards him on the tide, her t'gallants billowing in the fresh wind as she closed with the police galley. Tom waited until she'd passed before swinging round to come up on her lee.

'Ahoy, *Campion*, this is the police,' bellowed Tom, his hands cupped around his mouth. 'I wish to come aboard.'

'Last time I counted,' said the master of the West India brig *Campion*, 'there were close on thirty of us in the convoy. We was twiddling our thumbs off the North Foreland for nigh on a week waiting for the wind to change direction. Couldn't get nowhere. And all the while them bastard press gangs kept snooping round looking for hands.'

'But that's all changed, if I'm not sadly mistook,' said Tom, studiously ignoring the comment on the Navy's recruiting style.

The two of them were sitting in the Great Cabin in the stern of the brig, clouds of evil-smelling tobacco smoke billowing from a pipe clenched between the captain's teeth.

'Aye, it has right enough. Soon as the wind came round we lost no time weighing anchor and heading up the estuary, I can tell you.'

'Are the rest close behind?'

'Aye. I reckon there'll be one or two round yon bight in Bugsby's Reach. Rest of them and some colliers what joined us just before we left, won't be far behind.'

'Colliers?' Tom's eyebrows shot up. 'How many?'

'Oooh, 'bout a dozen, I reckon.'

The sun was just visible over the Plaistow Marsh when, fifteen minutes later, Tom took his leave of the *Campion*'s captain and dropped down the brig's starboard companion ladder to the police galley. Over forty ships. And all of them would be in the Pool well before nightfall. He thought about trying to stop them, make them wait until it was safe to go on, but dismissed the idea. The delay at the North Foreland had already cost money and it was unlikely the merchants would tolerate any further loss of revenue.

'I couldn't even give them a date when it would be safe,' Tom muttered under his breath. 'They could be stuck here a week, maybe two, before we find that bloody hulk.'

He settled himself down onto the arms' chest, picked up the tiller-guys and, for a long minute, gazed up the reach to Blackwall Point, conscious of the heavy responsibility that now rested on his shoulders.

'D'you hear there? We've got work to do. Away larboard ...' a pause, then, 'Give way together.'

Tom stood at the window of Harriot's office and watched the slow procession of brigs, snows and the occasional barquentine make their way up through the Pool, drop anchor and swing up into the tide.

'How is it looking?' said Harriot.

'The flood tide's just turned,' said Tom glancing over his shoulder at the magistrate. 'About half the vessels in the convoy have made it. The rest will have to wait for the next flood tide but they should all be here by this evening.'

'What time is high water?'

'Midnight,' said Tom.

'So what do you think? Will the attack come tonight?'

'I'd be surprised if it doesn't. Tomorrow more ships will leave the port. The French won't get another chance like this until the summer when the regular convoys arrive from the islands.'

Harriot grunted and turned back to his paperwork. 'I've told the Secretary of State about the convoy's arrival. He's asked to be kept informed. What's happening about the search for the hulk?'

'The Upper and Lower duty boats have been up above the Bridge since dawn, searching every likely craft they come across,' said Tom, watching a line of barges swinging round on their mooring. 'I've asked them to stay there until nightfall when the night-duty crews will take over.'

'Talking of which,' said Harriot, 'you're on night duty yourself, are you not? You best get home for some rest. Likely you'll have a busy night.'

'Aye, I think I will,' said Tom. 'But I've an errand to attend to first.'

CHAPTER 30

Peggy Tompkins glanced at the clock over the door of the ward. Another hour and she would be free to return to her room for a rest. She looked up, surprised by the sound of approaching footsteps. She was not expecting any new arrivals and the medical and surgical rounds had all been completed several hours before. She waited to see who it was. The door opened.

'Why, give you joy, Tom,' she managed, and felt a flush spreading up into her cheeks. 'I make no doubt you have come to see Toiler.'

'Joy, Miss Peggy. No, not me. I've brought someone else who wishes to see him.'

Peggy could have sworn he'd stammered. She looked beyond him as a second person entered the ward.

'Ruxey!' Peggy felt inexplicably relieved to have someone else to talk to. 'Your brother is over there. He still suffers from the fever but I make no doubt he is over the worst of it.'

She watched the girl hurry to Toiler's bedside and embrace him, laughing.

'They look happy, do they not,' said Peggy. 'They must have worried about each other.'

'Miss Peggy . . .' said Tom.

She waited, her stomach churning, wondering what he was about to say. He looked tired, she thought. She wondered when he'd last slept. From the other end of the ward a patient was calling for her. She tried to ignore it, saw Tom's head turn towards the sound and then back to her.

'I can see you're busy . . .' said Tom, as the thin, reedy voice called again. 'I must not detain you.'

'Tom.'

He stopped and looked back at her, waiting for her to speak.

'The man looking for Toiler? The Frenchman? He was here.'

'Aye, I know.'

'No, you don't understand. He was here today.'

'Where?' Tom looked alarmed.

'Miss Squibb saw him at the gate on the Whitechapel road. She thought no more of it until she again saw him in the orchard at the back of the hospital, beyond the quadrangle. I think he was trying to get to Toiler.'

'Two of my men are, as you know, at the door of the ward,' said Tom. 'He's quite safe while he remains here.'

'Will you stop and talk to the boy?'

'No. There are some pressing matters which I have to attend to. I'll return as soon as I am able. Would you be so good as to ask Ruxey to return to Wapping at her earliest convenience?'

'Of course. Will you be away for long?' Peggy looked down, unwilling to let him see what was in her eyes. She pushed a stray lock of hair back into her mob-cap.

'I . . . I don't rightly know.'

He sounded unsure. It was hardly surprising. She knew she'd not treated him well these last few months. She looked up and met his gaze, held it for a moment, a wan smile lifting the corners of her mouth.

'Please come back soon,' she said.

At shortly after midnight the Thames was bathed in the diffuse light of a full moon, the silvery beams reflecting off the last moments of a tide in flood. On either side of the channel, a few hundred yards downriver of the Tower, the recently arrived ships of the West India convoy rode at anchor, their bare masts and yards black against the starlit sky.

Further west, at Stanton's Wharf, a dozen fully laden colliers waited to be delivered of their cargo. Close by, fifty, sixty, perhaps more, lighters swung lazily in the water waiting their turn to be taken alongside the Custom House quays.

A sleek black shape slipped out between the line of ships close to London Bridge and fetched alongside a lighter, the splash and creak of its oars barely audible in the still night air.

'Take a turn with the bowline, Ruxey,' rasped Tom. 'We'll stop here a while.'

He looked over to his right, seeing nothing save the lights of the ships – a single lantern glowing over the companion ladder of each vessel like so many glow-worms spread out in a country field. Ahead of him, the bulk of London Bridge rose out of the darkness, its stone abutments washed in the pale moonlight seeming to frame the empty black arches like the mouths of giants.

He was uneasy about Ruxey's presence. Her injury had not yet healed. She would have to be careful not to strain it. He had told her as much, instructing her not to pull her oar with as much force as she had been used to. He could have saved himself the trouble. She had just smiled at him.

He slid off the arms' chest, unlocked it and opened the lid. Quickly unbuckling the leather straps holding a massive woodman's axe, he removed it and placed it on the bottom boards between his feet. Next he took out the four sea-service pistols and, retaining one for himself, handed the rest to his crew together with a small leather pouch of gunpowder and a quantity of shot.

'Load your pieces,' he ordered. 'And be careful. I don't

want any of you sinking the galley with a shot through the hull.'

Next he handed down the cutlasses.

'D'you hear there?' he said, when the crew had settled down again. 'You all know why we're here. I expect the hulk to make its appearance through one of the central arches of the Bridge between two and four hours from now. Any sooner and she'll not clear the arches. Any later, the force of the tide will be too great to control her. As soon as we see her, I intend to close with her. You, Kemp, will stay with the galley. Your job is to find a section of the hull, just below the waterline, that's rotting and attempt to put the axe through it.

'Ruxey and Sam will come aboard with me. You, Sam, will take control of the wheel and make sure the hulk doesn't hit anything.

'Ruxey. You and I will make a start on trying to control any fire there might be on board. Everyone clear about what's happening?'

'Aye, sir,' said Ruxey from her usual place at bow-oar.

'Clear it is, your honour,' rumbled Kemp's bass voice.

'Just one thing, sir,' said Sam.

'Yes?'

'Begging your pardon, sir, but I ain't never steered a ship afore, like what Ruxey has. And if she don't mind me saying, she ain't going to be a lot of use to you fighting the flames in her state.'

'You're quite right, Sam. Ruxey, you take the wheel and Sam will help with fighting the fire.'

'Very good, sir.'

'I don't need to tell you of the dangers we face,' said Tom. 'While we are not alone – Mr Harriot is in the Supervision Boat over by the legal quays and the Lower Boat in the charge of Mr Judge is a little further back – it falls to us to go in first. I've little doubt that others, including watermen and lightermen, will join us as soon as the danger becomes apparent. It's possible the fire will already have been lit before the hulk reaches the Bridge. But they won't want to light it so early that the flames are visible before the ship reaches the Pool.'

'Will they be using gunpowder, sir?' said Ruxey.

'It's possible but unlikely,' said Tom. 'Using gunpowder risks sinking the ship before she's done her job. That said, they may want to use a few small charges to accelerate the spread of the fire and dissuade anyone from trying to put out the flames.'

'How are we supposed to stop her, your honour?' said Kemp. 'What with the tide up her arse – begging your pardon, sir – I meant her stern.'

'Short of sinking her, we can't,' said Tom. 'I plan on giving ourselves enough time to steer her through the Pool and put her on the hard somewhere around Cuckold Point where the congestion is lightest. Depending on how quickly we spot her, there could still be a crew on board and we'll have to deal with them. My guess is that they'll be anxious to be off her as soon as possible and will have no stomach for a fight. Once on board our job will be to attempt to put the fire out while steering a course down the middle of the channel. As I said, we won't be alone. One of the other boats will take a line from the ship and help keep her to the centre of the channel. Any questions?'

There was silence in the police galley, a mood of apprehension amongst the crew. It was natural enough. Tom had suffered from the same taut nerves many a time, the gut-wrenching fear that invaded the soul in the hours before a battle. He could recall with utmost clarity the dread mood that presaged an action, when the guns had been run out, the decks sanded and the men piped to dinner and all that remained was the endless wait. It was then, when the mind played tricks and time seemed to drag by, that the fear was at its most acute. He had longed, in those awful moments, for the crash of the cannon to spell the end of the waiting, when the chaos and din and smoke of conflict would drown out all emotion and terror, and nothing mattered except the loading and the firing of the guns.

His eyes flicked over to the Bridge. Nothing was moving. Even the tide had stopped running; was waiting to turn. A thick blanket of cloud crossed in front of the moon, obliterating it and the stars, reducing visibility to less than two feet. The wind had veered to the north and was ruffling the surface of the Thames, nipping at the tips of Tom's ears. He lifted the collar of his coat. In front of him, Sam was blowing into cupped hands, trying to get the warmth back into them.

It was going to be a long night.

Dubois paced up and down the upper deck of the brig in St Saviour's Dock, occasionally stopping to watch the half-dozen crew complete the final preparations before the ship left the dock on her final journey. He turned aft and stared at the dilapidated specimen of a gig suspended between the stern davits.

'This had better float, *monsieur*.' He glanced at the hunch-backed figure of Silas Grant leaning against the taffrail, his arms folded.

The gangmaster shook his head and said nothing.

Dubois considered making an issue of it, thought better of it and turned away. It had been hard enough getting the men to come and he wasn't about to risk losing them before the brig had even slipped its moorings. Grant had promised he'd be at the dockside no later than dusk. By nine o'clock there had still been no sign of him or the six crew he'd negotiated. To Dubois's intense chagrin they had eventually arrived just before ten.

He wandered over to the ship's wheel. If the gig was in a poor state of repair, it was as nothing compared to the ship, a vessel in the last stages of her life, stripped of her masts, her paintwork flaking, her decks sadly ahoo, her chains and anchors missing. It reminded him of the corsair that had briefly been his, of the condition Pascoe had reduced her to in the space of a few short hours. Pascoe would suffer for what he'd done.

'I'll be taking the money now, mister.' Grant was still leaning against the taffrail.

'The work is not finished. You will be paid when it is done. Do the men know what they're doing?'

'They know enough. When will I be getting the money?'

'I've told you already.'

'How do I know you won't leave without you pays us?' Grant eased himself away from the rail and moved towards the other man, his hand dropping out of sight behind his back.

Dubois saw the movement and stepped away from the wheel, his fingers tightening round the handle of his knife. 'You don't. You will have to trust me. I am not so stupid as to have it on my person. If you want to see the money you will do what I say and stay with me.'

'Never you fret, mate,' said Grant, his empty hand reappearing at his side. 'I'll be doing that, for sure.'

'These men,' said Dubois gesturing towards the grime-ridden individuals standing beneath the fo'c'sle break. 'They've handled a ship before?'

'Hundreds of times. Done it every day for years.'

'You misunderstand me, *monsieur*.' Dubois's patience was

wearing thin. 'Are any of them sailors? Have they ever been on a ship at sea?'

'Why would they be going there?' said Grant, looking askance. 'Isn't it enough they don't get paid for the work they do here in the port without going to sea? Sure, they know how to steer a ship, if that's what's worrying you. But sailors? No.'

'It would be something if they are able to do that much,' said Dubois, rolling his eyes. 'They're drunk.'

'They'll do what you ask of them,' said Grant, his eyes narrowing dangerously.

Dubois was already regretting his remark. If the conditions of the men here were anything like those he'd experienced in Marseille, he knew what to expect. He was used to the ways of corruption where men were forced to work for no pay. The expectation on the waterfront was that you took whatever you could and sold it to buy food. The work you had was simply a means to an end – the opportunity to steal. He'd grown up knowing no other life.

'Yes, but ...' Dubois was anxious to be off.

'They're drunk cos that's the only way they can get work,' said Grant. 'Those that want to work goes to the man what can give it to them. And mostly he's the landlord of a tavern. So they buy him a drink and have one themselves and pretty soon they's drunk. See? There ain't no other way.'

Grant stopped talking, an angry flush in his cheeks. He was breathing heavily. For a moment or two, neither man spoke. Then Dubois turned away. Compassion was never his strong point. 'I hope, for all our sakes, they know what they're doing. It's time to go.'

'Sir?'

Tom's eyes snapped open. He realised he must have dozed off. The clouds of earlier in the evening had moved away, the reflection of the moon shimmering in the three-knot tide. He glanced along the police galley. Ruxey had turned, was looking over her shoulder.

'What is it, Ruxey?'

'Thought I heard something.'

Tom tilted his head and listened, his gaze sweeping along the arches of the Bridge. For a moment the only sounds he could hear were the gentle bumps of the galley against the side of the lighter and the occasional cry of a watchman out on the reach. He stared through the glimmering haze of ships' lights to the darkness surrounding the Bridge. He could see nothing out of the ordinary – the blackened outlines of some colliers close to Tooley Stairs, tiers of lighters, low in the water, the flapping of a seagull's wings disturbed from his rest. He lifted himself a few inches off the arms' chest for a better view.

'Can you see anything, Ruxey?'

'Main arch, your honour. Thought I saw something moving.' A note of doubt had crept into Ruxey's voice. 'No, I were right. There it is, sir.'

Tom saw it at the same moment, a shape that seemed to fill and devour the central arch of London Bridge. A moment later and it had emerged into the Upper Pool. A brig, by the look of her, a vast bulk of blackness. Tom scanned her upper deck, searching for any sign of a fire. There was nothing. He heard a loud thud and saw the hulk begin to swing athwart the tide. It looked as though she'd caught her stern on the starlings and was in danger of becoming stuck. Then she broke free and drifted down broadside to the tide.

'Cast off fore and aft. Away larboard. Give way together. Handsomely, now.'

The galley sliced through the ebbing tide, her bow wave creaming the water. A flash of yellow flame licked out from beneath the brig's fo'c'sle break. Then it was gone, as though it had never existed. A moment later, a shower of sparks issued from the same place. Then more flames, each larger and more aggressive than the one before. Tom stared. The fire seemed confined to one area – the fo'c'sle and perhaps the forward section of the upper deck. He breathed a sigh of relief. If it had taken hold anywhere else, it was still confined below decks. He had to hope he could keep it there. Once the flames reached the open air they would spread rapidly. A small craft, a gig, caught his eye, suspended from the stern davits. Someone was standing forward of the taffrail, shouting. They appeared to have seen the police galley. Men were running aft, piling into the gig.

'They're abandoning her.' Tom kept the excitement out of his voice. 'They're going to let her drift.'

He pulled hard down on the starboard tiller-guy bringing the galley sweeping round on a parallel course to the burning brig. She was drifting towards the Southwark shore. If he didn't get there fast, she'd collide with the dozen or so colliers moored there.

'We'll fetch alongside her larboard side and go aboard,' said Tom, raising his voice against the dull roar of a fire coming from inside the brig's hull.

'What about them scrubs what's the cause of all this, sir?' said Sam nodding towards the gig suspended from the ship's stern.

'We'll deal with the fire first,' said Tom. 'If the brig rams them colliers, there ain't no telling what'll happen.'

CHAPTER 31

André Dubois heard the crisp bark of orders and gaped at
the rush of white water curving in towards him. A chill
ran down his spine. You didn't need to be a sailor to recognise the voice of the quarterdeck. How they had got here
so quickly, he couldn't fathom. It was as though they'd
known all along and had been waiting for him. More voices.
More boats. Further away but closing fast. He could hear
the same clipped words of command.

He glanced aft. His men had seen and heard the same;
were running towards the gig suspended from the stern
davits. He looked on in shocked silence, as though a spec-
tator, the events evolving in slow motion. It wasn't
supposed to be like this. The colour drained from his
face. He stared at the small rowing boat lashed fast above
the taffrail. He could still hear Jim Clarke's voice. *No
point in swimming if you can use a boat.* The soldier in
Dubois would never have thought of that. He couldn't

swim. His only chance of evading capture was that boat.

A sudden sheet of flame erupted through the forward hatch. He leapt back from the heat. He'd forgotten about the fire, the thought of it driven from his mind by the sight of the approaching boats. He looked at the leaping flames. He hadn't expected them to take hold so quickly. Had assumed they'd not be visible until the hulk was in amongst the ships in the Pool. By then it would be too late for anyone to do anything about saving the port. He should have known. The men in the boats might still be able to put out the fire.

The line of foaming water was now much closer. He could just make out the shape of a rowing galley. Four men on board. Three rowing. He recognised the fourth figure in the stern sheets. He swore. He might have known it would be Pascoe.

He looked over the starboard rail. The brig was drifting towards some colliers close to the Southwark shore. It wasn't ideal. He'd wanted to remain on the brig for a little longer, steer her in amongst the tightly packed shipping further down. But there was no chance of that now. Even the wind seemed to be conspiring against him and was pushing the brig in the wrong direction.

The rowing galley was almost upon them. He glanced aft. His crew were at the taffrail, keen to be gone. Someone had unhitched the falls ready for lowering the boat. If he wasn't quick they'd go without him. He remembered the gunpowder. Most of it was in the Great Cabin, below the poop deck. He'd put it there deliberately, well away from the seat of the fire. He hoped the delay would mean the ship would not explode before she'd reached her destination among the ships and lighters in the Lower Pool.

The gig swung free on the davits. The men were clambering across the divide, risking all to escape. Dubois looked back over the larboard rail. The police galley was alongside. A few more seconds and Pascoe would be coming on board. He felt a hammering in his ears – recognised it as the violent beating of his heart.

He drew his knife. He'd missed a few opportunities to rid himself of Pascoe. It would be a simple matter to get him as he came up the side, a quick, clean stab to his throat.

The men were shouting at him. Wanted to go. Doubt seeped into his mind. The gesture was suicidal. Pascoe's crew would be close behind. He'd never get away. He rushed to the taffrail and leapt into the gig.

It started on its downward journey. Was travelling too fast, the falls running through the men's fingers, burning the palms of their hands. They hit the river surface with a spine-jarring crash, water slopping over the gunwales, threatening to swamp them, tangled ropes holding them to the drifting hulk.

'Cut us free, you dolts,' shouted Dubois, his voice drowned by the chorus of oaths around him. Panic and fear had done nothing to sober the crew. No one took notice.

Yet more shouts. The voices seemed close, were not those of his own men. He stared up at the ship, could see nothing beyond the light of the flames. The voices grew louder, more insistent. His nerves were as taut as harp-strings.

He drew his knife and slashed at the ropes.

Tom did not wait for the galley to come to rest before he leapt for the brig's companion ladder and raced up the side of the ship. He could hear Sam and Ruxey close behind as he reached the top and vaulted the rail.

The deck was deserted. And hot. No telling when it would collapse. He ran aft onto the poop deck and caught hold of the falls. They were slack. Dubois was gone. He wasn't surprised. He looked round. Sam and Ruxey were still on the upper deck.

'Take the wheel, Ruxey. Steer a course straight down the channel.'

He looked round for the water buckets that would normally be there. Miraculously half a dozen were still in place on the quarterdeck, complete with their hauling lines. Sam was already moving towards them.

More boats were beginning to arrive – Harriot and Judge amongst them. Others as well. They must have seen the flames. Most would be watermen, those whose livelihood was the port and the river that served it. They would know what was at stake. He doubted there was anything altruistic in their offer of help.

He saw Harriot climbing over the starboard rail. He was limping badly, one hand gripping his thigh, the result of an old bullet wound from his days with the East India Company. It wasn't often the magistrate let others see his pain. Tom nodded in salute and then turned to check on Ruxey. She was standing at the wheel, struggling to bring the brig onto a course that would take them away from the packed shipping. The drift of the smoke and the occasional leap of flame made it difficult to see where the brig was heading. A breeze caused the view to clear for a second. The ship wasn't answering to the helm. She was drifting with the wind towards the colliers on the Southwark shore.

'Mr Judge,' bellowed Tom, catching sight of his fellow surveyor climbing the rail onto the upper deck. 'Be so good as to return to your galley with your men. We have no steerage. I need you to tow us into the middle of the channel. Sam,' he said, turning to his friend, 'throw a line to Mr Judge and make it fast at the bows.'

'Aye, sir. A line at the bows it is.' Sam sprinted past a wall of flames and onto the fo'c'sle deck.

From the waist of the ship came the loud roar of escaping flames, quickly followed by the howl of a man in the extremes of agony. Tom spun round. Fire had erupted through the deck planks, aft of the fo'c'sle, close to where the mainmast should have been. Plumes of choking smoke billowed up into the night sky. He could see a man lying on the deck, writhing in agony, his clothing in flames, his hands tearing at the burning flesh of his face. Tom scrambled down the ladder from the poop deck and pulled him to the side of the ship.

He glanced at a waterman seemingly shocked into inactivity. 'God rot your soul, you infamous villain. Bear along with a bucket of water else this man will die.'

Dousing the flames, he crouched over the man and eased his blackened hands away from his face. Blisters had already formed around the lips and nose, his cheeks were a reddish pink and his eyebrows had gone. Tom had seen worse. The fellow would live. He turned to the man who had brought the bucket and raised his voice above the din of crackling timber and the hiss of steam.

'Get him ashore and up to the nearest accident hospital.'

'He ain't the only one, your honour.' One of the other men was pointing to a body lying under the fo'c'sle break. 'Found him on the main deck. He ain't one of ours. Looks to have been strangled.'

Tom looked at the corpse, at the empty sleeve of the left arm, and nodded. He knew who it was. He looked at the blackened face. He'd not seen it before, at least not properly. It reminded him of Stevy, the boy he'd been forced to shoot dead in Hastings. The similarity was striking, one an older version of the other.

'So that's why he came after me,' he murmured.

He looked round. A dozen men now ringed the blazing upper deck, throwing buckets of water in a losing battle against the inferno. Harriot was amongst them, his face smeared with soot and sweat. Beyond him, Tom could see the bows of the brig swing round as she was pulled back into the central channel. He glanced at the colliers. Less than thirty yards separated the nearest one from the burning hulk. Avoiding it was going to be close. He caught sight of Harriot. The older man looked exhausted.

'It's time you left, sir.'

'I am, sir, perfectly capable of deciding for myself when to leave this ship,' snapped Harriot, his face grey and twisted in pain.

'Sam,' shouted Tom, 'lay along. On the double. Get me a length of mooring line. Mr Harriot is going ashore.'

'I'm needed here, sir,' said Harriot, reaching for a water bucket.

Sam put a bowline round the protesting magistrate's chest and threaded it through a davit.

'This, sir, is gross insubordination,' shouted Harriot as he was bundled over the side and lowered, still protesting, to a waiting galley.

'Stand clear of the ship,' said Tom, waving the boat away.

He grinned in spite of himself. The old boy would doubtless have something to say about his forceful removal from the scene.

He thought of the Frenchman. Wondered where he was.

Dubois stumbled out of the gig and ran along the narrow passage leading from the river stairs to Tooley Street, the crew close behind. At the junction they stopped while Dubois looked up and down. He was surprised. Men and women were hurrying past from the direction of Borough High Street. He guessed they'd seen the burning ship and had come to gawp. He hesitated as a thought occurred to him. Any one of these people might remember a bunch of men running; might connect them with what was happening on the river.

More people hurried by. They were turning in towards Hay's Wharf. He was right. It was the ship that had, despite the lateness of the hour, drawn them here. Ordering the men to spread out, he pulled his hat down over his forehead and turned out of the passage towards Borough High Street.

At the top of the rise he stopped again and glanced to his right. More of the crowd were making their way onto London Bridge, lining the parapet, two and three deep. He turned and headed away from them, his thoughts on Pascoe and the police galleys that had been waiting for him. The bastard had an unpleasant habit of appearing when he was least expected. But how had he known? An image of Toiler came into his mind.

*

The young woman drew a blue shawl up over her head and watched the men. She had seen them coming ashore from a small rowing boat, run up into Borough High Street and turn down towards St Saviour's church. She wondered if they had had anything to do with the burning ship she'd seen emerging from under London Bridge a few minutes before. She thought for a moment and then followed them as they crossed the street and turned down a footpath alongside the church.

Arriving at the entrance to the passage, she stopped. It was as far as she was prepared to go. The men had disappeared from her sight. She turned and went back to her place on the Bridge.

Tom had deliberately left the Frenchman alone and made the conscious decision to focus on the hulk. The fireship was the greater risk. Hundreds might die if he did not deal with it.

He shot a glance at the colliers close to the Southwark shoreline. The gap had narrowed to a bare fifteen yards. Flames from the fo'c'sle deck were lighting up the night sky, leaping twenty, sometimes thirty feet into the air, fanned by a brisk north-westerly. Soon the fire would reach the quarterdeck. Then the poop. He eyed the approaching flames, trying to gauge how long they had before they'd be forced to abandon ship. Twenty minutes. Thirty at most. He guessed they were opposite the fish market at

Billingsgate. Thirty minutes might get them as far as Limehouse. It wasn't enough. They'd need longer than that to be clear of the port, somewhere they could put the hulk onto the hard where she'd do no damage. He glanced over the side. Kemp was still trying to hole the ship. He didn't appear to be having much success,

'Sam, order the men off,' shouted Tom. 'Including Ruxey. There ain't nothing more they can do here. Just you and me to remain.'

'You'll have a hard job getting Ruxey to leave, sir.'

'Throw her overboard if necessary. It's too dangerous for her to stay.'

He paced over to the starboard rail and looked anxiously at the last of the colliers. The sideways drift had stopped. The gap was getting wider. He felt someone's presence beside him. It was Sam.

'She won't go, sir. Says she'll go when we go. The rest of them are just leaving.'

'Damn the girl!' Tom leaned against the rail as he watched the last of the men slip over the side and down to a waiting skiff. 'Since she won't go, tell her to keep us in mid-channel for as long as possible. God willing, we'll find a gap where we can put this wreck ashore.'

'Aye, sir.'

Tom expelled a lungful of air, not sure they'd be given the luxury of being able to choose where to ground the hulk – or even the time. On either side of them he could see the ranks of ships, lashed three and four abreast, their hulls seeming to bend and gleam in the fierce light of the fire, frightened faces lining the rails, transfixed by the passing threat.

'Wind's veering south-west and picking up,' yelled Sam above the crackling, hissing noise of the flames. 'Gets any worse and it'll push us over onto the north shore. The line to Mr Judge's galley's gone. Got burnt. Ain't nothing we can do about steering this heap of disaster without that line.'

Tom didn't reply, his face set like stone. Off the larboard beam, the squat outline of the Tower appeared as a brief glimpse of dark grey before drifting slowly astern. Small gaps were beginning to appear in the seemingly solid line of ships but none large enough to let them through.

St Catherine's church came and went, followed by the huge edifice of the Wapping brew house and, just beyond, hidden by the night and the smoke, the black mouth of Hermitage Dock.

'Squall coming in,' said Tom watching the vessels on the Rotherhithe shore heel over as a strong gust blew in across the marshland. 'D'you hear there, Ruxey?'

'Squall it is, sir,' cried Ruxey. A moment later, 'Can't hold her, sir. She's broadside to the wind.'

Tongues of fire leapt from the larboard gun-ports as though in battle, the flames sweeping parallel to the surface of the water, seeming to caress the dozen or so barquentines moored off Parson's Stairs. Tom turned aft.

He felt rather than heard the initial rumble of the explosion; was aware of a slight tremble beneath his feet, growing in intensity. He had time only to glance up to where Ruxey was standing at the wheel. The blast knocked him to the deck, a wall of white flame engulfing the after section of the ship and sending shards of wood and iron scything in all directions. He looked up, searching what was left of the poop. A body lay on the starboard side, close to the taffrail, its clothing in flames.

'Ruxey.' Tom leapt to his feet and raced up the larboard ladder, the burning timbers scorching the soles of his shoes. He reached her and bent down, smothering the flames with his coat. He turned her over.

'Your Honour.' Sam's voice seemed to be coming from far away. 'Sir, ship's going to explode. They've got gunpowder below. We've got to go.'

Tom continued to stare down at the girl in his arms, the exposed flesh of her face blackened, her eyebrows and lashes gone, her lips swollen. He tried to cover the patchwork of reddish-pink and black where the heat and the flames had touched her. What was left of her clothes had been shredded by the blast and were hanging in tatters. He bent his ear to her mouth, listening for her breathing.

There was none.

He straightened up, strangely unmoved, as though the passing of her life had been that of a stranger met along the way. He felt no emotion. There was no change in the expression on his face. It was the only way he knew how to cope. She was beyond all human help. He remained kneeling beside her, unconscious of the heat or the danger he was in, aware only of the lifeless being that lay cradled in his arms. Grief would come later.

'Mr Pascoe, sir. For the love of God, come. The brig's about to blow.' Tom turned to look at Sam standing forward of where the mainmast should have been. Flames, higher and fiercer than before leapt through the torn fragments of the poop, the heat on his face and hands intense. He got to his feet, cradling Ruxey.

Another explosion. This time below the quarterdeck. The brig shuddered, her decks keeling over at a drunken angle. Tom grabbed at the rail, lost his footing and crashed to what remained of the deck, Ruxey's body slipping from his grasp. Smoke choked his breathing, obscured his view. He felt around, searching for her, found a huge rent in the planking where he'd last seen her.

She'd gone.

His eyes stung. He stepped to the jagged edge of the hole, the torn planks rising up as if to better allow the flames to escape. He waited. For what, he didn't know, unless it was to keep hope alive. He looked away. Perhaps it was for the best. There had been nothing he could have done for her. Nothing which would have meant anything.

Suddenly the brig jolted, pitching Tom to one side. He

looked across to the larboard bow. She'd run aground, slipping between the tiers of shipping to reach the foreshore, hard by Hermitage Stairs, flames licking at the wooden buildings of the Wapping waterfront. Within moments they, too, had caught fire, the flames quickly spreading from Brown Key to Oil Wharf, stacked with all manner of marine stores – hemp, sails, masts and pitch.

Another crash as the stern swung round in the tide and collided with a barquentine, close astern. Tom felt a hand pulling him towards the ladder up which he had so recently come. It was Sam, his grip vice-like, determined, yanking him to the ship's rail as the inferno reached the neighbouring barquentine trapped on the hard.

'Jump, sir!' He could hear Sam shouting into his ear, holding him by his elbow, thrusting him towards the ship's rail.

Peggy Tompkins gazed round the receiving room of the London Hospital in a state of shock. She had seldom, if ever, seen the room so crowded. Most of the people were coughing, their faces blackened with smoke or coloured a mottled salmon pink. Others appeared to have lost all their hair, their clothing burnt.

And the noise. She had been aware of the screams almost from the moment she'd left Harrison Ward on the second floor of the hospital and begun to make her way down to the receiving room – summoned there by a general call for all nurses to attend without delay. The cries of the suffering were the worst part, worse even than the sight of the injuries. A blaze down by the river, someone said. A fire so large that it had caught many people still in their beds. Many dead and over thirty houses destroyed, someone else had volunteered. A third claimed to have seen some ships on fire out on the Thames.

She pressed her way through the crowd, catching the odd phrase here and there between the cries of those in pain.

'He were brave ...'

'Should 'ave seen 'im. Like ten men he were ...'

'... ship were a ball of fire. Don't know how anyone could be alive, and that's the truth.'

Peggy touched the arm of the last speaker, his clothing hanging in shreds and smelling of smoke. 'Did the men you speak of escape the flames? The ones you saw on the ship?'

'Don't rightly know, miss,' said the man. 'There were an explosion. Sounded like gunpowder. Anygate that were when a great ball of fire catches them houses alight. Couldn't see nothing after that, on account of the smoke. Wouldn't surprise me none if they was all killed.'

'Can you describe the men you saw?'

'They looked no different to all the rest what work on the river, miss, 'cept ...'

'Except what?'

'Now that I think on it, one of them were wearing the King's cloth. An officer in the Navy, like. Big cully, he were, with yellow hair.'

Peggy steadied herself against the wall of the receiving room and struggled to regain her composure. Had it been Tom? Was he dead?

'Miss Tompkins?' She turned to see the duty physician beckoning.

The night dragged by. She could think of nothing but Tom, of what might have happened to him, of the shabby way she had treated him since the incident with Boylin last year. She saw him in the faces of the people around her, in their features, twisted in the agony of their suffering. She imagined how he must have died, the anguish he must have endured. And then her mind filled with the memories of the happy times they had spent together, and tears came to her eyes.

Suddenly she remembered the others of his crew. If Tom had been killed then perhaps Ruxey had been as well, and Sam.

She thought of Toiler. Wasn't sure she had the strength to tell him.

CHAPTER 32

Sam stared at the flickering silhouettes outlined against the bright orange glow of the flames soaring above the rooftops of Wapping Street. Long lines of men, women and children were passing buckets from hand to hand, their efforts hopeless, the fire sweeping along the waterfront towards Union Stairs.

It was his fault that she had died. It was he who had persuaded Tom Pascoe to swap their roles. It was he who should have been standing at the wheel of the fireship, not Ruxey. It was he who should have insisted she left the brig when ordered to do so by Tom. He felt the cold sweat of remorse break out across his forehead. When the explosion had come, he'd done nothing to save her; had left it to Tom to jump across the burning poop deck and attempt to bring her back.

For a moment, he thought he could see her. She was laughing, getting into the police galley, taking her place at the bow thwart. The image faded. She'd not often laughed, not to begin with, not when she had first joined Tom Pascoe's crew. Back then she had seemed morose, reluctant to engage in conversation, almost as though she was afraid of where it might lead, of the friendships that might develop. It was only later, after the revelation of her womanhood, he had learned a little of her past and come to appreciate the stresses and strains under which she had lived her life these five years since. He remembered his own welling anger when she had told him of her life in Hastings, of her relationship with Surly Will and what had happened that afternoon on the East Hill. Her tale had brought back unwelcome memories of his own and he had thought again of the Hannah Pinkerton he had known and loved and lost.

The image of Ruxey returned. She was standing behind the wheel, her face partially obscured by the swirling smoke. She saw him looking at her and smiled and waved. It was the last time he had seen her alive.

It should have been him at that wheel.

'Shift your bob, Sam. We've not a minute to lose.'

He turned. Tom was standing next to him, on the bridge over Hermitage Dock, his eyes red-rimmed, his face black. It had been a close call. Another two or three seconds on that hulk and they'd both have been killed. He'd been forced to push Tom off the brig and follow him into the Thames just as the explosion had ripped the hulk apart.

'Where to, sir?' he said.

'Christ, Sam,' said Tom, his voice betraying his tiredness. 'Haven't you heard a word I've said? We're leaving. I want to find the cant scrub that's responsible for all this.'

'What about Ruxey, sir? You ain't going to leave her.'

'What d'you suggest?' snapped Tom. 'She's dead and there's nothing we can do about that. We can't get to her body until the fire goes out and that won't be until after the next high tide. So, if it's all the same to you, we'll do something useful, like looking for that bastard Dubois.'

Tom stalked off the bridge, not waiting for a reply. The galley was waiting for them by Parson's Stairs where Sam had seen Kemp take it in the moments before he and Tom Pascoe jumped from the flaming brig.

'Give way together,' said Tom, after the three of them had settled down. 'We'll make for Custom House Stairs. It's the wrong side of the river but it's the only place we'll get ashore at this state of the water. I want to have a look round Southwark. See what we can find. I reckon that's where we'll find Dubois.'

It was a long, hard pull against the ebb, the galley hugging the south shore, where the force of the current was less. The wharfs came and went – Mr Butler's, Pearson's, Hartley's, and Davis's – the smell of spices and coffee, of wool and of wheat, drifting out over the Pool. Then came Gun & Shot Wharf at the bottom of Morgan's Lane, quickly followed by the stench of the dung wharfs with their flotilla of barges, each one heaped high with human excrement ready to be taken downriver and dumped.

Off Battle Bridge Stairs Tom altered course and steered the galley across the river towards a shallow flight of steps that served the western end of the legal quays.

'Make her fast, Kemp, if you please,' said Tom stepping from the galley, his clothes still wringing wet from his enforced ducking. He seemed to hesitate for a moment, then turned back and unlocked the black arms' chest in the stern of the galley. He took out four cutlasses, cursed quietly, put one back and handed them out. Then he did the same with the sea-service pistols, powder and ammunition.

'Don't know what we'll find but I'll not want to be bested for want of something to defend ourselves with,' said Tom, by way of explanation.

Leaving the quay they turned left into Lower Thames Street and then, almost immediately, left again onto London Bridge. It was still barely light, the bridge alcoves filled with the sleeping bodies of men, women and children, their emaciated frames covered in filth. Away to the east the sky over Wapping glowed red, and a towering column of smoke seemed to hang cloud-like over the rooftops.

'If you please sir.'

Sam stopped. The voice was familiar. He recognised the beggar he'd given some money to. She was wearing the same blue shawl that had so reminded him of Hannah.

'Are you, sir, the constable?' She sounded doubtful, her eyes running over his soaking clothes and muddy footwear.

'I am,' said Sam. 'Is there something you want of me?'

'You was here before. Gave me money.'

'I remember.' Sam fumbled in his pockets for a coin. The others were waiting for him.

The young woman shook her head and looked at the sleeping forms around her. Lowering her voice, she said, 'I ain't after no money, sir. But you're looking for the men what was on that burning ship, ain't yer? I saw it come through the Bridge.'

'Oh, aye?' said Sam, suddenly interested. He beckoned Tom to join him. 'Did you see the men on board, then?'

'Alas, I didn't, sir,' said the woman. 'I saw some men come ashore. Don't know them, like. But I'll warrant they come from that ship. Saw them at Tooley Stairs. I thought to myself, them scrubs ain't up to no good.'

'Where did they go, these men?' Tom was squatting beside her, his elbows resting on his knees.

'I followed them as far as the path through the church-yard at St Saviour's.' The woman jutted her chin towards the parish church. 'They went there.'

'But you don't know where they went after that?' said Tom.

The woman shook her head.

'Did you see how many there were?'

'Seven, maybe eight. They was in a hurry. Kept looking back. I were afraid they'd see me.'

They left the woman, crossed the High Street and made their way to the footpath she had indicated.

'This is where I found old Moses after Dubois had attacked him,' said Tom, as the three of them turned down the path. 'It could, of course, be a coincidence that it should happen in the path that leads to St Saviour's Dock.'

'The only place we never searched for the hulk,' said Sam.

'Exactly,' said Tom, looking rueful.

They pressed on, a low wall separating them from the churchyard, the still, silent headstones standing like so many sentries guarding the souls of the departed. At the junction with Church Street, Tom peered up and down a street deserted but for a stray cat foraging for scraps amongst a large pile of rubbish.

'Where to now, sir?' said Sam. 'They could be anywhere.'

'Over there,' said Tom, pointing to the Blind Beggar tavern. 'It's right on top of St Saviour's Dock. If that's where the fireship came from I'll warrant someone will know something. Wait.' He stepped back into the mouth of the footpath. 'Someone's coming out.'

Sam watched as the front door of the tavern opened and two men stepped out and began to walk along Church Street towards them.

'Get yourself behind the graveyard wall,' said Tom,

looking round at Kemp. 'Let them pass you and then cut off any retreat. You, Sam, come with me. We'll wait for them further along.'

A minute later, the two men rounded the corner and started down the church path.

'Belay there, in the King's name.' Tom's voice cut through the cold dawn air.

Startled, the pair stopped. Then one of them turned as if to run, saw Kemp and halted.

'The King's name be damned.' The speaker, a scrawny individual with lank shoulder-length hair and close-set eyes, sized up Tom with scarcely concealed belligerence. 'Will you be out of my way now, else you'll be sorry.'

'You can please yourselves, lads,' said Tom, a hard edge to his voice. 'It's a talk with us or Newgate with a rope round your neck. What's it to be?'

For a few tense seconds silence hung over the pathway.

'What is it you'll be wanting with us?' The second man was smaller and rounder than his friend. 'You've no cause to stop us.'

'That's as may be,' said Tom. 'It's what you were doing on the river these past few hours that's of interest to me.'

'Sweet Jesus, we've not been on the river since yesterday,' said the same man.

Tom smiled. He had no evidence. For all he knew, they were speaking the truth. Nor was the woman on the Bridge any help. She'd not seen the men on the hulk.

Would only say she'd seen them by the river stairs.

'You were seen on that burning hulk coming through the Bridge. I saw you myself, getting into the gig and leaving her. You were seen again as you came ashore. You were followed down this path and were seen going into the Blind Beggar. Now what's it to be? A talk with me or the hangman's noose for murder? It's a matter of no consequence to me. You can live or you can die but I want your answer now.'

'And if we talk?' The scrawny man was more hesitant now, less sure of his ground.

Tom considered him for a moment, needed his cooperation. 'I'm only interested in the cully who paid you to go on that ship.'

'Sure, it was like you said,' said the man who'd first spoken. 'We didn't know nothing about what was happening. We was offered work by Silas. We thought it were to lade a ship with straw. When we got here last night, there were a foreign looking cove what told us what to do.'

'And where is he now?'

'Don't know. He were in the Blind Beggar.' The man jerked his head back down the path towards Church Street. 'But he'll not be there now.'

'Anyone else in there?' said Tom, his face giving nothing away.

'Sure, there's the landlord.'

'Is that all?'

The man hesitated. 'Some of the boys ain't left yet.'

Tom nodded.

'Go with the constable,' said Tom, glancing at Kemp. 'Tell him everything that happened. When you've finished you can be on your way.'

'Kemp.' Tom took his crewman by the elbow and led him out of earshot of the others. 'As soon as you've taken statements from those two, put them in the cells until we're ready for them. Then I want you back here.'

'Aye, sir,' said Kemp touching his forehead with his index finger.

Tom waited until the little party was out of sight. Then he looked at Sam.

'Time we had a look inside that tavern, I think.'

CHAPTER 33

Toiler saw Peggy coming through the door of Harrison Ward. She'd been called away hours before. She looked exhausted, her eyes puffed up as though she'd been crying. He'd not seen her like that before. He thought of asking her if there was anything amiss. Decided against it. It was none of his business.

His fever had passed and he was well enough to leave. He supposed there was a reason for his continued detention. Peggy had explained it to him. He needed a certificate without which he'd not again be admitted to the hospital.

He turned over onto his side, wondering what was keeping his sister. He had only seen her once. He wasn't counting the first time when she'd found him in the treadmill on Hay's Wharf. He'd not been properly awake and what with his fever, the pain in his thigh and the fact that she was dressed as a man – well, he'd not recognised her. No, his first memory of her was when he'd seen her come through the door of this ward. She'd arrived with a tall, well-looking man, wearing the uniform of an officer in the King's Navy. Leastways, that was what it looked like to him, except that it was too old, battered and dirty to be an officer's uniform. His Honour, Mr Pascoe, she'd called him. It was obvious his little sister thought the world of him.

It had been difficult trying to squeeze five years of life into the half-hour they'd had together. There was so much to tell her and so much he wanted to hear of her life since she'd left Hastings. It hadn't been possible to get through it all. But there was plenty of time now.

He heard the chink of crockery. Breakfast. That would be followed by morning prayers. Then the rounds of the surgeon, the physician and the apothecary. In that order. Then lunch. Toiler rolled onto his back, his hands behind his head. The days in here didn't vary much.

She said she'd come and see him as soon as she could. Something was keeping her.

In Church Street, Southwark, a light shone from the ground-floor window of the Blind Beggar tavern, its yellow glow barely visible through the thick, tobacco-stained glass. It was the only sign of life within the decrepit building as Tom Pascoe and Sam Hart approached. Twenty yards short of the tavern, they stepped into the doorway of a house.

'Wait here,' said Tom. 'I'm going round the back. Try and see what's going on in there.'

Three or four minutes later, he was back.

'Difficult to see anything,' he said. 'Rear door was open. No one in the tap that I could see. There's a blanket pulled across the room. Couldn't see what was behind it but there seemed to be a light coming from there. That's got to be where they are.'

A shadow moved across the window of the tavern and, a moment later, the front door opened. A head appeared, looked up and down the street and then withdrew.

'D'you know him?' said Tom.

'No.'

'Nor me. Could be the publican.'

'What d'you want to do, sir?'

'We could wait for the others,' said Tom, grinning happily. 'Or we could go in by ourselves.'

'Just for a moment I thought you was going to wait. How d'you want to do it? Usual way? One in through the back and one through the front?'

'Exactly, Sam. You take the back way. I'll wait for exactly thirty seconds, then go in the front.'

They parted. Tom reached the front door and began to count down the seconds. Suddenly, the door rattled. The latch was being raised. He glanced over his shoulder. The nearest cover was over twenty yards away. He'd never make it. He faced the entrance and waited.

The heavy wooden door swung open and a man of about twenty-five, with long, swept-back greasy hair and an equally greasy broad-brimmed hat, stepped out. He saw Tom at the precise moment that the latter's fist connected with his mouth.

Tom caught him as he crumpled to the floor and propped him against the wall to one side of the doorway. He stepped across the threshold and looked round the apparently empty taproom. A single candle burned in its sconce on the bar, its presence largely redundant in the gathering light of day. From beyond the grey curtain he had seen earlier he caught the murmur of voices; quiet, disjointed snatches of conversation, as though the speakers had little to say to one another and were simply passing the time until the arrival of some other event. Tom glanced towards the bar. Behind it was the back door through which he had previously come. Its latch moved. He padded across and waited.

'Christ, Sam,' he whispered, as his friend emerged through the opening. 'A man could get himself hurt creeping about like that.'

He held a finger to his lips and pointed to the curtain. Sam nodded. They moved towards it. Abruptly, the conversation on the other side ceased.

'Joseph? Was it something you forgot, now?' The voice from behind the curtain was that of a young man.

A second or two of silence.

'Joseph? Will that be you?'

Tom swept the curtain aside, a cutlass in his hand, Sam beside him. Five men were sitting at a small table, the remains of food and drink in front of them. In the centre of the table, a single candle burned, melted wax gathering at its base.

Of Dubois there was no sign.

'In the King's name, stand fast there,' roared Tom, as the men leapt to their feet and rushed towards the two of them. He stepped to one side as the leading figure reached him, kicking his feet from under him. The man went down with a crash and lay still, apparently unconscious.

A howl of rage warned him of the approach of a second man. Tom spun round and saw the glint of steel in his fist, weaving from side to side. He was older than the others, a hunchback, his gaunt, calcified ruin of a face twisted in rage. Again Tom stepped aside, arching forward as the blade passed close to his stomach. The hunchback recovered quickly, came in for a second attempt. He was swift and agile despite his ungainly appearance, the blade of his knife flashing in the light of the candle. Tom caught his wrist and, pulling him forward, brought his knee up into his sagging jaw. There was an uncomfortable sound of teeth smashing into each other and the sight of bright red blood pouring from the fellow's mouth. He heard the knife clatter to the floor.

'You all right, Sam?' Tom was breathing hard. He turned to see his friend holding the point of his cutlass against someone's neck, his pistol pointing to the remaining members of the group, cowering against an adjacent wall.

'You,' said Tom, prodding one of the men with the toe of his boot. 'Where's Dubois?'

'I'll not be knowing nothing, your honour. We was told to come. Silas told us.'

'Who's Silas?' snapped Tom.

'Him,' said the man, indicating the hunchback sitting on the floor nursing a shattered mouth.

Tom picked up one of the half-empty beer mugs and upended the contents over the man's head. A groan, then silence. Tom repeated the exercise with a second mug. Silas Grant spluttered, looked up and groaned again. Tom bent down, caught him by the throat and yanked him to his feet.

'Where's Dubois, you uncommon blackguard?' Tom had his face close to Grant's.

No answer.

'Tell me, you villain, else I'll not answer for the consequences.'

'He ain't here. He's gone.'

'I can see that, you piece of shit. But where?'

Again, there was no answer. Tom drew his pistol, pulled back the cock and placed the muzzle against the man's forehead. 'I'll not ask you a second time.'

Grant's eyes bulged, his already ashen features paled some more.

'He said he were going to the infirmary.' Grant's eyes remained rigidly fixed on the barrel of the pistol, his words slurred, blood still pouring from his mouth.

'What infirmary?'

'The one in Whitechapel.'

'He's gone to the London? The London accident hospital?' A worried frown creased Tom's forehead. Toiler was still there. In the excitement of the moment, he'd forgotten about the lad, forgotten that he'd yet to tell him of his sister's death. And now Toiler was himself in danger. He thought about the constables posted outside Harrison Ward. They were reliable men but he doubted they'd be any match for Dubois. 'How long ago did he leave?'

'Not above two hours since,' mumbled Grant.

From outside came the sound of running feet. A moment later, Kemp barged through the tavern door, followed by another three watermen constables.

'I'm exceedingly glad to see you, Kemp,' said Tom, lowering the cock of his pistol and shoving it into a coat pocket. 'Help Sam get these four cullies back to Wapping. I've got something I need to do.'

CHAPTER 34

Dubois approached the London Hospital along the Whitechapel road, the building itself still partially hidden behind The Mount, a foul-smelling, forty-foot-high mound of rubbish that grew bigger, taller and more nauseous with each passing month. He crossed to the opposite side of the road. Two men were standing at the open gates of the hospital.

Dubois swore softly. There wasn't much doubt they were guards. He thought for a moment. There had to be a reason. Perhaps he was too late. Perhaps Toiler had told them everything he knew. If he had, it would explain a lot. The presence of guards was going to make things more difficult. But not impossible.

He turned at the sound of coughing. A large group of men, women and children was approaching the gates, their faces and clothing blackened with soot. They turned in to the courtyard and walked to the western end of the building, unchallenged by the guards. It took him a moment or two to realise who they were – victims of the fire he'd started. He shrugged his shoulders and melted into the shadows. Five minutes later, another group appeared. He chose his moment and slipped in behind them. He doubted anyone would recognise him as a stranger. Not in the pre-dawn light. But even if they did, they wouldn't say anything. Why would they? He was just another victim of the fire attending the hospital for treatment.

The group turned through the gate and approached the guards. The men were bigger and fitter than he'd thought. One was carrying a lantern. The first of the group had reached him. Dubois watched the man hold up his lantern so the light fell on the face of the newcomer. There was no challenge, no questions asked. The group moved forward. Dubois pulled his hat down over his eyes and stooped as though in pain. His right hand dropped to his belt, his fingers curling round the hilt of his knife.

He reached the first of the guards. The lantern was raised. Its light fell on his face.

'You there.' Dubois felt the blood drain from his face. He drew his knife, the blade still hidden beneath his coat. The person next to him stopped.

'Me?'

Dubois moved on.

The group reached the western end of the hospital and started down the steps to the receiving room. He watched them go. He had been here before; knew where he wanted to go and how to get there. He'd asked one of the porters who'd told him where Harrison Ward was. He wondered if there were any other guards, maybe inside the hospital. Perhaps even in the ward – where he wanted to go.

Toiler was one of the few people left alive who could identify him, place him on the *Mary-Anne* at the time of the killings. In a sense, it didn't really matter any more. He had done the job for which he'd been sent. In a day or two he'd be on a boat bound for France. But that wasn't why he was here. He was here because of Pascoe, because of the man who'd stolen his sloop. Dubois's face hardened. He didn't think the shame of that day would ever leave him – not until he had evened the score between them.

He left the group and circled round the back of the west wing of the hospital, into the garden quadrangle. At the far end, a door stood at the head of a shallow flight of steps. He'd used it before, when he and Moreau had last been here, searching for Toiler. He tried the handle. It was locked. He looked through the glass panel. There was no one about. He put his shoulder to the door. It gave way.

He crossed the threshold and looked up and down the corridor. If anyone had heard the door being broken, there was no sign of it. No one came to investigate. The sound of voices, low, muted, came from behind a nearby door. He hurried away. Likely it was some nurses in one of the wards.

He passed a series of doors on his left. Each one had a name plate attached to it. 'Bleeding Room', 'Surgery', 'Kitchen', 'Privys'. From somewhere up ahead he heard the sound of approaching footsteps clack-clacking on the stone floor. He ducked through the nearest doorway and quietly closed the door behind him.

The room in which he found himself was clearly used for bathing. It was equipped with five bathtubs, each sitting at right-angles to the long wall and each served by a single tap. At the far end was a window overlooking the front courtyard of the hospital.

He turned and put his ear to the door. There were more footsteps. It was too dangerous to move for the time being. He would have to wait for things to quieten down.

He had time. Pascoe would still be dealing with the fire-ship, would not be here for several hours yet. But come he would. He was sure of that. He smiled, remembering what Jim Clarke had once said to him. *She were a friend of Pascoe. A most particular friend*, the man had said. No, Pascoe wouldn't delay seeing her. Of that he was quite certain.

Dubois looked down the line of bathtubs. It wasn't an ideal place in which to wait, but it would do. He thought again about what Jim Clarke had told him.

Soon he would make his way to the ward where she worked.

Peggy listened with half an ear to the arrival of breakfast. It had been a long night, much of it spent in the receiving room, helping with the seemingly endless stream of people hurt in the Wapping fire. The hospital governors had taken the unusual step of ordering the gates to be left open throughout the night so the injured might be treated. People had been arriving in their droves.

Inevitably, fights had broken out amongst those waiting to be seen, and Peggy had been obliged to ask for the assistance of the two watermen constables posted to the door of Harrison Ward.

They were still down there, and would be for another hour or two.

She sniffed at the sleeve of her dress. It smelt of smoke. No doubt her face and hair smelt the same. She wished her relief would arrive so she could have a wash. She'd done her best to clean off the worst of the grime but the basin outside the ward had not been up to the task. She decided that nothing short of a bath would do. She walked down the length of the ward, looking at each of her patients in turn. Most were still asleep. She'd have to wake them in a minute and give them their breakfast.

'Miss.'

Peggy turned to see Toiler, his hand raised in the air.

'Why, Toiler, you're awake early,' said Peggy. 'Could you not sleep?'

'I slept well enough, thankee, Miss Peggy. I were just thinking ...' Toiler stopped in mid-sentence, his eyes turning towards the door of the ward. 'Who's that?'

'It's the servants with breakfast,' said Peggy, following the direction of his gaze. 'Milk pottage this morning.'

She turned back to him, feeling his forehead with the back of her hand. 'What were you thinking?'

'Them Frenchmen . . .' He gave another, fretful glance at the door. 'Have you . . . ?'

'No,' said Peggy, tucking in the blanket on his bed, 'they've not been back and I doubt they'll trouble you further.'

'Miss?'

'Yes?'

'When d'you think Josephine – I mean Ruxey – will be coming to see me?'

Peggy's heart missed a beat. It was the question she'd been dreading; had done nothing to prepare herself for. 'I regret it extremely but I've not seen her since she was last here,' she replied. 'Doubtless she will come as soon as she is able.'

The ward door opened. The two nurses who were to relieve her and Charity Squibb came in carrying the breakfast.

'I'll leave you now,' she said. 'Whatever happens, I want you . . .'

Peggy's voice choked up and she looked away, afraid Toiler would see her. But he wasn't listening, his face turned towards the approaching mug of milk pottage.

'Miss Squibb,' said Peggy as soon as she and her room-mate had left the ward and entered the room they shared on the landing, 'should Matron ask where I am, please to tell her that I shall be in the cold bath room. Every part of me smells of that horrid smoke.'

Picking up a towel and a change of clothes, she left her room and ran down the stairs, her mind on Tom and what might have happened to him. All she knew for certain was that he had been on a ship in the Thames which had caught fire. What he had been doing there and how the fire had started, no one could tell her. She was sick with worry, the words overheard in the receiving room during the night, playing and replaying in her mind.

Ship were a ball of fire. Don't know how anyone could be alive, and that's the truth . . .

Wouldn't surprise me none if they was all killed . . .

Now that I think on it, one of them were wearing the King's cloth. An officer in the Navy, like. Big cully, he were, with yellow hair . . .

She reached the ground floor and turned down the central corridor. The bathing room was at the other end of the building. She hurried along, past the door to the quadrangle. A cold breeze ruffled her hair. Surprised, she stopped and looked. The door, normally locked, stood ajar. She pushed it closed. Something was wrong. It wouldn't fit properly. She examined the lock. It was broken. There were splinters of wood on the floor. She looked up and down the corridor. There was no one about. She would tell someone as soon as she'd finished her bath. It was curious that she'd not noticed the damage earlier; she'd passed this way returning to the ward from the receiving room. She continued along the corridor, stopped at the door marked 'Cold Bath Room', opened the door and went in.

She'd not be disturbed.

It was the click of the door handle he heard first. Dubois dropped to the floor between the window and the nearest bath. Someone was coming into the room. He lay perfectly still. There was a gushing noise as one of the taps was turned on. Then the rustle of a dress being removed followed by a period of silence. Dubois raised his head. It was a woman. Young and beautiful, her long black hair tumbling to her shoulders. He watched her gather it in her hands and twist it into a loose knot at the nape. She turned towards the bath and stepped in. His pulse quickened at the sight of her body, her small firm breasts, the curve of her hips. He heard her gasp as the cold water touched her skin. He looked back at the pale, oval-shaped face and realised he'd seen her before, when he and Moreau had been looking for Toiler. It had been night time and the woman had come to the gate of the hospital to speak to them, the lantern she had been carrying lighting her face. She'd even given her name.

She were a friend of Pascoe. A most particular friend. Jim Clarke's words hammered into his brain. He sank to the floor of the bathroom, his mind focusing on what had to be done. He heard her moving about in the bath. It sounded as though she was getting to her feet. He raised his head again, wanted to see her one last time, his excitement rising.

She had turned away from him, the light from the window on her back, a towel in her hand. She was beginning to dry herself. Soon she would be dressed and gone. His hand dropped to his coat pocket and withdrew a length of cord. Without a sound he climbed to his feet and moved towards her, his heart beating unusually quickly.

CHAPTER 35

Tom left the Blind Beggar and ran down the length of Church Street before turning into the footpath that would take him to Borough High Street. He wasn't as fit as he thought, his breath coming in laboured gasps, his thigh muscles beginning to ache, the sweat adding to his discomfort. He slowed to a walk and searched for a chaise. There were few about at this hour. He'd reached the middle of the Bridge before one came along.

'The London Infirmary in the Whitechapel road, driver. With all speed, if you please, and there's an extra shilling in it for you.'

He sat back and thought of Ruxey and her brother Toiler. One was dead and the other in mortal danger. He should never have involved the girl in such a dangerous task; should have sent her packing the moment he'd discovered the truth about her. Now it was too late. The chaise rumbled over London Bridge, up Fish Street Hill and right into

Fenchurch Street. He had tried. He smiled in spite of himself, remembering how Ruxey had stood in front of him, hands on hips, fiercely arguing to be allowed to continue as a member of his crew.

He stared out of the side of the chaise, the noise of the horse's hooves loud in the early morning stillness. Death was so final, so brutal a reminder of the brief span of human existence. Even for him, no stranger to the mark that sudden death left on those who remained, Ruxey's passing had hit hard. Her safety and her welfare had been his responsibility. And he'd failed her.

The chaise passed through Aldgate, the houses on either side smaller, more decrepit as the carriage headed east, the people thinner, their clothes more ragged, the children barefoot and rickety. Soon they had reached Whitechapel where the road broadened and the houses became little more than hovels within which a person might shelter from the wind and the rain.

Tom mentally urged the driver on. He would not rest easy until he had satisfied himself about Toiler's safety. Even the presence at the hospital of four of his watermen constables was not enough to assuage his fear. Dubois was capable of anything.

He dug out a plug of tobacco from his coat pocket and bit off a lump. For a moment he let the comforting taste fill his mouth. Then his mind returned to thoughts of the Frenchman and the double murder that had been the starting point of the investigation. He'd never quite under-stood why Surly Will and Bulverhythe George had died. With their deaths had gone the ticket home for the Frenchmen.

'Unless Dubois just lost his temper over something that went wrong,' said Tom, below his breath. 'It just don't make sense, else.'

''Ere we are then, guv'nor.' The driver's voice interrupted his thoughts.

'Thankee, most kindly.' He alighted and paid the man off, relieved to see two of his men still by the entrance gate. If anything had happened they would've told him by now. He hurried across the courtyard. He was looking forward to seeing Peggy. He could see her face now, smiling at him. His heart soared. She seemed to have put behind her the unhappy events of last year, putting to an end the long months in which their friendship had appeared to be over.

He ran up the stairs to the first floor and opened the door to Harrison Ward, wondering where the guards had got to. He'd make some enquiries later.

'May I, sir, be of assistance?' Tom looked round. The speaker's voice was not familiar.

'Why, thankee, miss,' said Tom, hiding his disappoint-ment at not seeing Peggy. 'I've come to see young Toiler.'

He stayed with the boy for about thirty minutes. There had been nothing to say beyond the obvious – that Ruxey had died quickly and without pain; would have known nothing about it. In a way, the long periods of silence that had followed the brief announcement seemed to help the boy come to terms with what had happened. Tom had learned, on the hard road of experience, that grief could not be stemmed by any words of his, however kindly meant. Better that Toiler be allowed to grieve in his own way and in his own time. Doubtless he would, in the fullness of time, wish to return home to Hastings and pass on the tidings of Ruxey's death to his mother. But until that time, Tom would remain close by, would offer his comfort and support.

He left the boy, dry-eyed, staring at the foot of his bed, and promised to return the next day. He walked to the door of the ward and caught sight of the duty nurse.

'By your leave, miss,' he said, 'is Miss Tompkins off duty?'

'Miss Tompkins, sir?' The nurse hesitated. 'Might I ask who's enquiring?'

'My name is Tom Pascoe. Miss Tompkins is my particular friend.'

She looked flustered.

'Wait here, I beg,' she said, turning and hurrying out of the ward. He watched her go. Had something happened? Was Peggy unwell? The nurse returned three or four minutes later, her eyes red as though she had been crying.

'Will you come with me, sir.'

CHAPTER 36

There is a path on the Isle of Dogs. It runs close to the banks of the Thames from Limehouse Hole to the southern tip of the Isle opposite Greenwich before tracking up beside Blackwall Reach, to Blackwall Point. It is seldom used except by the herdsmen who tend the cattle that graze the flat-lands and, on Sundays, by those who pass that way to escape, for an hour or so, the foul air of London. But very few, if any, trouble to follow the route to the far side where lapwings, curlews and snipe wade in the shallow water and the wind blows across from the bleak marshes to the east.

'Why?' Tom slammed his fist into the stunted trunk of a tree and stared at the sky. He looked across at Sam, his lifeless eyes set within a gaunt, unshaven face. 'Why did the bastard have to kill her?'

A week had passed since he'd been taken down to Blizard's office and given the news. He'd not taken it in at first. Refused to believe the words he knew had been spoken.

She died of her injuries less than an hour ago. I'm very sorry.
She'd been strangled.

No, we have no idea of who might have been responsible.

The surgeon's words kept running through his head.

May I see her?

Blizard had gone with him to one of the empty wards on the second floor where her body lay, Charity Squibb weeping silently at her bedside. A sheet had been drawn up over her neck, shrouding the marks he knew would be there. It was then he had broken down, great sobs of grief overwhelming him as he knelt beside her, his head buried against her cold body.

He'd left the hospital soon afterwards, driven on by a blinding fury and a desire for revenge. Throughout the days that followed he'd not been home, travelling instead to the south coast and searching the beaches from Pevensey to Ramsgate for the man he meant to kill.

'Come home, sir,' said Sam, laying a hand on his shoulder. 'You've done all you can to find him. Let the lads help you. They want to. And it ain't just them what's offered. We've had men from all over the port asking after you, wanting to help, like.'

'He's gone. Can't you understand?' Tom's face twisted into a snarl of anger and hatred, a barely supressed fury in his voice. 'The bastard's gone back to France.'

Tom lapsed into silence for a moment and when next he spoke, the fury had left him. 'He were seen in Rye the day after ... the day after Peggy died. A boat was stolen that night and the scrub ain't been seen since. I were going to follow him but it were too late. I'd never find him.'

'I know what you is going through, sir.'

Tom looked at his friend, remembering that he, too, less than a year ago, had suffered in much the same way. He put out his hand and gripped his arm.

'How did you know where to find me?'

Sam shrugged. 'It weren't difficult, sir. Every villain this side of St Paul's knows you. I had only to ask and they told me where you were.'

Tom turned away, his mind tortured by what had happened. Peggy had died because of him, because she knew him, because Dubois had recognised the pain it would inflict on him. He'd failed her, had not been there to protect her when she most needed it. It had been the same with Boylin. He'd not seen the danger she was in then, and he'd not seen it now. He raised his head and gazed up to the Point where a dozen or more East Indiamen were riding at anchor, their tall masts seeming to touch the formless grey of the sky. He thought of the past he and Peggy had shared and the future that was to be forever denied them. There had been so much he wanted to know about her, so much he had wanted to say to her. He was conscious of an aching regret that he had never really known her.

'He'll come again, sir. There's no way the French won't send him back once they learn the port weren't burned to the ground. And when he does ...'

The ghost of a smile crossed Tom's face. He nodded, slowly.

'Yes, Sam, when he does ...'

HISTORICAL NOTE

Readers familiar with modern London and modern Hastings may question why the names of certain streets and places appear to have been changed. The truth is that the names that appear in this story are accurate for the period and were only subsequently changed as London (and Hastings) developed. Southwark Cathedral, for example, was, in 1799, the parish church of St Saviour while the nearby St Saviour's Dock is no more. London Bridge was a few yards further east than its current position and passed down the side of St Magnus the Martyr church.

Hastings – now a thriving town spread over a considerable acreage of East Sussex – comprised two main streets (both of whose names were changed in the nineteenth century), and a few others that connected them. The Bourne Stream has wholly disappeared beneath a busy street while the White Rock, a huge promontory jutting out into the sea, was blown up over 150 years ago, its former existence acknowledged now only in the name of a local theatre.

As to the story, it is, of course, a mixture of fact and fiction. French agents were known to have made several unsuccessful attempts to fire the Port of London during this period. The fire in Wapping did actually occur in March 1799 although there is no evidence that it was caused by a fireship, and there was also an outbreak of typhus in the same month to add to the misery of Londoners.

And the bodies in the fishing boat? Slightly later than 1799 and further down the Thames than in my story, a sunken lugger was discovered together with the bodies of a whole family, battened below deck. The culprits, who were never caught, were believed to be pirates, their motive, greed. The story surrounding the loss of Jim Clarke's arm at the Battle of Antrim in June 1798 is also accurate in its salient points. There was a charge by the 22nd Light Dragoons against a rebel army in Antrim leading to the deaths of many and doing much to undermine the reputation of the military at that time. Many of the injuries suffered by the cavalry were due to an old brass cannon used by the United Irishmen and filled with grapeshot wrapped in silk stockings.

PJE

GLOSSARY

Bourne Stream   now flows beneath a busy street in the Old Town of Hastings

Bridge, the   London Bridge was simply known as the Bridge at this time although there were others, including Blackfriars and Westminster

Cannon Street   changed to Cannon Street Road in more recent times

Ceiling boards   the 'floor' boards of a vessel

Chain pennant   the lighter's equivalent of a painter or mooring line on a dinghy

Clubbing   means of controlling a ship while dropping downstream. The kedge anchor is cast astern and allowed to dredge the bottom, reducing the ship's speed

Coaming   the raised lip round the hatch of a ship, lighter, etc

Crimp	a man whose business is the production of men (often by force), for payment, to serve as seamen
Crutch	an H-shaped contraption, one each side of a lighter's stern. Used to support the long sweep-oar or 'paddle' with which the vessel is steered
Devil's Tavern	until about 1802, the name of the public house now known as the Prospect of Whitby, in Wapping
Falls	the tackle by which a boat is hoisted to or lowered from a ship
Fo'c'sle	forecastle, the raised deck towards the bows of a sailing ship
Jurat	a sworn officer – as with a magistrate
Lettre de cours	French equivalent of the British Letters of Marque – the Admiralty authorisation to take, as prizes, enemy shipping
Mistral	I am aware the French regard their ships as masculine but I have referred to Dubois's corsair as a female out of sensitivity to the English ear
Orlop	lowest deck of the ship
Slough	a pond at the northern end of the Old Town of Hastings from which the town drew its water

Stade	the stone beach at Hastings, now largely under concrete but still occupied by fishing luggers
Starlings	timber posts designed to protect bridge abutments and/or a passing vessel from collision damage
Strakes	Horizontal planks making up the hull of smaller vessels
Taffrail	Ship's rail running round her stern
Trows	Short lengths of greased timber placed below the keel of a Hastings fishing lugger being hauled over the pebble beach
Waterside	officers were (and still are) posted to the waterside and made responsible for all matters relating to the safety and condition of the patrol boats

ACKNOWLEDGEMENTS

One of the great pleasures of writing is the opportunity it presents, in the general course of research, to meet people in those walks of life that are hidden from most of us. It is a great privilege and one that I am acutely aware of. Amongst those to whom thanks is due are Daniel Dover and Malcolm Cohen for their help and advice on the Judaic faith, David Mott for my visit to Dover House in Whitehall (Melbourne House in the early part of 1799) and Rob Jeffries and John Josslyn who, together, run the Thames Police Museum in Wapping.

Those who write or who have ever tried to write will know that no book is ever the work of a single person and this is particularly true in the final stages of its production. My thanks, therefore, also go to Jane Wood, my superb editor, and to Oli Munson, my agent.